RAWHIDE JAKE:
LEARNING THE ROPES

THE LIFE AND TIMES OF DETECTIVE
JONAS V. BRIGHTON, BOOK 1

RAWHIDE JAKE:
LEARNING THE ROPES

JD ARNOLD

WHEELER PUBLISHING
A part of Gale, a Cengage Company

LIBRARY OF CONGRESS CIP DATA ON FILE.
CATALOGUING IN PUBLICATION FOR THIS BOOK
IS AVAILABLE FROM THE LIBRARY OF CONGRESS.

ISBN-13: 978-1-4328-8920-3 (softcover alk. paper)

Published in 2022 by arrangement with JD Arnold

Printed in the USA
2 3 4 5 6   28 27 26 25 24

To my life pardner, Diane, and my
brother, Johnny, and especially,
Patricia Burkhart Smith, who was
of so much help to many authors.
May she rest in peace.

FOREWORD
BY MARSHALL TRIMBLE

The key to writing good historical fiction is to include enough historical truth to convince the reader if events didn't happen exactly this way, they are authentic enough that they *could* have happened this way. Truth and legend are inseparable partners in the history of the West.

Many years ago, when I was a young man teaching Southwest history, one of my students showed me some of his western drawings. He was, like me, a big fan of cowboy artist Charlie Russell. I believed he might have a bright future as an artist. He confessed that he hated history, but he loved to illustrate the Old West.

His name was Jack, and I said, "Jack, I'll give you an A in this class if you'll draw some Old West pictures that I can hang on the classroom walls. There's only one catch. Your renderings must be historically authentic. The clothes and tack must also be period. The firearms must also be period. Don't draw an 1894 Winchester on an 1880 rendering. Don't place a Colt Peacemaker in the hands of mountain men."

Jack agreed and proceeded to make drawings. At the end he got an A in Southwest History. He smiled and said, "Mr. Trimble, I think you tricked me. While making sure these illustrations were historically accurate, I studied ten times harder than the other students."

I replied, "And you learned ten times more. Jack, I think you're going to make a dang fine western artist."

Almost fifty years later Jack and I are still best of friends, and, yes, he is, in the words of Charlie Russell, *"Makin' dead man's wages,"* as an artist. His illustrations have graced several of my books.

It's the same with historical fiction. Critics and colleagues will let you know if your history is bogus. It isn't often I have a chance to read good historical fiction, but on this one I've struck pay dirt. Author JD Arnold is a master storyteller. Much of Brighton's early years have been lost in time, but JD has done an amazing amount of research to write authoritatively on his life and times in Kansas and presumptive Texas adventures during the early 1880s.

All those Texas ranchers in Books One and Two were historically inspired, as are the locales, weather, towns, fencing wars, Panhandle strike, and brands and their owners. He's written a riveting, fast-moving, well-crafted story that had me hooked from the beginning. This is a tome about a real-life range detective named Jonas V. Brighton. Through the author's descriptive narrative the reader *"Gets the dust of the herd in their nostrils."* To borrow an old cliché, it's a real page turner.

During the early 1880s large cattle ranches dominated the plains of northwest Texas. It was open range country just prior to the introduction of Joseph Glidden's *Devil's hatband,* mass-produced barbed wire, that would soon enclose the ranges and change ranching.

In the business of ranching the Eleventh Commandment was *"Thou shall not covet thy neighbor's cows,"* but it was frequently broken, especially if the owner was an absentee, or if, in the eyes of the thief, *"He had too many dang cows."*

Most of the livestock rustling was perpetrated against the big outfits. Many of these ranchers themselves had gotten their start by swinging a wide loop, and it wasn't unusual for some of their cowhands to *"steal a start"* by pilfering some of the boss's cows. He might even get away with it if he didn't get greedy. Settlers took advantage of the open range to do the same. Nesters who weren't stock thieves were sympathetic to the rustlers, making it almost impossible to find a jury that would convict.

Throughout the West the big outfits established stock grazers associations and hired stock detectives to administer justice to those caught in the act before they had a chance to see a lawyer.

Cowboy author Ramon Adams wrote, *"The rustler's greatest nemesis was the stock detective, a man with nerve and a thorough knowledge of cows, hired by the cattle associations to trap and run down them thieves."*

Thanks to author Rita Ackerman, Jonas V. Brighton, aka Rawhide Jake, is better known as the range detective who gunned down the notorious Arizona livestock thief Isaac "Ike" Clanton. For several years Clanton had been able to cleverly evade the long arm of the law. He boasted the reason his ranch made such a profit was he didn't have to pay for his cows.

Book One takes the reader through Brighton's early years. The author has managed to flush out the mysterious detective's checkered past. He was born in Portland, Indiana, on February 15, 1847. He ran away from home when he was sixteen and joined the Union Army during the Civil War. He was captured and placed in the notorious Confederate prison at Andersonville.

Our story begins in October, 1875, when he was sentenced to five years in a Kansas prison for grand larceny. He stole a span of mules and five horses. The following August his wife and daughter were killed in a Kansas tornado. His two sons were taken in by relatives.

Prison life would prepare him for his career as a detective. One of the fringe benefits of doing time with outlaws was he learned to think like one.

Upon his release from prison Jake was planning on becoming a freighter, wagon maker, or a blacksmith. Those plans were thwarted when he hooked up with a beautiful, free-spirited detective named Jennie Hudson. They solved a couple of crimes including a murder. He still managed to get cross-wise with the law. After being arrested for tampering with the U.S. mail in 1882, he actually shared a cell briefly with the outlaw Frank James.

So how did Jonas V. Brighton pick up the more suitable sobriquet "Rawhide Jake"?

Well, that's one fact we can't pin down as were most of his experiences as a stock detective in Texas. Brighton certainly isn't the only notorious Western figure whose early years are a mystery. But how much of the so-called "Real West" is actually partly truth and partly fiction?

As for me, I can't wait for Book Two when Rawhide Jake gets into the fencing wars, hauls in more rustlers, marries his sweetheart, and then, in Book Three, heads for Arizona.

Marshall Trimble
Arizona State Historian
True West Magazine's "Ask the Marshall"

CHAPTER ONE
KANSAS: PRISON

"Prisoner ten-eighty. Name?" The prisoner took note that the man spoke in a deep, commanding voice. He sounded and looked like a person who was clearly not to be trifled with. He wore black trousers and a black coat over a plain black vest, a white shirt with a high turn-down collar, and a black tie in a large Windsor knot. The collar and cuffs of the shirt were bleached white, and the suit coat looked recently brushed. He wore a silver watch chain and fob on his vest. Except for a neatly trimmed but full mustache he was clean shaven, and his fingernails were dirt free. His well-barbered black hair was parted on the right side and brushed left and right from the part.

They were in a square room with stone walls and floor. One end wall had a thick wooden door in the center, and the other end had an iron-bar door. There was no heat, and the spring morning chill was in the room. The man sat at a small desk positioned to one side in front of which each prisoner had to pass. On the desk were two small piles of files, one on his left and one on his right. In the middle was a single open file over which he hovered a pen. He dipped the pen nib in an ink bottle to his front and poised to write.

"Jonas V. Brighton, sir," prisoner ten-eighty answered. The man looked up at the convict and studied him with shining, steady, penetrating brown eyes. Brighton noticed the man's facial skin was white with the shadow of a beard showing through. His mouth was set hard, and there were no laugh wrinkles, but, almost imperceptibly, just a hint of a smile showed. And then it disappeared.

"You may refer to me as Warden Hopkins, convict Brighton." His tone was reserved and icy.

"Yes, Warden Hopkins."

He returned his attention to the file. "Date and place of birth?"

"February 15, 1847. Portland, Indiana."

"That checks out," Warden Hopkins said as he checked a box on the paper in the file folder. He nodded to one of the guards, who held a measuring stick to Brighton's back. "Stand up straight," he said.

"Five foot eight and one-half inch," the guard announced.

"Okay. Husky build. Black hair. Look at me."

Brighton looked at the warden for one second and then dropped his gaze. He didn't want to cause any kind of a confrontation. He had been told many times by many others that his eyes naturally held a look of challenge in them, and so he was always conscious of that, especially at a time like this.

"Dark-gray eyes." The warden made a few more notations in the file and then said, "Grand larceny, eh?" Again, with that penetrating stare. "What did you steal?"

"A span of mules and five horses."

"Why?"

"Needed them."

"Why?"

Although it was none of his business, probably best to explain. "Me and two other fellers were gonna start a freight hauling business between Dodge City and Wichita. I am a blacksmith and wagon maker and mule skinner by trade, so we had a wagon I made but needed the animals to pull it. I wanted to save up to buy 'em, but one day my partners showed up with the horses, and I went along with it. So I really didn't steal

15

them per se."

"Uh-huh. And the mules?"

"Well, yeah. I stole them. Better to pull the wagon. But I am not a horse thief."

"Uh-huh. You are a mule thief then?" The warden cracked a slight smile and glanced at the guard, who was also smiling. Brighton smiled, too, even though he didn't think it was funny. What did the warden know about how hard it is to make do for a wife and three children when you ain't got a cushy job like him? Every once in a while when a feller is down to the blanket, he has to do what he has to do to get by. Besides, this is the first time he got caught, and he wouldn't have if it weren't for Meeks and Mills getting the fat in the fire.

"What about the escape from jail in Hays?"

"Yes, Warden. That's a fact. Caught us again in Ellis County. I am here to pay my dues, Warden. I won't be trying to escape or cause any trouble."

"Mmmm. Well I see you have five years to think about it. That'll be a release in October, 1880. Might be a little earlier for good behavior. You can read and write?"

"Yes, Warden Hopkins. We had a country school near where we lived, and my parents sent us each year until we moved to Springfield. I went until I joined the army in '63."

"Union?"

"Yes, sir, er, Warden."

"How old were you when you joined?"

"Almost seventeen."

"Parents give you permission to join?"

"No, Warden. I ran away."

"After the war?"

"I apprenticed at Studebaker Brothers in South Bend, Indiana. That's where I learned blacksmithing and wagon making."

"When did you come to Kansas?"

"Sixty-seven."

"Wife? Children?"

"Wife, two boys, and a little girl, two years old."

Warden Hopkins made notes in the file, blotted the wet ink, then looked up and stared at Brighton for a minute. He nodded to the guard, who hooked Brighton's arm at the elbow and led him through the iron bars to the cell where the other newcomers waited. As he went his ankle chains clanked loudly.

The warden gathered up the small pile of files, stood, and addressed the prisoners in the next room through the bars. "Convicts, with the addition of your souls to this institution there are now three hundred seventy-nine prisoners housed here. I make it a point to process every new inmate because I want to get a look at you, each and every one of you. We have walls that are eighty feet high. All our correction officers are crack shots. I strongly advise you to not attempt to escape. You will not be successful and most likely be killed in the process. We observe the strict silence system here in Lansing. That means you are not permitted to talk among yourselves for any reason. No talking for any reason. Punishment will be meted out to violators. That is all. Enjoy your stay."

He turned and exited the room through the wooden door they had all come in through.

And we got a look at you, Warden, Brighton thought as he was prodded into the single file line of five inmates.

He was in the middle of the line as they shuffled and clanked their way through another iron-bar door where they were ordered to sit on a bench against one of the walls. There was another guard watching them through the bars. He held a sawed-off shotgun at the ready across his chest. Both guards were dressed in black like the warden minus the collar, tie, and watch chain. Brighton noticed their cuffs were a dull white and not bright like the warden's. The first guard said, "Unshackle yerselves, and leave them shackles on the floor." He tossed a key to the prisoner on the end of the line closest to him. With their handcuffs still on their wrists they each in turn removed the shackles from their ankles as ordered.

"Now with yer left foot slide the shackles across the floor. That's good. Now you, convict in front there with the key, unlock yer handcuffs and let 'em drop to the floor. That's good. Now with yer left foot slide 'em across the floor like you did the shackles. Yer other left foot, convict. There you go. See, you ain't all that dumb. Now each a you do the same down the line, and then you hand the key to me." He directed his last instruction to the prisoner at the end of the line closest to him.

"All right, on yer feet and turn to yer right." The guard went ahead of them and opened the door, stepped through, and said, "Let's go, convicts."

The guard walked beside Brighton as he herded the little group down a long, narrow corridor with barred cells on one side. He was a big man, tall and husky, with brown hair, brown eyes, and a calm face with no facial hair except for a mustache. "What was yer unit in the war?" he asked Brighton.

Jonas glanced over at the guard to be sure

he wasn't falling into a trap of some sort. He ventured forth. "Twenty-first Regiment, Illinois Volunteer Infantry."

"Me, I was Second Kansas Militia Infantry. Jayhawker through and through." He smiled as if Jonas should realize the import of that revelation. "Too bad you gotta be in here."

"I survived Andersonville.[1] I guess I can handle this place."

"I heared a that place. Pretty damn bad from what I heared. How'd you survive?"

Jonas hung his head and said, "There was a group of prisoners who called themselves Andersonville Raiders. They went around and stole anything they could from the other prisoners, usually clubbing them to death in the process. Big Pete Aubrey formed up a group called the Regulators. I joined up with that group." Instinctively,

[1] Andersonville, Georgia, was the infamous Confederate prisoner of war camp officially named Camp Sumter, where nearly thirteen thousand Union soldiers either starved to death or died of communicable diseases or disease related to unsanitary conditions. There was little or no clean water or food, no latrine and no bathing facility. The prison opened in February, 1864 and was liberated in May, 1865.

Jonas glanced around to see if anyone was listening or watching. He continued, "We caught and tried the Raiders, and a jury set punishment. We Regulators took care of each other, and we did a lot to stop the Raiders thieving and killing. Guess that's how I got through. Being a Regulator." He glanced up at the guard, who was staring straight ahead.

"So, you're saying that Union soldiers were attacking their own?"

"Yeah. It was pretty low down." Brighton went quiet, and so did the guard.

"My name is Rodgers. You need anything, you come see me."

They arrived at the cell block designated for prisoner 1080. "Make yerself at home," Rodgers said as he gestured for Jonas to enter the cell. Another prisoner was on his bunk and sat up when Jonas came in. "Bell, you show this fella yer fine Kansas hospitality. He's gonna be yer roommate for a while. But remember, no talking."

A week later prisoner 1080 stood with his back to a gray stone wall. He was in the hot and humid laundry supply room. He stood straight with broad shoulders laid back and muscular arms, made strong by years of swinging a blacksmith's hammer, hanging loosely at his sides. Yet, every muscle in his sinewy body was as taut as a drumhead. In front of him, three other prisoners, wearing, like he was, black and white stripes, formed an arc and pressed in toward him. Beads of sweat were on their foreheads and the backs of their hands.

He felt the sweat drip down his sides from his armpits as he focused on them, alert to the slightest threatening movement. It was a matter of pride with him. He would not touch his back to the wall because he was not about to allow these addle-headed snakes to think he was afeared of them. Well, anyway, two of them were snakes — skinny and slithery, each of average height. He was relatively unconcerned about them. Still, it would have been nice to have a pistol in his hand.

The one with a pox-scarred face was the giggler and stood on the left. The other snake on the right just drooled. But the hard case in the middle was big and looked like a bull all heated up and mean, straight out of hell. At least seven inches taller than Brighton, he glared down at him with black eyes full of malice. His brow was heavy and dark. His face was wide, and his jaw looked like a smithy's anvil. He smelled like death-a-coming. He was a killer for sure. Maybe a crazy killer.

"I heared yer been sidling up to the guards, Mister Jonas V. Brighton," the bull grunted like a feral pig. "That's yer name ain't it?"

"Reckon so." Brighton's steely dark-gray eyes turned stony, and he met the bull straight on, eye to eye, with a hot and intense stare.

"Yeah. Well, we think yer got things confused."

"How's that?"

"Yer must be a asinine dullard." The bull moved in closer, and the snakes on his flanks moved with him.

"Not necessarily."

"I thinks yer is," he said with a grin and twinkle in his eye. The stink of his breath from the rotten teeth he bared in the grin was enough to make Brighton gag, but he didn't.

"Yeah. We gonna get you straightened out," the left snake hissed with a big grin and the devil in his eye. "You gonna give us pleasure after Will here softens you up a bit." The other one started rubbing his hands together as if he were preparing to eat.

"An' yer gotta larn who's boss in here, an' that's me. If'n yer want to sidle up to someone it best be me. I takes what I want whenever I want it. So we gonna give you a little sumthin' to help you 'member that. Then we gonna take what we want." He stepped closer.

"Best not bother me," Jonas said in a low and calm voice.

The bull gave a grunt and rushed in with his huge right fist cocked back to unload a massive blow into Brighton's face. He started the punch but never finished it. He doubled over, racked in pain from the kick Brighton delivered to his groin. He started to reel into the wall headfirst, and Jonas stepped aside to let the massive body pass by him. He added to the momentum by pushing hard on the bull's back. When he hit the wall headfirst, there was a loud crack, and he fell slowly with his head sliding down the wall in an unnatural flop to one side. He was dead before he hit the floor. The two snakes stood with their mouths hanging open and their eyes as wide as saucers.

Brighton raised up straight and took a step toward the snakes. "If you want to live," he said again low and calm, "you better follow the prison rules and keep your mouths shut. You talk to no one about this. You got that?" he snapped. They both nodded their heads up and down. "Now git on outta here," he barked. They ran from the supply room in the laundry where they had cornered Brighton, and then he hurried out behind them trying to look casual. He checked to make sure nobody was around to notice their departures and double-checked for guards. Looked like he was in the clear.

Later in the day Rodgers walked up to one of the cells on the ground floor and said through the bars, "All right, Spivey, where's Teasley?"

The skinny pock-faced man was flat on his back in his bunk twiddling his thumbs. "Uh, I dunno," he said meekly. "Uh, I think he said a while ago he was headin' for the laundry." He shot a furtive glance at the guard and then quickly looked away.

"I'm lookin' for him. He missed supper. If you see him, tell him he better get in his cell now."

"Yes sir, boss."

Rodgers went to the dining hall first to make sure Teasley hadn't come in late for supper. He rounded a corner and unlocked an iron-bar door, then went into the hall that was full of long wooden tables with attached seat benches. It was void of personnel. He crossed to the kitchen door and shoved it open. "Anybody seen convict Teasley?" he hollered. There were men working at the sinks and stoves, but they all shook their heads or answered *no.* Now Rodgers was getting a little nervous and thought about sounding the alarm. Might be an escape. He thought he would check the laundry first just to be sure.

It not being a regular wash day, the laundry, too, was empty. He walked around the big hampers full of dirty and clean linen poking them with a mop handle in case the big ox was hiding in one of them. He called out, "Teasley! You in here? Better come out if you are." And then he noticed the supply room door was ajar. He stepped carefully over to it and swung the door open. Rodgers stopped dead in his tracks when he saw the huge lump of black and white stripes on the floor against the wall. Slowly, reluctantly, he came around to the side where he could see the face. No doubt about it. He was dead.

Rodgers fished his watch out of his vest pocket, flipped open the cover, and noted the time — 1805 hours. Too late now. The warden was gone for the day, and his rule was that he only returned to the prison if the governor or a director of the prison board showed up for some reason. Not even a break-out attempt, successful or otherwise, or a conflagration or riot could force his return. Deputy Warden Hanks was in Wichita. So Rodgers walked back to the guard station, and, after explaining what he found, he said, "Gimme that stretcher. I will need at least four strong convicts to carry him outta the laundry to the morgue."

Finished with the removal of the corpse, Rodgers said to one of the guards, "Come on. I need to fetch Spivey and Hicks outta their cells." He took the inmates to the laundry supply room and pressed both of them against the wall where Teasley died. "Now, I'm gonna give you one chance to tell me what happened here. If you lie to me you will dearly regret it. So, Hicks, you go out there with Mister Hadley. When I am ready for you I'll bring you back in here." He squeezed Spivey's arms tight against his sides so that Spivey's pocked face twisted in anguish. "Now, tell me from start to finish what happened." Rodgers let go of Spivey's arms.

"Sheesh. You coulda busted my veins," he said as he rubbed his biceps up and down.

"Talk." Rodgers speared Spivey's eyes as he looked away to the floor.

"What makes yer think I was even here to see the killin', huh?" He looked a challenge into Rodgers's eyes. "I was never here atall."

"Who told you there was a killin' here?"

"Wal . . . you did."

"No. I never did. So, how'd you know there was a killin' here? Because you were here and saw it. That's how. And you know who got killed, too. Because you were always attached to him like a Siamese twin. Where he went you went, didn't you?"

"Who you talkin' 'bout?"

Rodgers grabbed Spivey by the coat front and pressed his forearm into Spivey's Adam's apple so that it cut off his air supply. He let him start to turn blue and then said, "Now are you gonna quit wastin' my time and talk?"

Spivey's eyes were popping out, and his mouth was trying to gasp for air like a fish out of water. But, he managed ever so slightly to nod his head. Rodgers released the pressure, and Spivey bent over, coughed, sputtered, and sucked in big gulps of air for a good two minutes. Through his stringy brown hair hanging over his face he looked up sideways with hate in his eyes. Rodgers ignored the look, cocked his head, and with his eyes indicated for Spivey to start talking.

"Wal. It's hard, yer know. Rattin' off 'nuther convict."

"Harder than six months in the hole?"

"I wanna talk to the warden afore I say

'nuther word."

That evening Brighton sat on his bunk in the cell he shared with another prisoner named William Bell, who sat across from him. It was late, and the two of them were somewhat obscure figures in their cell in the shadows cast by the newfangled arc lamp further down the corridor outside the cells.

"You hear about the murder today?" Bell whispered like it was big news.

"I heard," Brighton growled in a hushed tone as he sat on the edge of his wood plank bunk and twirled a strand of cornhusk that leaked from the hole in his mattress. He fell back on the bunk, and the husks in the mattress crackled like popping corn in a hot skillet over which he said quietly, "Best keep quiet 'less a guard overhears you jawin'."

"I know. Just big news is all. They can't hear us whisperin' like we are."

Jonas rolled over with his face to the wall and did not answer. He hoped his cellmate would shut his trap. He was certain the guards would like to use the strict silence system as an excuse to whip up on violators.

"Heard anythin' about who did it?"

Brighton jumped up from his bunk and, in his stocking feet, padded to the bars of

29

their cell. He craned his neck to see left and right. No guard in sight. So he tiptoed to the center of the cell between the bunks and whispered, "You better shut up, or you are goin' to get us in the hole."

"Sure." Bell stayed quiet for all of two minutes. "Things are gonna change around here now that big Will Teasley is dead. I wonder who'll step in and take charge."

"Maybe his two reptile lackeys," Jonas whispered.

"How'd you know about them? You only been here a week."

"I got eyes. I watch things real close. And I take care of things. Don't forget that."

"What's your meanin'?"

"Better hope you are never obliged to find out."

He got up and checked again for guards. "Must be playing poker down at the end," he muttered, then continued, "Now that's it. No more talk." Jonas pulled off his coat and pants and hung them on a peg on the wall and flopped back onto his bunk and pulled the blanket up to cover his shoulders.

In the shadow of the night, flat on his back, eyes wide open, Brighton was thinking. If it hadn't been for Meeks and Mills he might not even be there. Then again, how was he to know that farmer had tattooed the inside of the lips of those mules? Took that farmer three months to find those mules, and here he was in a zoo because of it. A zoo full of animals like Will Teasley. What an ape. Him and all the ones like him and those two snakes in the prison were very bad men and needed to be killed. Beating and buggering men. They all should be hanged out of hand. Bad men. Worse than the raiders at Andersonville. Teasley had prodded the wrong man.

But now what? If Spivey and Hicks talked they'd lie about it to save their own skins. It was self-defense through and through, and that was the honest truth. Just because Teasley got shoved hard into the wall didn't change anything. Maybe it might though. They might say that was overkill and charge him with murder. Teasley needed killing anyway. Spivey and Hicks, too. They were all three coming at him, so he had to be sure Teasley was out cold so he could deal with the other two. That settled it. Brighton let out a big sigh, relaxed, rolled over onto his side, and was asleep in two minutes.

Early the next morning before breakfast Hadley had Spivey and Hicks sitting in handcuffs in the center of a row of six straight-back chairs in the warden's outer office. There was a door near the corner of the wall against which they sat and another one next to the secretary's desk. It was through that door Rodgers went not five minutes past. Light from a window behind the secretary was augmented by oil lamps on the walls and a lamp with a white shade on the secretary's desk. She shifted in her chair and picked up a writing pad from her desk. Warden Hopkins came out from his inner office with Rodgers following him. He went across the room to the door in the corner, opened it, and went in with the secretary right behind him. Rodgers motioned for Hadley to bring the prisoners in. The room was about twelve by fifteen with no windows, and the walls were plaster painted gray. A wooden table was centered at the end of the room farthest from the door with three chairs on one side of the table. The warden sat in the center chair and the secretary to his left with a pad in her hand. She twirled a green Dixon pencil in her right hand, and there were several more freshly sharpened pencils on the table in front of her. A brass spittoon sat on the floor next to the rear table leg on the warden's side. Otherwise the room was empty.

Spivey and Hicks were brought in by Hadley and stood in front of the table about eight feet back. Rodgers stepped to the side of the table by the warden and spat a stream of tobacco juice into the spittoon. The secretary made a look of disgust as the juice splatted in the spittoon. Rodgers failed to notice her discomfort as he folded his arms across his chest, spread his legs, and glared at the prisoners.

The heavy manacles forced their hands down in front of the two men, and they hung their heads as well. Warden Hopkins stared at them for a very long and uncomfortable two minutes. He pulled a Corona from his inside coat pocket and a match from his vest pocket. He scratched the match on the tabletop, and it flamed. Carefully he lit the cigar, blew out the match, and dropped it in the spittoon. He puffed blue smoke toward the ceiling, licked his lips, and smiled at the prisoners, who repeatedly glanced up and then quickly back down.

Finally, Warden Hopkins spoke. "Tuesday, November 9, 1875." He paused as he retrieved his watch from his vest pocket and snapped it open. "Zero seven ten hours," he continued. "I have before me two convicts. For the record state your prisoner number and full name." The secretary busily wrote everything said in shorthand. Warden Hopkins nodded toward Spivey. "You first."

"Yes sir. Prisoner number six five two, Ronald J. Spivey." Hopkins looked at Hicks.

"Prisoner six five two, I mean six two five, sorry, sir. Everett Peter Hicks, sir."

Warden Hopkins glanced at Rodgers and Hadley, who were ever so slightly smirking and then immediately went serious when they met the Warden's eyes.

"Also in the room are correctional officers Rodgers and Hadley along with my secretary, Miss Alice Johnson, who is recording these interviews. At approximately eighteen hundred hours yesterday, Correctional Officer Rodgers discovered the body of prisoner five three, Wilford Teasley, in the laundry supply room. The death did not appear to Officer Rodgers to be of natural cause. Prisoners Spivey and Hicks allegedly have information regarding the circumstances of prisoner Teasley's unnatural death. Prisoner Spivey, state in your own words what happened."

"Yes, Warden sir."

"Just a minute," the Warden said. "Mister Hadley, please remove convict Hicks to the outer office where he cannot hear convict Spivey's testimony."

"Testimony?" Spivey blurted out. "I didn't know this was any law court."

34

"Just another word to describe your story. You are not testifying in a court. This is a warden's inquest, is all." Warden Hopkins waved his hand through the air as a sign of relative unimportance. "Now, will you please get on with it."

"Wal, I guess so. Not much to it though. Me and Teasley and Hicks was talkin' with convict Jonas Brighton in the laundry supply room. Lettin' him know about Teasley and he bein' the yard boss and all." Through his stringy hair Spivey glanced at Rodgers and back at the warden, apparently to see if they were upset about what he said. "Wal, all of a sudden this feller Brighton explodes and kicks Will in the balls and then shoves his head into the wall. Broke Will's neck. Me and Hicks got the hell outta there then. And that was it."

"You didn't see fit to report it."

"No, sir. We was sceert. I was anyways."

"All right. Have him wait outside, and bring in Hicks." On the way out, Spivey gave the Warden one last sideways glance and then looked away quickly when he was met by Warden Hopkins's flinty stare. Then he caught the eye of Hicks as they passed and made a look of silent threat.

Rodgers closed the door, and Hopkins said, "Convict Hicks. Convict Spivey just told us that convict Brighton without provocation attacked convict Teasley and threw him into the wall. Is that what happened?"

"Uh, what's provakashun mean?"

"It means that Teasley did nothing and that Brighton attacked him out of the blue."

"Yes, sir. That is what happened. Yes, sir. Shoved him right into the wall. Yes, sir." Hicks's head bobbed up and down like a drinking duck.

"What was convict Teasley saying?"

"Well, he was sayin' how he was the boss and Brighton better larn that."

"And?"

Hicks twisted a little and pawed the floor just a touch with one foot. "And how he takes what he wants when he wants it." Hicks grinned big as if he had just delivered a pot of gold.

"And what did he want?"

Hicks pawed the floor more as the grin disappeared and his eyes showed fear. "Uh . . . I dunno. He didn't say."

"Did he say something to you and Spivey about giving Brighton a beating and then buggering him?"

Hicks puffed out his cheeks and formed an *O* with his lips as he turned his head from side to side. "No siree. He never said nuthin' like that."

"Convict Spivey says he did."

"He did?" His eyes went wide in wonderment, and he lifted his head higher.

"Sure did. So you better come clean and not lie to me because Spivey has already spilled the beans." Hopkins blew a cloud of cigar smoke to the ceiling and gave Hicks a no-nonsense threatening look. "Nothing will happen to you if you tell the truth."

"Uh-huh. Well, gosh dammit now that I think about it, he did say somethin' 'bout that."

"And that you and Spivey were going to get some, too."

"Now that ain't the truth. I was just watchin'."

"Hicks?" Warden Hopkins rolled the name off his tongue. "Tell the truth. As long as you didn't do anything you won't be charged. If you did do something it will go easier for you if you tell the truth."

Hicks's shoulders drooped, and he stared at the floor. "Okay. Gosh double dammit. We were all gonna jump him."

"Okay, take him away, and then come back here."

Rodgers took Hicks out, sat him down, and went back through the door. Hadley stayed with the prisoners.

"Fetch Brighton, and let's get his side of

the story."

"Yes, sir."

Rodgers appeared at Bell and Brighton's cell door. He inserted his big key in the lockset, and as he turned it he said, "Warden wants to see you, Brighton".

Jonas was lying on his bunk with his hands folded behind his head and was already dressed in his stripes. When he heard the words from Rodgers's mouth he felt like he had just taken a slug in the gut. Sure enough the two snakes talked. Now what?

He tossed his feet over the edge of the bunk, sat up, and pulled on his boots. He turned a hard stare at Rodgers and said, "What's he want?"

Rodgers did not smile when he said, "I think you know."

Brighton stabbed a sharp scowl at Bell, who sat on his bunk blinking his eyes in rapid succession.

Along the way to the warden's office Rodgers stopped Brighton in a small room and snapped handcuffs on him. Then they continued a silent walk out of the secure section and into the administration wing of the prison. At the warden's door in a hallway containing a line of doors on both sides, Rodgers stopped and knocked on the door, opening it at the same time. Brighton felt the moisture pop out on his forehead as the door opened. But then he saw Spivey and Hicks sitting there, and he cursed them silently and shot an intense death stare at them. They talked for sure, and by their sheepish look he knew it.

"Prisoner Brighton," Warden Hopkins began and paused while he stared at Jonas as if he was surprised to see him. Then he continued, "I am disappointed. At in-processing you told me you weren't going to cause any trouble. Now look at the mess you're in."

Jonas kept quiet. He was not about to volunteer anything. This was a touchy situation, and he needed to make the right play, or he could be spending the rest of his life in prison. But at the same time he didn't want to appear uncooperative or dishonest. Obviously, the warden had already talked to Spivey and Hicks, who no doubt spilled their guts. So, he better just tell it more or less like it happened. It was delicate.

"You have nothing to say?"

Should he, or shouldn't he? He decided to commit.

"I see Spivey and Hicks outside. I suppose you are askin' about what they probably said about Teasley?"

"I am."

39

"It was self-defense, Warden. They came at me." Brighton drilled the warden with his dark-gray eyes, so intense was his conviction.

"They?"

"Yes. All three of them. They are bad men. Teasley led the way." Warden Hopkins gave a knowing look to Rodgers.

"Tell me exactly what happened and what they said."

"I was in the supply room straightenin' everything out on the shelves like I was told to do when the three of them came in behind me. I sensed they were up to no good, so I managed to get around to get my back at the wall, and they surrounded me. They were sayin' that Teasley was the boss, and they were gonna give me somethin' to help me remember that, and then they were gonna take what they wanted. They were gonna whip up on me and then . . . bugger me. I wasn't havin' any of that, so when Teasley cocked his fist and charged me, I kicked him in the groin and let him fall into the wall. I guess he broke his neck."

"Did you shove him into the wall?"

"No, Warden," Brighton lied. "I might a pushed off him a little to keep my balance. I don't know. It all happened so fast I don't rightly recall."

"Why do you say they are bad men? Aren't all the convicts here bad men?"

"Well, under the law we are all criminals. But I think there is a difference. Bad men murder and rape and bugger and such as that. Not that we are good men, but we are not bad men like those three. They are barely one step above animals. We are just men, basically, usually upright, who did bad things."

"Uh-huh. Why didn't you report it?"

"I don't know. Scared I guess. I'm new here. I didn't know what would happen with the other convicts. How they would take it and what they might do."

"All right. You can go. Mister Rodgers." The warden motioned to Rodgers to take Jonas out, which he did and then came back in.

"Sounds like self-defense to me. What do you think?" Hopkins said to Rodgers.

"I agree, sir. Spivey is a known liar, and Hicks is so slow-witted he says and does whatever Spivey says. Teasley, well we know he has been trouble since he first was taken in. This fits his MO to a *t*. And it's not the first time he's been accused of beatin' and buggerin' prisoners. Remember convict Herschfeldt? That was a sad one."

"Yes, I do. All right, the incident under

41

investigation is officially determined to be an act of self-defense by prisoner ten eighty, Jonas Brighton, when without provocation he was threatened and attacked by prisoner fifty-three, Wilford Teasley. Time is zero eight hundred hours. That is all, Alice. Thank you. Has the deputy warden returned yet? No? Okay, thank you." The secretary gathered up her things, stood, and left the room.

Warden Hopkins tossed his cigar butt in the spittoon, slid back his chair, and stood up. He looked at Rodgers. "Just between you and me, Brighton did us a big favor. Made things a lot easier for us. Teasley was a huge pain in the ass. Caused much more paperwork than he could ever be worth."

"I am with you there, sir."

"Three months solitary confinement for Spivey and Hicks."

"Yes, sir."

First of the year, 1876, Jonas was called to the warden's office. "Convict Brighton," he said, "we are going to put you to work. There is serious talk about opening a coal mine and using prisoner labor to work it. But don't get yourself all contrary. You won't be going into the mine. You are going to be part of the crew building wagons and carts and what have you that will be needed for the mining operation. You'll be earning top convict pay." He smiled and puffed his cigar and leaned back in his leather desk chair. "How's that sound?"

"Sounds fine to me, Warden. When do I start, and who do I report to?" Jonas was expressionless but stood straight and rigid, not quite but almost defiant.

"Well, I thought you might be a little more appreciative." He blew a puff of blue smoke to the ceiling, watching it as it ascended.

"I am appreciative, Warden. I guess we are doing each other a favor. You need wagons, and I need activity and money. Sounds like a fair trade."

Hopkins let his chair come to upright, leaned forward, and crossed his arms on his desk top. "There is no trade, convict Brighton. I can pull you off that crew any time I am so inclined." His face turned hard, and he glared at Brighton with eyes that held a threat.

Jonas needed to fix this misunderstanding. He wanted to stay on the warden's good side and stay on the wagon building crew.

"Understood, Warden. Didn't mean to sound uppity. I do appreciate the work."

Hopkins appeared to relax and soften his

43

expression. "All right then. Report to Mister Rodgers, and, convict Brighton . . . I do expect you to keep your promise and stay out of trouble with no escape attempts. You'll be working every day outside the walls."

"Yes sir, Warden. As far as it depends on me, I will keep my promise."

Jonas V. Brighton kept his word, and all was moving along routinely as each day passed and brought him closer to his discharge date. Each passing month brought him another five dollars held in his prisoner trust account. Even the cold and rain could not dampen him, and the heat of summer could not sweat him out completely as, with delight, he watched the balance in his prisoner account grow. He bought nothing from the commissary, and the prison provided tobacco for everyone, so he was in need of nothing. He calculated that by the time he was discharged he would have close to two hundred fifty dollars providing there were no hitches along the way. With that money he figured he could move the family further west and homestead a farm. He already had his eye on two old broke down wagons in the back of the shop where he worked and knew he could have them fixed up as good as new within a week after his discharge. Two wagons would handle all their belongings. Or he could take the wagons further west, sell them, and open a shop in the trade he was trained — blacksmithing. One option. But, he always did want to try his hand at farming. He thought about trying to make a deal with the shop foreman to acquire the wagons and sneak some time to work on them. But he decided against taking the risk of getting caught. He thought he should be patient and conservative and stay on the right side of Warden Hopkins, no matter what.

Jonas was not a sentimental man, but he couldn't help but think about how pleased Matilda would be to see him pull up with two new wagons and a team of mules, especially since she was so angry with him for being thrown in prison. Harry would be eleven years old and able to help work a farm. Edgar would be nine, so he could handle the chores. Martha could help her Ma, as she would be seven. Heck, they all already were working hard to make ends meet while he was in prison. They were laboring at chores and domestic help for the Wilsons up in Kill Creek, Osborne County. For that they got room and board and cloth and thread and such to make their clothes and a new pair of shoes every Fall.

Wilson had the biggest farm in the three-county area but lived in the township. Jonas was relieved to have made those provisions for them. Course it was Matilda who had most of the influence in that one, since she was good friends with Mrs. Wilson. But Jonas did insist the children attend school, and everybody was in agreement. The Wilsons were known as fine people, and they were. Anyway, Matilda would be happy to see him with those wagons and learn he intended for them to bust out on their own. A new beginning. But it was not to be.

On August 21, 1876, Jonas received a telegram from James Wilson. It read:

SORRY STOP WIFE MATILDA DAUGH-TER MARTHA KILLED BY TORNADO STOP SONS HARRY AND EDGAR STILL HERE STOP PLEASE ADVISE STOP

Jonas V. Brighton was a man not easily shocked and not what one would call a family man, but a first reading of the telegram took the starch right out of him. He fell seat first on his bunk and stared at the yellow paper with black bold print.

"Bad news?" Bell queried.

"None of your damn business," Jonas growled.

His wife and daughter ripped to death in a cyclone from hell. He didn't want to think about it. He didn't think about it. He stood and gazed absently through the bars of their cell. "Well, guess I won't be a farmer after all," he whispered to himself. "Two boys to look after on my own now. Got to make provision for them."

Brighton did not want to pay for a telegram or postage stamps, so he answered the telegram with a penny postcard. He also sent one to his older brother, William, in Independence, Kansas, asking for him to retrieve and care for his sons until he was released from prison. William made arrangements and accommodated his younger brother.

December 19, 1879, Jonas stood in front of Warden Hopkins's desk. He was attired in new brown wool trousers, a navy-blue flannel shirt, and brown, ankle-height lace-up boots. Over his left arm was draped a blanket-lined brown-duck coat, and in his left hand he held by the rim a brown farm hat in the Cuban shape made of brown duck cloth with a leather sweatband. He was bathed, freshly barbered, clean shaven, and mustache trimmed. Deputy Warden Cross and Mister Rodgers stood off to the side.

"Well, Mister Brighton, you are a free man, renewed and ready to re-enter society. Have a cigar." Warden Hopkins smiled admiringly like Jonas had never seen before. He picked up a Partagas Corona from his desktop and held it up for Jonas.

"That is not a cheap cigar," Deputy Warden Cross said. "And Warden Hopkins doesn't give them to just any discharged convict." He smiled and cocked his head in a knowing way.

Jonas took the cigar and said, "Thank you, Warden Hopkins. Much appreciated. I'll save it for later."

"You kept your promise, and the result is you are released a year early for good behavior. I trust the new clothes compliments of the state of Kansas are acceptable." The warden leaned back in his chair and blew a cloud of cigar smoke up to the ceiling. "I have two hundred thirty-five dollars for you, which is the balance in your prisoner trust account, plus your possessions on your person on the date of your incarceration. Please inventory your possessions and verify receipt thereof plus the two hundred thirty-five dollars. Sign here at the X." Warden Hopkins handed him a sheet of printed paper with inked entries and a signature line. Brighton went through his personal items quickly. He didn't have much, just a jackknife, an old watch, and a few coins, including a half eagle five-dollar gold coin. He counted the cash, a five, tens, and twenties, folded the bills in half, and stuffed them into his front pants pocket. The knife and coins he put in the other pocket and the watch in the little pants pocket made for that purpose. Then he glanced over the affidavit and signed with the pen handed him by the warden.

"Can't say it was a pleasure stayin' with you, Warden Hopkins, and can't say I hope to see you again," Jonas said with a wry little smile. "Maybe under different situations, who knows?" He turned to the other two men and nodded. "Gentlemen."

"Mister Rodgers will show you out. Good luck." Warden Hopkins stood and offered his hand, which Jonas shook, and then he also shook the hands of Cross and Rodgers.

"Come on, Brighton. I'll show you the gate. It ain't pearly, but I expect you'll like it just the same," Rodgers said as he grinned big.

"Thank you, Rodgers." Jonas smiled with an ironic look in his eyes as the two of them took note that he left off the "Mister" in his response to Rodgers. They walked down a hall and a flight of stairs that emptied into a large unfurnished room. Rodgers opened a heavy door, and the outside came in with a gust of cold, snowy air. Jonas buttoned up his coat and jammed his hat on his head. "Now, I would be obliged if you would direct me to the train station. I know it is close because I heard the whistles day and night."

At the gate, Rodgers pointed and said loudly over the wind, "Right down thataway about five hundred feet and turn right. Follow the road about a quarter mile where it intersects with Main Street. You'll see on your right Jones General Store. It's a yella clapboard with a porch and a big hitchin' rail out front." He spat a stream of tobacco juice that made a little brown crater in the snow. "You buy your ticket there and other things if you want," he said with a curious grin. "Train platform is another hundred yards down the road. Where you headed?"

Brighton reached up to grab his hat and hold it on against the wind. "Independence," he shouted.

"Missouri?"

"Kansas." Jonas tipped the brim of his hat and turned to walk down the road.

"Good luck!" Rodgers yelled after him.

It was midmorning with a gray sky. The snow was still frozen and crunched under

Jonas's boots as he walked along in the iced-over wagon ruts of the road. Light snow was in the wind. Beside the road, the snow was a foot deep. He held his head down to keep the freezing wind from his eyes. It was but just a few minutes before the coat provided him by the state of Kansas proved to be inadequate against the cold wind. He jammed his hands into the coat pockets and began to shiver. So, he walked more rapidly, almost trotting.

He came to the main road, looked up from under his hat, and saw his destination. Hurriedly, he entered with the wind on his heels and shut the door quickly. Jonas stomped the snow off his boots on the wood plank floor and surveyed the establishment, noting all the usual shelves, tables, glass cases, and countertops full of sundry goods. He spotted a fairly large sign of a gloved hand with the index finger pointing to his left with a sign under it that said Train Depot indicating a path of travel through an archway in a wall dividing the store and the depot. There was a man behind one of the counters and a young woman in a dark-blue gingham dress straightening merchandise on the tables. "Good mornin'," the man called out. He was clearly the clerk of the store, as he was in his white apron over a white shirt with no collar and red garters on his shirtsleeves. "Can I help you?"

Jonas nodded and moved off in the direction of the depot and waved his hand in a gesture of thanks.

"You have to buy your ticket here. That's just a waitin' room through there."

As Jonas turned and approached the counter, the clerk took a small step backwards. "You just been released from the prison?"

Jonas pulled off his hat and slapped the snow off it. Glancing up at the clerk with a steely and steady scowl and then looking down at his hat he said, "I have. Does that bother you?" And he looked up with a friendly smile on his face. Then showed the same smiling face to the young lady at the tables, who had stopped moving and was watching them intently. She smiled back and straightened some stray strands of hair at the nape of her neck with a coy look back at Jonas. She wasn't necessarily pretty but attractive in a way. Jonas could see her long, black hair and bright, cobalt-blue eyes from across the room. Her features were soft. She was full-bodied, and he liked the way she moved and held herself. While still smiling, he nodded slightly like a gentleman in acknowledgement of her silent communication.

"No. I reckon not as long as you don't cause no trouble. Margaret, you about done there?"

"I just need a ticket to Union Depot in Kansas City and through to Independence, Kansas."

"Yessir. And when it stops at Union Depot you buy your ticket there for Independence. Except it ain't leavin' for 'nuther four hours. Two o'clock, and it is usually on time."

"That'll be fine."

"Fifty cents."

Jonas pulled the gold coin out of his front pants pocket and tossed it on the counter. "I'd like my change in paper money."

The clerk picked up the coin and bit into the edge. It was soft enough. He punched a button on the cash register, and a drawer opened into which he dropped the gold coin in a cup and retrieved four one-dollar United States notes and two silver quarters. Brighton stretched over the counter and craned to see inside the cash register drawer. The clerk reacted by slamming the drawer shut and jumping back, clutching the bills and coin in his hand pressed to his chest and covered by his other hand. Jonas froze the clerk in place with a stare full of business from his dark-gray, shining eyes. "Just want to see how much you got there," Brighton said in a menacing low growl. The clerk began to quake. The ex-convict did not blink and did not move. He stood there boring an imaginary hole into the clerk's head. Then he said, "All right, give me my ticket and my change" and turned to smile handsomely at Margaret. He could tell she was impressed and flushed all over with excitement.

"You working all day?" She nodded her head *yes.*

"Why don't you give Margaret the rest of the day off?" Jonas said to the clerk while he kept his eyes on Margaret. She smiled big and lowered her eyes demurely.

"I . . . I . . . I can't do that," the clerk gasped.

"Are you the store manager today?"

"Yessir."

Jonas turned back to the clerk and drilled him again with a hard stare. "Then you can do it," he said.

"Wal . . . Margaret are you all done?" She nodded *yes.* "All right then. If you want you can take the rest of the day off."

Jonas held out his hand, palm up. "My change and ticket, please."

"Oh. Sorry. Here you go."

Brighton stuffed the money and ticket into his pants pocket, turned to his left, and held his arm for Margaret to take. "Shall we?" he said with a come-hither look. "You know a place for a good cup of coffee?"

"Yes, let me get my coat. I'll be back before two, Mister Jones." Her voice was all sweetness. The two of them sauntered out into the wind arm in arm.

Presently, a half a block up, they came to a small café. Margaret turned in, and Jonas followed. They got comfortable and ordered two coffees. Small talk ensued, and in less than a half hour they were finished.

"You live close by?" Jonas queried directly.

"Up the road a little in a boardin'house."

Two hours later they were putting their clothes back on when Jonas said, "How much do they pay you at that store?" He wanted to see how Margaret was going to play the con.

"Oh, not much. But it is enough for what I need to get by."

"How much?"

"Fifteen cents an hour. We open at seven and close at five." She dropped her gaze to the floor and fluttered her eyelashes.

"Well, you took half the day off for me. Here's a buck to cover it." He pulled the four U.S. notes from his pocket, peeled off one, and put it on the dresser.

"Oh, no. I couldn't do that."

She was playing innocent. And doing right well at it.

"Yes, you can. You earned it."

She fluttered more. "Well, if you insist." She eased around the bed toward the dresser and stopped halfway. "It is hard to get by these days," she said as she looked up at Jonas, flashing her brilliant blue eyes with just enough woe expressed.

Jonas laughed in barrel rolls coming up deep from within. He hadn't laughed like that in over four years. Margaret looked confused and annoyed. After a bit, Brighton regained control.

"Miss Margaret, if it is 'miss,' " he said, still chuckling, "that is the best act I've seen in a long time, but you ain't gettin' any more than a buck outta me. I do like your style, and you may now know my whole life story. It ain't worth more than a buck though."

Margaret scrunched up her face, quickly stomped to the dresser, snatched up the dollar note in her gloved hand, and stuffed it in her little clutch bag. She grabbed her coat off the bed, threw it around her shoulders, jerked the door open, and went through. Jonas called after her, "You gonna leave me alone in your room?"

"It ain't mine," she hollered back as she sped down the stairs. With that Jonas glanced around the room and realized it was somewhat barren and absent any evidence of a full-time resident. He shrugged his shoulders and left.

Coming out onto the boardwalk, he pulled up his collar and pressed down his hat as he looked up and down the street through the blowing snow. Only a few people were out and about leaning against the wind as they trudged through the weather. Margaret was nowhere to be seen, so Jonas headed back to the general store. He walked in purposefully through the half-glass double doors and shut them behind him with just a little slam. He again surveyed the store. Jones was at one of the tables with a female customer and looked up at the sound of the doors closing. Margaret was not there. Brighton walked over to the counter in front of the liquor shelves and waited for Jones to come over, which he did after a couple of minutes.

"Yes, sir? You're back. How can I help you?" he said from behind the counter.

"I'll take a half-pint of brandy and some matchsticks."

"Well, you are in luck. I just got a shipment in yesterday and have plenty in stock. Sure you wouldn't want two or three bottles? I imagine you're pretty dry after what? Five years behind bars? Got some fresh dime seegars, too." He grinned big.

This feller was acting a lot different from the first go around. Pretty bold now. Margaret must have told him about Jonas. What she didn't know though was that he had killed a man. A bad man. This feller was not a bad man. So, he could let his smugness go by. And then he saw the reason for the storeowner's boldness as a tall deputy United States marshal walked from the depot through the archway into the store. He twirled his watch bob in one hand and let the other hand linger about the butt of the pistol holstered on his right hip. He strolled around the store a little and then back into the depot. Jonas guessed he was waiting for the train to arrive to escort someone to or from the federal prison at Leavenworth.

"None of your business where I been and how long," Brighton said flatly and again penetrated Jones eye to eye.

"Uh sure. No offense. That's thirty-five cents. There ain't no consumption allowed on the premises. Don't have a license. No charge for the matchsticks," he said as he looked in the direction of the deputy in the depot. Jonas laid down two quarters, picked up the bottle, and put it in his coat pocket. He scraped his change off the counter and ambled over through the archway to the depot just as Margaret stepped out of the back room into the store proper. He saw the movement out of the corner of his eye and turned to look.

"Margaret," he said politely and tipped his hat. She glared at him for a brief few seconds and then whipped her head up and to the right away from him as she turned her back to him. Jonas chuckled. "So much for sweetness."

The lawman was standing with his back to the black pot-bellied stove in the center of the room. There were empty wooden benches lining three walls with a break in one wall for the door to the outside on the main roadway. On either side of the door, there was a big window, and the deputy was facing them. He was the only person in the room. Jonas walked in and stopped at the stove to warm himself as well.

"Cold one today, eh?" he said.

The deputy turned to face Brighton and said in an official tone, "I ain't in the habit of jawin' with ex-convicts." He stared threateningly at Jonas, who felt a flash of anger and then let it go. He stepped over to the window, turning his back on the law-man, and in ten minutes he heard the train whistle. He hurried out the door and down the road to the platform at the side of the tracks. There was no place to get out of the wind, and so he hunkered down and waited the three minutes for the train to come in, screeching and steaming and huffing and puffing with bell clanging. Then it stopped with a big blow of steam off the drive pistons. A conductor jumped down from the lead car, blew his whistle, and called out, "Five minutes. Departure in five min-utes." Jonas climbed up the car platform steps and went through the door. He asked a porter for directions to the smoking parlor. He wasn't in a mood for conversa-tion, and he intended to smoke his fine cigar and sip his brandy just like a regular gentle-man. He had to step off that car and hurry down the platform to the last car, where he stepped up and entered a nicely appointed car that held the aroma of cigar smoke.

The train whistle blew twice, and it lurched forward. Slowly it pulled away from the platform with steam blowing, deep throaty chugs, and bell clanging. Jonas wiped away the frost and looked out the window at the eighty-foot-high walls of the prison. He saluted a fierce farewell and sighed. It was over.

He retrieved the cigar from his shirt pocket, pulled his coat tight across his chest, leaned back in the seat, and lit the cigar, then pulled the brandy from his coat pocket. As he puffed, he sipped a little brandy from the half-pint he bought in the store. It was an excellent cigar, and the brandy wasn't that bad at the cost of thirty-five cents. At last he relaxed and felt free. A fine cigar and brandy and a nice woman were all things not to be had in prison, even though the woman was a pro and not happy with him.

Thinking of Margaret brought him around to muse over his first four hours as a free man. The thing that annoyed him was that everyone seemed to know he was an ex-con. Of course, that wouldn't be too hard to figure for Jones, the storeowner, and Margaret. His clothes were standard issue for all the released prisoners who no doubt made their first stop just like he did at the store for a train ticket or a bottle or what have you. Jones and Margaret had probably seen hundreds. But, even though they had a good game going, there was no call to be so nonchalant. And then that deputy marshal. My, wasn't he uppity. Maybe they all should try doing a few years themselves before they started looking down their noses at people. That was why he was gruff with Jones, scaring him to think he might rob him. Put him in his place. Maybe he wouldn't be so superior acting. But what a setup they had. A quarter mile from the prison with a train depot, a store with liquor, and a sweet little whore doing double duty as a clerk and a purveyor of delight. Oh, he knew right off she was a lady of ill repute as they call them. Like he said to her, she had style. Kept her out of jail, never suggesting anything or asking for money for a romp in the hay. Just being so sweet. He wondered how much Jones's cut was. And from the way he was acting, maybe Rodgers was in on it.

Jonas sipped more brandy and then put the bottle away. He had a long way to go, and he needed to make it last. He started figuring again. About seven hours actual travel time on the rails and ten hours changing trains and waiting time. And then he needed to look up his brother's blacksmith shop in Independence, gather up Harry and Edgar, and relocate north. He didn't plan but to spend a few days visiting in Independence. It was going to be tiresome but far better than seventeen hours at Lansing.

It was snowing again, and Jonas barely saw

the black-on-white railroad sign that announced the town of Independence just as the conductor came through and called it out twice. Presently, the train crept into the station, and he hopped off before it stopped. He pulled his collar up and hurried into the depot station house. He held the door open for a lady and an older gentleman followed by a young woman, whom he presumed was their daughter. He smiled, she smiled, he held his admiring stare, she flushed and looked away. Not his type. He shut the door. They bustled over to the stove, and Jonas espied a ticket agent and telegraph operator sitting at a desk with his back to an open sliding window in the plank wall between the ticket office and the waiting room.

"Excuse me," Jonas said. "Could you direct me to the Brighton blacksmith shop?"

"Nope."

"Uh, beg your pardon."

"Ain't the Brighton shop no more."

"What do you mean?"

"William Brighton up and died of apoplexy a year ago."

Jonas stood staring without seeing. Why hadn't Mary sent word? What about the boys?

"Is Mary, his widow, still in town?"

"Mighty nosy, ain't yer?"

"William was my older brother."

"Well, how come you didn't know 'bout his passin'?"

The agent was giving the real squinty eye to Jonas and looking him up and down. Jonas gave him a hard stare and said, "I've been out of touch. They were carin' for my boys, Harry and Edgar."

"Oh, so yer the black sheep brother that's been in prison, eh?"

Brighton felt a real urge to jump through the window and ring the little varmint's neck but held his temper in check.

"Yer better check in with the marshal, 'cause I ain't tellin' yer nothin'."

Jonas watched him slowly slide his hand to his top desk drawer and was mildly humored as the agent pulled out a Colt Double Action Army revolver with a five-and-a-half-inch barrel in forty-five caliber. Brighton hadn't seen this particular pistol before. He smiled and said, "That the new Model One Eight Seven Eight I heard about?"

"It is, and I don't know whether or not yer heard about it, but I reckon you better git on outta here now." He waved the pistol toward the door but apparently was savvy enough not to point it at Jonas.

Jonas smiled and tipped his hat. "Good

day to you, sir. Kindly point me to the marshal's office."

Brighton forced the door against the wind to close it. The office was warm as it was being heated by a potbellied stove against the wall on the left. The man at the desk was obviously napping, as he suddenly dropped his boots to the floor, sat up, and sputtered before he declared, "What the hell? Er, what can I do fer you?" He wore a star on his vest that said *Deputy.*

"Reckon the marshal ain't in?"

He folded his arms on the desk top and leaned forward. "You reckon right, mister . . ."

"Brighton."

"You related to Mary and William since passed?"

"Yes. William was my older brother. I am here to fetch my boys and visit a little with Mary. Thought I would spend a little while with William, but, as you said, he is passed. Be obliged if you could show me the way to their house."

"Wal, why don't I take you there, and she can verify your identity. You armed?"

"No, sir."

"Don't mind if you were to open your coat just to be sure you ain't packin' a pistol."

Jonas unbuttoned his coat and spread it

wide. "Can't trust an ex-con, eh?"

The deputy stood, pulled a coat and a hat off pegs in a row on the wall, shrugged into the coat, and smashed the hat on his head. "Ain't no never mind to me. Just doing my job." He opened the door and said, "Let's go."

They stepped up to the covered porch of a white two-story house, and as they stomped the snow off their boots, the deputy twisted the knob on the brass rotary doorbell. Within a minute, Jonas heard footsteps inside coming toward the door. It opened about a foot to reveal Mary, who poked her head through. "Albert?" she queried the deputy, and then her eyes rested on Jonas. The door swung open a little more, pushed by the wind, and Mary pulled her shawl tighter around her shoulders. Jonas and Mary hadn't seen each other in eight or more years, and there was no immediate recognition of him on her part. They both had aged. Strands of gray were in her brown hair, her face a little more wrinkled, but her blue eyes were still sharp and intelligent. Of medium height and posture, she showed herself to be, as always, a quite capable woman with no undue frills. She wore a green dress with white apron and a dark-green knitted shawl.

The deputy tipped his hat and said, "Mornin', Mary. Sorry to bother you. This feller claims to be William's younger brother and your boys' father."

Jonas removed his hat and smiled at Mary. She smiled back pleasantly and said, "Jonas." She reached out and took his arm. "Come in, come in. Thank you, Albert."

"Shut the door and come in here to the parlor. Here, give me your coat and hat. Sit right down in this chair. I'll be right back. I want to put a pot on to boil for tea. You just missed the children. They are all off to school already. I'll be right back."

Mary went out to the kitchen, and Jonas sat in the chair looking around the parlor. Not anything remarkable what with the gold-colored wallpaper and window drapes except for a somewhat large daguerreotype photograph of William and Mary on their wedding day that hung on the wall opposite him. It was surrounded by a cream color mat, shaped in an oval and framed in fine-looking dark walnut. William would have been about nineteen or twenty years old then. He was old enough to join up for the war, but he already had a wife and two children, so the family all thought it best that he stay home. And he did.

Jonas caught the movement in his peripheral vision as Mary came down the hall. She sat on the divan across from him. "Water'll be ready in just a bit. My goodness, you should have let me know you were coming. So sorry for your loss of Matilda and Martha. I can well sympathize with how you must feel. Poor William. Just about a year ago now. Apoplexy. Right down there at the shop. Matter of fact it was Albert, the deputy, who found him. Slumped over the anvil. Well, you're out of prison now. What are your intentions?"

Just then the teapot tooted. "Oh. Here. Hold on for a minute." A few minutes and she returned with a tea service on a tray. "Let's let that steep a bit. Now, you were saying?"

Jonas smiled, as he hadn't said anything as of yet. "First, I must say I was highly surprised to hear of William's passin', and I am sorry. Didn't know about it until I walked into the train depot. How have you managed?"

"Oh, I sold the shop for a very good price. I own this house free and clear. And I just recently have been seeing a gentleman. He is a widower as are we, Jonas. He is the postmaster in town. You know we are now nearly three thousand souls here in Independence. So, we are a good-sized town. I have

68

the children to keep me busy. Speaking of which, I presume you will want me to continue to care for the boys."

"Well, I was thinkin' of takin' them up north with me. Shouldn't they be with their pa?"

"Not necessarily. Especially a pa with no wife. The boys need a mother at this tender age, and it is true they need a father, too. They've been here three years now and are well-established in school. They are best of friends with their cousins, and I just think it best they stay here for me to look after. What are you planning to do up north, and where exactly will that be?"

"I have a referral to a feller who is makin' wagons for the army at Fort Riley. That's up near Junction City."

"Who will watch over the boys while you are on the job?"

Jonas hung his head and stared at his feet. "Suppose I'll need to hire someone to do that."

Mary poured tea into blue and white china teacups and handed one to Jonas. "Sugar? Cream?"

"Sugar. No cream."

"Two lumps?"

"Three." Mary raised an eyebrow, and Jonas smiled. "I got a real sweet tooth."

"I see that. Probably would fill those boys full of candy, too. No, I think it best they stay here with me. If the Lord smiles on us, I expect Johnathan, he's the postmaster, will be proposing soon. He is a good Catholic man, and the boys already like him."

"Well, I understand what you are sayin'. Why don't we wait and see what the boys have to say before makin' a decision?" He smiled and sipped his tea.

"Yes. I suppose so. No offense, but I am pretty sure they will want to stay here. And either way, you will stay for Christmas. You been attending Sunday Mass?"

Jonas dropped his gaze to the carpeted floor and slowly shook his head *no.*

"Well, you can come with me and the boys and Johnathan while you're here."

CHAPTER TWO
KANSAS: LEARNING DETECTIVE WORK

Mary was right. Jonas decided it probably was best for the boys to stay in Independence, where they wanted to stay anyway. It would be very difficult for him to care for them on his own. He bought everybody Christmas presents, stayed until after New Year's, gave Mary a hundred dollars and his furniture and household goods she already had in her possession, promised to visit as often as he could, and boarded the train for Junction City.

The train made its last major stop in Manhattan before Junction City. It was a bright and clear afternoon that Jonas took advantage of to stretch and rejuvenate, as he had been sitting on the train for nearly eight hours. He stepped off onto the platform and breathed in the air. He guessed the temperature was above freezing but not by much. Strolling one way and then the other on the platform he stretched his legs and then ambled into the depot building. Jonas spied the pot of coffee sitting on top of the large potbellied stove in the center of the waiting room. There was a stack of tin cups on a table against the wall across from the stove. He noticed that other passengers in the depot had helped themselves to a cup, so he did likewise and nearly choked on the beverage that must have been sitting on the stove for hours. But it was hot, and he had drunk worse.

Next to the table of cups was a stack of *The Nationalist* newspaper that was local to Riley and Geary Counties. He picked up one from the stack and saw that the issue was for that week, so he fished a nickel out of his pants pocket and dropped it in the cup with the five-cent emblem on it. Then he folded the newspaper in half and placed it under his arm. He took his time, sipping the coffee and moving in the general direction of the door when the conductor's shrill whistle pierced the air and the call of "all aboard" came loudly across the platform. As he headed for the door he was jostled by a stern woman with two children in tow. A little coffee splashed on his fingers, and he was holding the cup away from his body when it was nearly spilled by a large man who pushed past him. But Jonas took it all in stride. After all, he was a free man, and he intended to stay that way.

Back in his seat he leaned back and kicked his feet up on the seat across from him. There was no mud on his boots so he figured he wasn't hurting anything. He unfolded the newspaper and began to peruse the articles. It was another hour to Junction City. Should be plenty of time to delve into the local society.

One particular article caught his attention. It was about the continuing court action in Junction City of an arrest for murder that was made three months prior by the city marshal, assisted by a private detective who worked up the case. What was interesting was that the detective was a woman and according to the article quite effective in digging up the evidence against the accused. Her name was Virginia Hudson. She was from Missouri and hired directly by Captain Charles Ross. Jonas wondered what private detectives were paid. A salary, per diem, percentages of reward money, or maybe even the entire reward? Might be interesting to be a detective, however they did it.

Before the train came to a full stop in Junction City, Brighton hopped off to get ahead of the other passengers heading for the station. It was too late in the day to hitch a ride up to Milford, where the wagon maker he sought was located, so he needed to find out from the agent where he might acquire inexpensive room and board for the night.

"Hello," he said to the agent seated behind the arched opening in the wall across from the door. "Can you tell me of a nice room and board? Not too expensive. I'm headed for Milford and need a place for tonight." He swatted his cold hands against his coat. The fellow did not even look up from the schedules he appeared to be reviewing. He just pointed in the direction behind Jonas, where there was a bulletin board on the wall with all kinds of notices of various sizes and colors pegged to it. Jonas swiveled his head to see what he was pointing at and then back to the agent he said, "Thank you, my good man," and tipped his hat.

On the bulletin board he found two boardinghouses with their addresses and looked at the agent to ask for directions but then changed his mind. The man was probably mute anyway. So he stepped back out onto the boardwalk, pulled up his coat collar, pressed down his hat, and started walking. He came to a barber shop and went inside. Come to think of it he hadn't been barbered since leaving prison, so he hung up his hat and coat and sat in one of the waiting chairs.

The barber stopped his snipping on his customer and looked his way and said, "Good afternoon. You just come from the train station?"

"Yes. How'd you know that?" Jonas looked at him quizzically.

"Well, I seen the direction you came from. There ain't nothin' down that way past the train station for a gentleman such as yourself."

"I see. Well, this gentleman needs a shave and a haircut or he ain't gonna be lookin' like any sort a gentleman anymore." He chuckled, and the barber and the other customer joined in.

"Would you give me directions to this establishment?" Jake showed him the slip of paper with the name of the boardinghouse on it.

"The Jenkins House? Sure. You're only about five blocks away," he said as he continued to snip hair. "Head west right here on Tenth to Clay. Turn north. Be there on your right. There we go, Bob. That should do you for another month." He dusted vigorously with talc and a brush, removed the hair cloth around the man's neck, then the chair cloth, and continued to brush his customer's clothes.

"Here you go," the customer said. "Thirty-five cents." And he shrugged into his coat and put on his hat, then went out.

Jake stepped toward the barber chair and said, "What happened to shave and a haircut, two bits?"

"Oh that was just a song. Long since gone."

"Uh-huh. You know or ever heard of J. T. Morgan's wagons?"

"Sure. That's Jeremiah T. Morgan up in Milford. He builds wagons for the army at Fort Riley."

"I heard he's lookin' to hire on extra help. You hear anything like that?"

"No. Can't say as I have. Where'd you hear that?"

"Oh, just around. You know of any boardinghouses in Milford?"

"No boardinghouses but lots a folks take in boarders. In fact, Jerry Younkin was in just the other day and said he's got room for one more boarder. He's farmin' up that way. If I remember correctly Morgan's shop ain't but a couple miles down the road from Jerry's place."

"All right, I'll look into it. Much obliged. Now, how does one hitch a ride up to Milford?"

"Well, there again you're in luck. The

mailman's leavin' tomorrow in his buckboard on his route north. Probably hitch a ride with him, and the post office is right around the corner and down a few blocks from Jenkins. Down at Seventh and Adams."

About noon the next day Jonas hopped out of the buckboard and then pulled out his valise from the back. "Thanks again, Denton. Be seeing you around," he called out to the mailman, who was good enough to drop Jonas right at the Younkin farm mailbox, which was a half mile from the farmhouse. He covered the distance in ten minutes on the snow-packed drive through the white desert of winter. He was exhaling steam when he came to the front door and knocked. A dog started barking and didn't stop even as he came charging around the corner of the house, spraying snow off his churning feet, and slid to a stop next to Jonas. His tail was wagging, and he wasn't showing teeth, so Jonas held down his hand for the big mutt to sniff. As he did, a teenage girl in a thick, full-length brown coat came around the same corner the dog did.

"Yes, sir. Can I help you?" she said with a hint of challenge.

"I understand you have room for a boarder. Is this your place?"

The girl grinned and said, "No, sir. This is the Younkin farm. It belongs to Jerry and Elizabeth. I'm their daughter, Sylvia." She held out her hand for a shake. Jonas took her strong grip and shook hands. "Ma's collectin' eggs. I was just goin' to help her. Would you mind waitin' here on the porch until Ma comes? You can sit right here in that chair. Would you like a glass of sweet tea?"

"A glass of sweet tea would be wonderful," Jonas said as he set his valise on the floor by the chair. "No ice, though," he added with a big smile and a little chuckle.

The girl giggled and said, "Course not. I'll just be a minute." She opened the screen door and then the front door and disappeared inside the house.

A few minutes later the door opened, and a young woman came out with a glass of sweet tea. She was pretty, and Jonas's eye wandered for but two seconds as he took note of a well-endowed figure. Probably about five foot six in her shoes. She had clear, milk-white skin with a hint of rouge on her cheeks and red, succulent lips. Her brunette hair was piled high on her head, and she wore thick bangs across her forehead to the top of her brow almost into her eyes. She looked out from under the bangs with bright, blue-gray green eyes that had flecks of cinnamon around the pupils. That alone would have been enough, but everything combined gave her a very exotic appearance. Her movement was slow, measured, and suggestive. Her voice, when she spoke, was low and smoky. She was without a doubt an allurement, and she knew exactly what she was about.

"Hello. Sylvia said I should give this sweet tea to you," she said as she held out the glass of tea. Jonas took it from her, and she pulled her gray wool shawl tighter around her shoulders and tight across her chest. She wore a navy-blue paisley day dress.

Jonas doffed his hat and said, "Thank you. Name is Jonas V. Brighton. And you are?"

"Virginia Hudson." She held out her hand. Jonas took it and held on for longer than was the custom. "You can call me Jennie like all my friends do."

"That name is familiar to me. Where have I heard it?"

"You probably read it. I'm a detective. Solved a murder in Junction City," she said, all businesslike.

"That's right. I read it in the paper."

"What's the *V* stand for?"

"Beg your pardon?" Jonas said, clearly clueless about what she was asking. There was no connection to the topic of their conversation.

"Your middle initial. What's it stand for?"

"Oh. Well that's a secret."

"Maybe I'll pry it out of you someday." She smiled mischievously with a hint of wickedness.

"Well, you bein' a detective and all maybe you will. But you'd be the first." He grinned.

Her eyes danced mirthfully, and her smile widened and then disappeared just as Mrs. Younkin came around the corner of the house. She wore a canvas long coat over her brown dress and was carrying a basket of eggs.

"Hello. Elizabeth Younkin," she said as she held out her hand. "Here, let's get inside out of the cold. I see you have some tea. That's good."

They all moved into the house. Virginia was last, and she closed the door behind them. She came up close behind Jonas, almost touching his back. He felt her but pretended he didn't notice. "Sylvia said you are looking for room and board."

"Yes. That is correct. The barber by the train station in Junction City said he thought you had a room with board available."

"Well, he thought right. Are you employed?"

"I hope to be after tomorrow. I am a wagon maker, and I heard J. T. Morgan is hiring. I have money saved up to carry me over."

"Well, you heard right again." She smiled graciously and said, "Fifty cents a day for room, breakfast, dinner, and supper. We're up early for the chores, but the table's set by six. You do your own laundry including sheets. Sylvia can iron for you if you need some done. We're right friendly folk here. Ain't that right, Jennie?"

"Oh yes. Very friendly. I've been here a month and enjoyed every minute of it." Jonas took note that she seemed to be overplaying it a little.

"Well fine, then. Let me pay a month in advance." He glanced at Virginia and saw her perk up and take note of what she just heard.

"Let's first see how you fare at Morgan's tomorrow."

At the supper table, Jennie sat next to Jonas and almost immediately had her knee pressed against his under the table. Coyly, when nobody else was looking, she smiled at him as if they were sharing some secret. Jonas was naturally intrigued, but he was more interested in the sleuth business.

"Tell me, Jennie, have you had many other

cases that you've investigated? Detective work sounds real interestin' to me," Jonas asked, and he was immediately flashed on by all the other eyes at the table. They looked from him to her and back again.

Jennie scowled and said, "Mister Brighton, please if you would, refer to me as Missus Hudson. I am a recent widow, and we hardly know each other well enough to be on an informal first-name basis." She glanced at both Elizabeth and Jerry Younkin. Jonas nearly choked on his biscuit and quickly took a long drink of water.

"I am sorry," he said with a polite smile and an expression of regret. "I did not intend to be forward."

"Yes. I accept your apology." Again she glanced at the Younkin seniors and even quickly at Sylvia. They all seemed to be appeased and returned their concentration to their plates. She tapped Jonas's knee twice with her knee and again, while nobody was looking, shot a glance at him that seemed to say *play along.*

"As to your question, Mister Brighton, I am from Saint Joseph, Missourah, where my husband and I were private detectives. So, yes, I've investigated more than a few cases before my husband was killed. He was run over by a freight wagon." She fell silent and dropped her gaze to the tabletop. After a minute, she resumed her story. "We were known to Captain Charles Ross of Junction City. When he heard of my husband's demise he wired me to come and help with a case. That's the one you read about. Well, there was so much publicity after the arrest that I was overwhelmed and escaped up here to live with the kind Younkin folks. That's about the long and the short of it."

"About how many cases?" Sylvia asked.

"Oh, I don't know exactly. Close to fifty I would say."

"My goodness. That's quite a few." Sylvia looked startled. "You must've started investigatin' cases before you were sixteen, since you're only eighteen now." She obviously was feigning earnest inquiry.

Also obviously perturbed, with a sideways glance at Jonas, Jennie said, "Well, maybe it was fewer than fifty. I don't remember exactly, but at least I was married at sixteen unlike someone else who has very poor prospects of ever marryin'." She shot ocular daggers at Sylvia.

"Oh, I think my prospects are pretty good for a *decent* marriage."

"Ladies, please," Mrs. Younkin said. "Pass the peach cobbler around, Sylvia. Thank you."

"I am a widower too," Jonas said, somewhat subdued. "My wife and daughter were killed in a cyclone back in seventy-six over in Osborne County."

"I think I remember reading about that in the newspaper. Quite tragic. We are sorry for your loss," Mrs. Younkin said, and the silence loomed only to be broken by the clinking of utensils on plates.

"Elizabeth tells me you are a wagon maker, Mister Brighton," Mr. Younkin said.

Jonas tapped Jennie's knee like she did his and said, "Yes. I intend to visit Morgan's tomorrow and see about a job."

"Yes. Fine fellow, Jerimiah Morgan." Younkin cleaned his plate and wiped his mustache and beard with the red and white checkered napkin.

"Care for a cigar?" Jonas asked.

"No, thanks. John there and I need to get the stock fed and button everything up for the night." With a nod he indicated the older teenage boy sitting on the side to his right.

"Can I be of any help?"

"No, John is my hired man. David'll pitch in, too. We can handle it. Much obliged just the same for the offer."

Mrs. Younkin said, "David is our oldest son. Twelve years old. You already met Sylvia. Fourteen. And then there is Belinda.

84

She's eight. And our baby boy, James. He's five." Each of the children smiled at Jonas as they were introduced.

"Well, all right. Call me if you need any extra help. I am also a blacksmith by trade."

"Well now. I might take you up on that. We got a forge and anvil and tools out in the barn. I got a lot of things needin' repair and other things to make I got ideas for. Maybe we can make some arrangements. Let's talk about it tomorrow when you get back from Morgan's."

"All right. Do you allow cigars, Missus Younkin?"

"I don't mean to be inhospitable, but I would appreciate it if you could smoke out on the back porch."

Jonas saw the look pass between husband and wife and with a pleasant smile said, "Certainly. My pleasure."

About half the cigar was smoked down when Jonas heard the door creak behind him. He turned around to see Jennie slip through the door, shutting it quietly. She pressed up against him and whispered in his ear, "I hope you don't mind. I intend to sneak into your room tonight." She didn't wait for a response and seemed to suddenly disappear. Jonas shrugged his shoulders and chuckled to himself.

Sure enough between ten and eleven Jonas awoke to the feeling of weight on top of him. It was Jennie in her nightgown that she had hiked up to her waist. His blankets were thrown back, and she was fumbling for his manhood under his nightshirt. She was breathing heavy, and Jonas felt her breath on his face. The fragrance of her perfume was intoxicating, and he let himself rise to the pleasure of the moment. Jennie began to moan, and Jonas covered her mouth with his hand. Meanwhile, Sylvia watched the moonlit couple through the keyhole.

When Jennie had tiptoed but a few steps in the dark hall away from Jonas's door she gasped with surprise as Sylvia struck a match to light a candle and stepped from a shadow to confront Jennie. She, too, was in her white nightgown with a sleeping bonnet on her head. She held up the candle, put a hand on her hip, and demanded, "What'er you doin'?"

"Shh! I am goin' to the privy," Jennie whispered.

"You might want to put some shoes on then. And you better wash that nightgown in the mornin'." She held the candle down lower. "You got stains on it."

Jennie involuntarily looked down to see

wet stains around the middle portion of her nightgown. She looked back up with her face all pinched up in anger, and in a loud whisper she said, "You little brat. I'll —" Sylvia blew out the candle and was behind her own bedroom door before Jennie could finish her sentence.

In the morning Jonas sat with Jerry, John, and David at the breakfast table. They were all finishing a last cup of coffee when Elizabeth came in with the pot. "Anyone for another cup?" she said. No one responded, and she turned to return to the kitchen when Jerry said, "Just a minute, Liz."

"John. You and David go on get started. I'll be right with you." They scraped their chairs back and went out to the back mudroom. "Jonas, me and Liz were talkin' last night, and if things don't work out right away at Morgan's we'd like to offer you room and board in exchange for smithin' and farrier'n. You do shoe horses don't you?"

"Well, no. Sorry I haven't learned that skill."

"That's all right. I got plenty else for you to do."

"Much obliged for the offer. I'll see how it goes today."

Jake turned out the Younkin lane to the

road and crunched the snow for the two miles to J. T. Morgan's to find out that he was two days too late. Morgan filled his last opening but said to keep checking because his orders changed all the time. Jake looked around the operation for a little while and then tucked his hands in his coat pockets and trudged back to the farm faced into the wind on the return trip. He kept pushing with his head down. He had his face and ears wrapped in a long, plaid, wool scarf to avoid frostbite, and his hat was jammed down tight on his head. It took him an hour to traverse the distance back to the farm, and he was so glad to be warming his hands in front of the fire.

The next day he went about the barn setting up his shop. He was anxious to get the forge hot and warm the air so he could stop blowing steam from his mouth. It was a good ACME forge of cast iron, with a hand-levered fan, standing on four legs, with a hood and flue over half the bed. He was not successful the first day, but on the second day he was, and he pumped the hand-levered fan as fast as it would go to get up a good bed of red-hot coals. Then he started shaping parts from the steel Younkin had in stock.

It was about an hour after the noon dinner when she glided through the smaller door of the barn and over to Jonas's shop. He was at the forge and saw her coming out of the corner of his eye. He set his work-piece aside and stepped back from the forge to face her. "What're you doin' here?" he asked with a half smile.

She wore a long brown coat and a black wool scarf over her head. She pulled off the scarf and let it fall around her neck and down her front. "I miss you," she said with a little pouty look.

Jonas pulled off his gloves and held his palms up, shrugged his shoulders, and said, "It's only been two days. We don't even know each other. How could you miss me? I've been real busy with this shop."

"Too busy for this?" she said as she opened her coat flaps to reveal her naked-ness.

Jonas sucked in a deep breath, flashed searching looks to his left and right, and said, "Are you tetched? You're gonna get us evicted." But he could not restrain himself. He quickly untied his apron and let it drop to the ground. Then he stepped over to her and slipped his arms inside her coat and around her body. She lunged at him and hungrily captured his mouth with hers. Then she pulled back and moved over to a barrel that was on its side. She lifted her coat flaps, wrapped them around her waist and laid over the barrel. "Come see about me," she said in a husky voice dripping with seductive tones. Jonas looked furtively left and right again and then moved in.

He buckled his britches belt and said, "What was all that knee bumpin' about at the supper table my first night here?"

"Oh, just tryin' to get you to go along with me. I knew you weren't the goody two-shoes type a fella."

Jonas pumped the handle for the forge fan and said, "You ain't no widow, are you?"

Jennie sat against another barrel smoking a little cigarette. Her coat was wrapped around her so as not to reveal any of her nakedness. She picked a piece of tobacco off her tongue and said, "What makes you think that?"

"Well, you sure ain't in mournin'," he chuckled.

"You're right. I just say that to keep the flies away and get sympathy from Elizabeth Younkin. That daughter of hers, Sylvia, is on to me though. I gotta watch her real close."

"So what're you doin' out here on the farm?"

"I got in some trouble in Missourah. I'm

90

lyin' low here for a while."

"What kind a trouble?"

"Private matter."

"Uh-huh. Meantime you did that detective job in Junction City."

"That's right."

"Tell me about it."

"Not much to tell. Ross knew who did it but couldn't prove it. I went undercover and lured the feller into a confession."

"How'd you do that?"

She stood and tossed the cigarillo in the forge. "I have my methods, Mister Nosy," she said with a devilish little smile and gleaming dance of the cinnamon flecks in her eyes.

"I'll bet you do."

Jennie was just at the barn door when it opened and Sylvia stepped through. "Where have you been?" she demanded. "I've been lookin' all over for you. What're you doin' in here?" She said as she looked past Jennie to see Jonas at the forge pulling on his gloves.

"I had business to discuss with Mister Brighton." She smiled impishly.

"I bet you did more than discuss."

Jennie feigned a shocked look and said, "Whatever do you mean by that?"

"You know what I mean. Never mind. Ma

wants to see you right now!" She stamped her foot on the ground with the word "now." Jennie went through the door first, and Sylvia followed, but before she was out she turned her head to see Jonas and smiled at him in a curious way.

The months rolled by, and the weather changed from winter to spring. Jonas worked in the blacksmith shop, and Jennie helped with the household chores. They managed to keep their affair a secret from everyone except Sylvia, who was constantly spying on them and finally caught them. She repeatedly blackmailed Jennie for little things all the time until Jennie caught her and John in the hayloft. That levelled the playing field. The last thing Sylvia could ever have happen was for her father and mother to find out about her experimentation.

One day in May, Jennie came into the shop with a letter in her hand. Jonas put down his work and listened to her summarize the letter. It was from Captain Ross. "He needs a married couple to work under cover and catch a con artist who's sellin' real estate he probably doesn't own. Naturally, I volunteered us."

"But we ain't married," Jonas stated as a

matter of fact.

"That don't mean anything. All we have to do is say we are married. Who's gonna ever check?"

"I don't know," Jonas said as he rubbed his chin.

"I thought you wanted to do detective work. That's all you been talkin' about. You got that correspondence course and all. Don't you want to put all your book learning to good use?" She chided him like a haughty brothel queen. "Or were you sayin' that just so as you could use me for your sexual pleasure?" She laid a pouty glare on him and thrust out a hip.

"Me? You're the one who runs around here like a bitch in heat," Jonas said a little too loud.

"Well, I declare. Listen to you. Keep your voice down. Honestly, you know you are just as much a sexpot as I am. So, let's get back to business. You gonna do it, or do I need to find somebody else?"

"Oh, all right."

Two days later they caught a ride back to town with the mailman. All his buckboard had in the back were empty mail sacks that Jonas made a seat cushion out of to sit on to soften the jolts of the road along the way.

Jennie rode on the spring seat next to the mailman. The weather was threatening, and, as luck would have it, about halfway to town, the sky opened up, and sheets of rain pelted them. Fortunately, there was a large elm tree on the side of the road, and the mailman reined the horse over to pull the buckboard under it. The thick canopy of leaves stopped much of the shower but not all. Jennie pulled the hood of her coat over her head, and Jonas held his hat down by pulling on the brim with both hands. Lightning crackled, and thunder boomed all around them. They managed to not get soaked until the wind pushed the rain horizontal. By the time the thunderstorm passed they were drenched to the bone, and the sun stubbornly remained hidden behind the clouds. They came into town looking like drowned rats, and thunderstorms were still busting out all around them.

"I only brought one dress," Jennie said as she pressed her back against the board wall of a building to maximize the protection afforded by the overhang covering the boardwalk. A little puddle was building around her shoes as the water drained from her petticoat.

"I only got this one suit," Jonas said.

"I got an idea. C'mon. Follow me," Jennie

said breathlessly.

They dodged the rain as best they could as they ran for the Chinese spa and laundry. It was the only place in town that kept a dry heat sauna going around the clock. There they could warm their wet bodies while they waited for their clothes to dry and be pressed by the shop owner.

The next morning they sat in a small office across from a stout fellow with a full brown beard and bushy eyebrows. He sat behind a desk that had a safe and file cabinet behind it. His name was James J. Brinkman. "So you're saying you can sell more lots than me because you know more people in town. Is that right?"

"That's right," Jonas said. "We take a ten percent commission on all the lots we sell. You provide the title, and we collect the money for you."

"Uh. I'll collect the money, if you don't mind."

"All right. Long as we get paid."

"Well, I'm just starting out here, so I guess I don't mind giving y'all a whirl." He grinned, which was hard to see through his beard, but his sparkling eyes told the tale.

"You have title to the land, don't you?"

"Yes, sir. I have a deed signed over by the

former owner. See here." He turned around and retrieved a sheaf of papers from the safe, untied the official looking ribbon that bound it, and displayed a fancy looking deed all signed and dated properly.

"May I see it?" Jonas studied the deed briefly and compared the legal description to the meets and bounds subdivision plat Brinkman had tacked to the wall. They matched all right, so he memorized the name of the seller and handed the deed back to Brinkman.

That evening they met secretly with Captain Ross. "The deed was signed by Helen T. Montgomery," Jonas said.

Ross backhanded the piece of paper Jonas had given him. "That's her, all right. I couldn't remember who owned that land. She's an old spinster that lived here nigh onto twenty years ago. Owned a lotta land around here. Sold it all and moved back to Chicago. I suppose it's possible she sold it to that Brinkman fellow. But it just doesn't feel right to me. I got her lawyer's name and address somewhere around here. I'll look it up and send a letter to him to verify the sale."

Jonas and Jennie sold five lots in a week. Brinkman put the money in the safe and handed them pre-printed deeds with the correct lot number filled in and signed by him. Try as they would, neither Jonas nor Jennie could catch the safe combination because he always hid the dial with his bulky body. So they decided to get him drunk and make some excuse to get in the safe.

"With those kind of sales we should celebrate. Will you join us, Mister Brinkman?" Jonas said as he pulled a pint bottle of whiskey from his inside coat pocket.

"Don't mind if I do. Got some glasses right here, and if we run out I got another bottle down here in my desk drawer." He grinned, and Jonas poured a good amount into Brinkman's glass and about the same in his own but less in Jennie's.

After they refilled and everybody seemed to be loosened up, jabbering away about real estate deals and opportunities, Jonas said, "You know Mister Brinkman . . ."

"Call me James, please," he said as a plea and tipped his glass to them.

"All right, James. I was gonna say me and Virginia been sellin' real estate all over this state and Missourah, too, for a lotta years now. Some deals legitimate and some shady. It was always the shady ones that made us the most money. Wasn't it, Virginia?"

"Sure was. Remember all the deals we were workin' with the Corrigans in Kansas

City?" She nodded her pretty head know-ingly and said, "There was some good money there."

"You were in deals with the Corrigan brothers?"

"Yeah. We were their principal brokers," Jonas said.

"Well, well. I'll drink to that."

"Yeah. They acquired a lotta land with forged deeds mixed in with their right-of-way purchases for roads and their streetcars, then we sold it at high profit for them. Ever do anything like that?"

"Me? No. All my deals are on the up and up." He avoided eye contact and took down a big slug of whiskey.

They finished off Jonas's bottle and almost all of Brinkman's. Try as they could though, they could not get him to confess anything incriminating or obtain the combination to the safe. So, they decided to give it up and stumbled back to their room at Jenkins's boardinghouse. Brinkman went his own way.

The next week, on a sultry Wednesday afternoon, Jonas sat down heavily in the chair in Brinkman's office. "Well, that's five more," Jonas said as he swathed his face with a big white handkerchief. He loosened his tie and collar and unbuttoned his vest. Brinkman sat at his desk pouring over papers spread all over the top. "I have to go up to Milford for a day or two, but Jennie will stay down here and work." He sneaked a look at Brinkman to see if what he said had any effect. He couldn't tell. The plan while he was gone was for Jennie to seduce Brinkman and try and get information out of him. He wasn't really going to Milford though. He intended to shadow Jennie to make sure she didn't get herself into any trouble. She took offense at that, saying she was experienced and could handle herself. He wasn't quite sure what she meant by that, but he intended to watch over her anyway. "Well, all right. I'll see you in a day or two." Brinkman waved his hand over his head without saying a word or looking up.

That evening Jennie came in the office and slapped signed contracts on Brinkman's desk. "Well, that's two more. Makes an even dozen now. At two hundred dollars down you should have about twenty-four hundred smackers. Of which, I may remind you, our take is two hundred forty bucks. So, if you don't mind I'll take our cut right now." She stood with one hip thrust out and her hand pressed into her narrow waist. She wore her hat at a jaunty angle on her pile of hair and smiled suggestively at Brinkman.

"Well, I can pay you right now if you take me out to supper." And *he* smiled suggestively.

"Why don't *you* pay me and *you* take me out to supper since you are the money bags around here?" She grinned coyly and moved in close to him.

"All right, you silver-tongued devil. You talked me into it." The safe door was unlocked, so he turned his bulk around and opened the door. For just an instant she could see some money, and then he scooted to the left and hid the opening while he counted out the cash. Then he shut the door and spun the combination dial. "Here we go. Two hundred forty dollars. Normally, I don't pay until the end of the month but since you're gonna be real nice to me, well . . ."

Jennie quickly thumbed through the cash of four fifties and two twenties. All through supper and all the way to his room, Jennie flirted with him. They had a lot to drink in the saloon as they ate their supper, and Brinkman had a bottle in his room that he pulled out as soon as they went in. Jennie sat in a chair and he on the edge of the bed. "Well, I'd say you are a really smart man, James. Probably makin' a lot of money on these lot sales."

"Why don't you come over here, and I'll tell you all about it," he said as he patted the mattress beside him.

"Well, I don't know about that." She took on a real innocent look.

"Oh, come on. I ain't gonna bite you. Wouldn't do anything you don't want to do."

"Well, all right. So did you buy that land real cheap?" she breathed into his ear in passing as she sat down next to him. He reacted, and she saw it.

"Let's just say, I got it for a song." And he lunged at her. She leaped off the bed before he could get a hold of her, and at that moment Jonas burst through the door.

"What's goin' on here?" he demanded.

"Oh, we were just talkin' business," Jennie said, tongue in cheek.

"Looked like more than real estate business to me. Monkey business I'd say."

"Now just a minute, sir. I can assure you your wife's honor was never in doubt." Brinkman tried to look indignant.

"Well, let's see what the police have to say about that."

"Wait a minute now. Don't be in such an all-fired hurry. We don't any of us need that kind of bad publicity. Let's talk about this for a minute." His forehead began to show tiny beads of perspiration. "Suppose I compensate you for your perceived threat to your honor. Would that calm you down?" With eager anticipation he looked from one to the other.

"He's got the cash in the safe. I saw it," Jennie said with a threatening look at Brinkman.

"Yes. I could pay you another two-forty right now."

"Well . . ."

"Let's go to the office," Brinkman said as he bent over and picked up his hat.

Next morning, Jonas was feeling pretty good. He and Jennie sat at a table by themselves and were drinking coffee and eating slices of toast with bacon strips on them. As he basted a slice of toast with a thick spread of raspberry jam, he said just above a whisper, "I think I'm takin' to this detective business real good if this is what we get for it. Four hundred and eighty bucks in two weeks."

"Unless that's a phony deed Brinkman has." And, just as she finished saying that, Captain Ross walked in the dining room. He had a letter in his hand and set it on the table as he sat down without invitation.

Jonas and Jennie stared at him with blank looks on their faces.

"Well, we got him. With your testimony and this letter he'll be indicted sure."

"What's in the letter?" Jonas asked.

"It's from the old spinster's lawyer. He says everyone more or less forgot about the land but that he still holds the deed for her. She never signed over any deed. In fact she's been mentally incapacitated for months."

"So he did forge it," Jennie said with irony in her voice.

"Yep. You wanna be there when I pick him up?"

"You bet," Jonas said for both of them.

The office door was unlocked. and the first thing that grabbed their eye as they walked in the door was the safe with its door standing wide open. It was empty.

"Oh m'gosh. Tarnation and damnation. He's run off with the money," Captain Ross said.

Jonas and Jennie exchanged glances and quick, very quick, little smiles. "Whatta we do?" Jonas asked.

Captain Ross turned real grave with a threatening look in his eye. "First thing we do is not say a word to anyone. Anyone! You understand me?"

"Yes, sir." Both the Brightons, as they

were now holding themselves out, looked a little scared.

"Last thing we need is a panic by folks over their money gone and illegitimate deeds in their hands. Let me see if I can find out where he might be headed and how he's traveling. If he took the midnight train he's gone. We won't ever see him again."

The Brightons were sitting in the dining room of the boardinghouse sipping coffee. They shared a piece of apple pie as it was still another couple of hours before the noon dinner was served. They were talking real quiet.

"What if they catch him?" Jonas whispered. "After we blackmailed him, you know he'll for sure tell that we got the four hundred eighty bucks." He looked left and right to make sure no one was overhearing what he said. There was only one other couple in the room, and they were clear on the other side.

"I know. But, if we give it back when they catch him, Ross'll charge us along with Brinkman as accessories. If we give it back now, he might let us off seein' as how we overcame our temptation and did the right thing. I don't know. What do you think?"

"It's a crap shoot either way. Four hundred eighty bucks in two weeks. That's double what it took me four years to earn in prison."

"You were in prison? What for?"

"Yeah. I just got out last December. Grand larceny."

"Damn. You should've told me. I need to know who I am workin' with. If he finds out you're a ex-con . . . We better give it back right away."

"Well, we don't need to give it all back. Far as anybody knows he only collected twenty-four hundred dollars. Our pay was ten percent of that. Or two-forty. So, we give that up right now and keep the other two-forty. We can always say it wasn't part of the land deal. It was private payment as compensation for the insult to you. That'd be our defense. Whatta you think?"

Jennie shrugged her shoulders and tossed her head a little. "It might work. Besides we were workin' undercover for Ross at ten bucks a day. That's a hundred right there. You have the money on you don't you?"

"Yeah. Always keep your money on your person or in a safe. Don't trust the banks. They go bust all the time, and everybody is just out. Zero. Nothin'. Here. Take this two-forty and stuff it in your purse. We'll use the excuse that he took off so fast we didn't have a chance to tell him about the money, and besides we were supposed to turn it in to him at the end of the month." He winked at Jennie, and she kissed him full on the mouth.

"You are brilliant," she said, breathing into his ear. "Let's go up to the room."

Jake scraped his chair back and stood to pull back Jennie's chair so she could stand when at the same time Captain Ross came in. He started to speak, but Jonas cut him off.

"We were waitin' for you to return. You left in such a hurry we didn't have a chance to turn over the money Brinkman paid us as our commission. Two hundred and forty dollars. That's ten percent of the twelve down payments he collected. Probably better to turn it over now rather than at the end of the month as planned. Don't you think?"

"Yeah. Yeah. I didn't think of that. Thanks. Bring it over to the office, and I'll make out a receipt. Found out he left on the five a.m. eastbound train. Nobody's seen him since. But, the Manhattan marshal wired back to say that one of his deputies saw a big, portly fellow get off the train this mornin'. Say, you wouldn't want to track him down for me, would you? Still the same ten bucks a day."

"That's interestin'. Let us think about it and get back to you later today," Jonas said, looking real interested.

"Make it quick. The longer we delay the farther he gets away. If you decide to do it, I'll give you badges and a letter of authorization."

As they walked back to the boardinghouse they spoke in barely audible voices to each other. Jennie said, "Guess we oughta do it. Heck, ten bucks a day is still good. But, if we catch him we gotta be sure he's got more than two thousand one hundred sixty on him so we don't get into bad straits for the two-forty we collected from him as compensation for the insult to me, as you put it. Twenty-one sixty and the two-forty we already gave back equals the twenty-four hundred he collected from the victims."

"Yeah. Because you know Ross will insist that it's money that belongs to the folks who were duped. I need to buy a pistol. You go on to the Jenkins House. I'll be there directly."

Jonas returned to the room, and Jennie leapt up from where she had been stretched out on the bed thumbing through the newspaper. "Did you get it?" she said eagerly as she perched on her knees on the bed. "Let me see it." Jonas removed the small pistol from his vest pocket and held it out for her to see. "Kind of small, ain't it?"

"It's supposed to be small so it can be concealed in a vest pocket. See?" He slipped the little pistol back into his vest pocket. "It's a thirty-two caliber, so it's enough to make a feller stop if he gets shot by it."

"I guess so. But you coulda got at least a thirty-eight in a shoulder holster under your coat. I could carry that peashooter in my purse."

"You want one, too?"

"Nah. One is enough, I guess. Don't think you'll ever have to use it anyway. We can share." She smiled jokingly.

"There's a three o'clock eastbound train. We better check in with Ross and board that train."

Jonas stepped out of the passenger door and down to the platform. He turned and held out his hand for Jennie. She took it and smiled coyly, saying, "Here we go. Our first big case."

At the sound of thunder, Jonas glanced at the sky. "Might be a wet afternoon. Why don't you procure us lodging? I'll go check around." He pulled out his pocket watch from his vest pocket and said, "I'll meet you at the Manhattan Palace at six for supper.

Once you get the room you can start askin' around about Brinkman. See if anybody's seen him."

"Who made you the boss?" She tossed her head indignantly.

"You got any better ideas, I am willin' to listen."

"Guess not."

"All right see you at six. Stay dry." He winked at her with a smile, and she reluctantly smiled back.

Jonas turned around and went into the depot. He walked up to the agent's window and said, "Excuse me. I am Jonas V. Brighton, detective for Junction City police." He pulled back his coat to reveal the badge pinned to his vest.

"What can I do for you, detective?" The agent eyed the badge closely.

"I'm looking for a man. Stout fellow with a big bushy brown beard and eyebrows. Probably wearing a three-piece suit. He boarded the five a.m. eastbound out of Junction City. Did you happen to see him come through the terminal?"

"The mornin' eastbound out of Junction City was delayed by an unscheduled stop at Ogden. Guess they was low on water. So it didn't arrive here 'til seven. Half hour late."

"Uh-huh," Jonas said and tried to look

interested.

"So I was anxious. It bein' late and all. I was watchin' for it out on the platform. Normally, I wouldn't make no never mind and tend to my business here at the desk."

"Uh-huh."

"So you're in luck. I watched the passengers detrain. Three a them."

"Did you see a man fitting that description?"

"No."

"I see. Well . . ."

"But I did see a big stout feller get off. He didn't have no beard, but his eyebrows were bushy enough." He grinned. "And they were brown."

"All right. Thank you. Will you immediately contact the police if you see him again? Did he come into the terminal and buy any other train ticket?"

"Nope. He just hauled his carpetbag off the platform and headed into town."

"Thanks again." Jonas hurried away and cursed under his breath. "Playin' games with me."

He went to the city marshal's office and reported his presence and mission. Then he went to the stage depot and asked around. Nobody had seen a big stout fellow with bushy brown eyebrows. So he started down

the line of shops and offices on Leavenworth Street and found that a man fitting
Brinkman's description bought boots, canvas pants, a denim shirt, and a broad-
brimmed hat in the late morning at the
general store.

"Did he happen to mention anything
about where he might be headed?"

"No, sir. Just said he needed to provision
himself for more primitive travel."

Primitive travel. What could that mean?
Jonas walked briskly to the livery and asked
around there. Nobody had seen him. And
then the big and angry black clouds of the
thunderstorm swept in and changed day
into night. The storm was right over the top
of them and boomed hissing lightning all
around with an avalanche of rain that
changed to hail the size of walnuts. In no
time the street was covered in white. A
deafening crack and a huge electric bolt of
blinding silver lightning struck the rod of
the church steeple two blocks over. Jonas
ducked away involuntarily and instinctively
slipped further back into the livery barn.
The hail changed back to torrential rain,
and it went on like that for twenty minutes.
Then, suddenly, it was all over. The thunder
grew faint, and the rain subsided to leave a
mud-filled street with hailstones still banked

up against the boardwalks. A rush of muddy water ran down the middle of the street filling depressions with large puddles, overflowing them, and then continuing on down toward the river. Rainwater dripped from everything and rolled over the sides of the catch barrels.

Jonas ventured closer to the door and cautiously looked out. He surveyed the street and then retreated when a large blob of a drip caught him full on the back of his neck. He leaned against a stable post and chewed a piece of clean straw. The afternoon eastbound train was the one he and Jennie came in on, and there was no ticket sold to Brinkman to continue east. But, that had to be the direction he was headed because he was from the East. If you were running away from something, usually you ran back to the place with which you felt most familiar. At least that is what Jonas reasoned. No train ticket. No stage ticket. No horse or buggy rental. He said "more primitive travel." What could that be?

While he was still deep in thought he pulled his watch, checked the time, and decided to venture out again toward the Palace. He sloshed his way to the nearest boardwalk, mentally cursing the mud, and then started walking while keeping an eye out for a place to cross the fast- moving stream of water in the street when he stopped dead in his tracks. The drainage was to the river. A light bulb went on. The river. Brinkman hired a boat to take him down the Kaw to Kansas City. He walked in fast, long strides to the Manhattan Palace Saloon. Jennie sat waiting at a table with drinks already poured. Jonas rushed in and downed his drink in one toss. "C'mon," he said. "Gulp that drink if you want it. We got to go, now."

"What the hell?"

"C'mon. I'll tell you about it along the way." He pulled a silver dollar from his pocket and set it down firmly on the table. Jennie put the glass to her lips, threw her head back, and took down the whiskey in one swallow. As they passed in front of the bar, he said to the bartender, "Dollar's on the table."

"That's fifty cents too much," said the bartender in a surprised expression.

"Keep the change."

"My, my. You are in a hurry," Jennie said.

He explained his theory as they hurried down the street to the boat landing. "Now we have to find a boat that looks like it is preparing to launch and get in position to catch him as he's boarding. Night's not too far off. Moon's out though," he said as he eyed the full moon rising out of the east in a sky full of broken clouds. It was in competition with the sun that, with the passing of the storm cloud, was free to shine through the clouds, too, as it slipped steadily to the west.

"I checked all the hotels, boardin'houses, saloons, and whorehouses. He wasn't stayin' at any of 'em. Why don't we ask around to see if anyone's fixin' to leave any time soon?" She talked in between slight gasps for breath as Jonas trotted and pulled her along by the hand so that she had to run to keep up. They ran down the boardwalk and jumped from plank to plank that had already been laid out in the muddy street where there was no boardwalk.

"Don't want to take the chance on alerting anybody. He could've been stayin' anywhere. See what we find when we get to the landing."

When they came to the road that paralleled the river's edge they stayed on the shore side of the road where the grass spared them having to walk in the mud. There were several little boats tied off and one small steamer. On the downstream end of the line of boats there was a keelboat tied to the bank. It had a single mast, a cabin, and a giant oar for a rudder. The low cabin was about half as long as the boat and centered in the middle. Probably about a forty-footer, both the bow and the stern were pointed, and the motley brown sides looked old, rustic, and leaky. There was a wagon parked next to the boat in the muddy road with two mule teams hitched to it. Three men were unloading crates from the wagon and pushing them up the gangplank that ran at an angle down from the gunwale of the boat to the side of the road. Two men on the boat muscled the crates into stacked rows on the forward deck. The aft deck was already stacked with crates three high.

Jonas pulled a cigar from his vest, bit the end off, spat it out, and snapped a match with his thumbnail. He lit the cigar while Jennie caught her breath. "Let's walk slowly like we are on an evenin' stroll along the riverbank. We'll stay here on the grass so we don't look daft by walkin' in the mud."

"Speakin' of which. Look at my shoes. Already wet and muddy. Ruined."

"I'll buy you a new pair," Jonas said as he took her arm and wrapped it around his. They ambled along, and Jonas pointed at various things to look like they were talking about this or that. "Doesn't look like that steamer's got any real steam up, so it probably ain't leaving any time soon. I'd say that keel boat is the best chance. Course, he could've hired any one of these smaller boats, too."

Slowly they strolled down the roadside and stopped at the keel boat when they came abreast of the aft deck. The last crate came off the wagon, and what Jonas assumed was the bill of lading was signed over to the man who looked like he was in charge of the boat. He was shabbily dressed in beige canvas pants and a dirty white shirt, stained brown around the neck. He wore a wide leather belt in which he had a pistol tucked. Looked like a Navy Colt. Despite his wide-brimmed hat, his face was well-tanned and creased under a three-week growth of salt and pepper scruff. His features were mild and unremarkable. His hair was graying, thick, and in need of barbering. Looked like he was about Jonas's height.

After the wagon was driven off and down the road a ways Jonas saw that the in-charge feller was staring at him and Jennie. Jonas waved a silent greeting and tipped his hat with a big smile to go along. He said, "Me and the missus are just strollin' along the river. We like the smell and the feel of the river after a storm." That perked the man up, and he came down the gangplank but jumped off into the grass between the river's edge and the road before he came to the end of the plank.

"You're river people, are yer?" He spoke to them from across the narrow road.

"You could say that. Yes. Name's Jonas V. Brighton, and this is my wife, Virginia."

The man removed his hat and said, "Pleased to meet yer." Then he looked at Jennie and said, "Ma'am," with a nod of his head. "I'm Albert Riggs, master of this here tub. Folks up and down the river jest call me Jigger 'cuz I am always jiggin' this boat up and down the river. Been doin' it thurty years now. Ain't many folks come down to the river 'specially after a humdinger like the one that just went through. It got the river bouncin' real good. Had to double tie the boat. I like folks that like the river."

"Well, it's sort of our pastime. We're new to town so we just started visitin' the river."

"Uh-huh. Wal, I don't git up this far much. Usually, runnin' cargo between Topeka and Kansas City. Pickin' up what I can since the big steamboats quit the river. Trains takin' over everthing. I can still beat 'em on charges. But I ain't got the cargo space like a train of boxcars. Now I got this army contract outta Fort Riley."

117

"You ever take on passengers?"

"Pretty rough livin' on this tub. Ain't got but four stiff bunks and a galley in that cabin. But, I'll take on one or two ever now 'n then. Wouldn't recommend it for a lady though." He touched his hat. "If'n yer thinkin' 'bout today, I already got one passenger booked so only got room fer one more."

Jennie shot a quick knowing look at Jonas and he back at her.

"Well, we're thinkin' about it someday just for the joy of a cruise down the river. Mind if we take a look at your accommodations?"

"Sure. Here let me drop a plank across that mud fer you."

Jennie squealed as she lost her balance just before she hopped off the plank. The skipper caught her arm and spared her a splash in the mud. "Here now, missus. T'wouldn't do to get all muddied up." He helped her off the board, and she held onto his arm as she skipped onto the grass.

"Why thank you, kind sir," she drawled and batted her eyelashes at the skipper.

"At yer service, ma'am. Please, this way to yer cabin." He helped her up the gangplank to meet up with Jonas, who was standing at the door to the cabin. They all went inside.

"Well, it ain't the Britannic. But I guess it

would do," Jennie said as she glanced around the compartment and smiled prettily at the skipper. Jonas saw the carpetbag on top of one of the lower bunks. He gave a signal with his eyes to Jennie for her to occupy Riggs and get his back turned to Jonas. When she did, Jonas sneaked a look at the nametag on the bag. It was Brinkman's.

"Yes, I agree," Jonas said as if he were some sort of critic. "Shall we return to shore, my love?" Jennie gave him a quick sideways smirk in response to his playacting.

Riggs emerged first from the cabin and held his hand out to assist Jennie. She stepped clear, and Jonas came out, leaning over so as not to bump his head on the door header. As he went through the passage, he glanced left to see none other than Brinkman coming up the gangplank. Jonas came out all the way and leaped in two steps to the gunwale. "Ho, Brinkman," he called out. "Hold on right there. You're under arrest." Jennie back-peddled out of the way and came to an abrupt stop as she bumped into a crate. Riggs stood by where the gangplank was tied to the gunwale, and, rotating his head from one to the other, he looked with wide eyes from Jonas to Brinkman. The big, stout fellow stared in surprise at Jonas but for only two seconds. Then he did an amazingly nimble pirouette and started to run down the gangplank. Jonas jumped onto the gunwale, leaped off, and like a cougar pounced on Brinkman's back only to be carried by the big feller to the bottom of the gangway. Then Brinkman wound his body up to the right, gave a mighty bellow, launched his body back to the left, and tossed Jonas off his back into the mud. Then he pulled a pistol from a shoulder holster and pointed it at Jonas.

Jonas fumbled for his pocket pistol but couldn't get a hold of it because his hands were muddy and slippery. Jennie screamed a shriek that could have raised the dead. "Save my husband!" And then the Navy Colt boomed as the percussion cap flared and ignited the gun powder. The thirty-six-caliber ball caught Brinkman in the right shoulder, knocked his pistol from his hand, and sat him down in the mud. Jennie was screaming. Riggs held the smoking pistol still aimed at Brinkman, who howled, "You son of a bitch. I'm gonna kill you." He bent over onto his knees and one good hand to crawl the few feet to where his gun was stuck in the mud.

"Don't do that!" Riggs called out.

"Brinkman. Stop!" Jonas yelled as he

wiped the mud off his hands and palmed the little pistol.

"You ain't never gonna take me in, Jonas Brighton. I ain't never going back to prison," he shouted as slobber flew from his mouth. He got to his gun, reached for it, grabbed it, and raised it to point at Jonas, who was standing with his little .32 in his shooting hand. Jonas pulled the trigger, and the gun went off almost simultaneously with the Navy Colt. Riggs shot him in the chest, and Jonas shot him in the head. Jennie was still screaming, and Brinkman grunted, rolled over like a big walrus onto his back, let out a big whoosh of breath, and died. Then it was quiet.

Jonas stood staring at the corpse for a full minute, then turned and stepped over to the boat. He held up his hand and said, "Thanks, Captain Riggs. You saved my life."

"Yeah, I real fast figgered out he was some kinda bad man. 'Sides, I don't cotton to no one killin' my river friends." He grinned.

"You look like you could use a bath, Jonas," Jennie quipped. "Guess that suit's about done for, too."

"Just drop it at the cleaners. Good as new," he said as he pocketed his pistol and brushed mud off his pants. People were running toward them, and in one minute a crowd gathered. They sloshed in the mud like a bunch of hogs trying to get a close look at the dead man. Someone said, "Call the marshal. Been a shootin' here sure."

"Nobody needs to call me. I'm right here." The city marshal, a tall and lean man dressed in a black suit and derby hat, pushed his way through the crowd that had formed in an arc around the corpse. He stroked his bushy brown mustache as he looked from Brinkman's body to Jonas to Riggs to Jennie. Two of his deputies came running up, and he said, "Get this crowd pushed back so I can interview these folks and examine the scene. Get 'em outta earshot." He waited for the crowd to retreat, and then he turned to Riggs. "What happened here, Jigger? Tell me in detail. Don't leave nothin' out."

"Marshal, I'm Jonas V. Brighton, and this is my wife, Virginia. We are both detectives with Junction City Police." He pulled his coat aside to reveal the badge pinned to his vest. "That deputy over there can attest to my checkin' in with your office earlier today. This man is a fraud suspect who Captain Ross sent us to capture."

"Uh-huh. Wilbur! Come over here," the marshal hollered to the deputy. "I still want to hear the story from you, Jigger. Then we'll see where we go from there, Detective Brighton." The deputy came up. "Wilbur, Detective Brighton here claims he checked in with you earlier today. Is that correct?"

"Yes, sir. He's from Junction City. Has a letter signed by Captain Ross."

"You have that letter on your person?"

Jonas retrieved the letter from his inside coat pocket and gave it to the marshal, who read it over quickly front and back.

"All right then. Welcome to the city of Manhattan, detectives." He tipped his hat to Jennie. "So, Jigger, what happened here?"

Riggs told him the whole story with colorful additives here and there. "All right. Sounds like a justifiable homicide. You all be at the courthouse at ten a.m. ready to testify before the coroner on this death."

Jennie stepped down the gangplank at the hand of the marshal, whom she of course flirted with. "Marshal, may I leave? I am in need of privacy," she said like a helpless maiden.

"Of course. Of course. I trust you'll be with Mister Brighton at the hearing tomorrow."

"But marshal," Riggs protested, "I got a contract I have to meet. I got to launch in an hour."

"Marshal, can we just take his affidavit to

123

the coroner?" Jonas asked.

"What's a affawhatever you called it?" Riggs said.

"It's your written statement about what happened."

"Cain't read or write."

"You can tell me it, and I'll write it for you word for word. Then you can sign it," said Jonas. "Marshal, you or one of the deputies can witness it. Isn't that true?"

"Yes, I suppose we can do that. All right, the undertaker here yet? There he comes. Let him through. Stand aside. Let him through."

"Marshal, we might want to search him first. He was believed to be carrying a large sum of money on his person," Jonas said encouragingly.

"All right. I'll search his person. You search his bag. Oh, right off. Here's a thick envelope in his inside coat pocket. Whew, there's some cash here."

"How much?" Jonas said while looking over the marshal's shoulder.

"Well let's see. Bring that bag over here so we don't lose any a this. Looks like mostly all hundreds. One, two, three . . . two thousand on the button."

"Nothing in the bag, so that must be it. Can you impound that money for us, Marshal, and Captain Ross'll give you disposition by wire."

"Sure thing."

"Jigger, shall we go to the marshal's office so I can take your affidavit?"

Jennie went to procure a room for her and Jonas in a hotel that had hot bath facilities on the first floor. She didn't wait for Jonas, as she was the first of the day in the tub luxuriating. She hadn't bathed in a week and was feeling the need. She put her shoes out for drying and conditioning and her dress for cleaning. Then she rang for the housemaid and ordered a bottle of champagne. She figured Jonas would have extra money after he searched Brinkman. But when Jonas came in she got a surprise.

"Two thousand. That's all he had on him," Jonas said as he shut the door behind him. "What's all this?"

"I thought we could celebrate, but I guess there ain't any extra money, huh?"

"Aw, we got money. Why not?" he said as he poured a glass of champagne for himself.

"Yeah, but we have to give a hundred sixty back to make twenty-four hundred to pay back to people Brinkman swindled."

"No, we don't. Now that Brinkman's dead, nobody knows about that but you and me. You want to give your half back?" He smiled devilishly.

"Noooo." And she smiled the same.

They left after the inquest on the noon westbound train. In all the business of the inquest and everything they somehow forgot to pay their hotel bill. The next morning they met with Captain Ross. "You didn't pay your hotel bill in Manhattan," he said flatly.

"Oh, that's my fault," Jennie said. "I was supposed to pay it, and I just forgot in all the hubbub. There were newspaper men nearly assaulting me and coroners and undertakers and lawyers. Why the Riley County Attorney almost charged us with murder and probably would have if it weren't for the marshal. Can you believe that? We'll wire them the money for the bill."

"Yes, I can believe it. In fact, the Geary County Attorney is convening a grand jury to look into the missing hundred sixty bucks. He thinks you might have it. So be prepared to testify tomorrow morning."

"That's crazy. We gave you what he paid us in commission. How would we have any more?" Jonas said with a cross look on his face.

"I don't know. Maybe he wants to get it on the record."

"On the record? That's only fourteen dollars per victim. If it weren't for us they'd be out a hundred eighty each."

"I know. I know. Far as I am concerned y'all did a right fine job. Let me have your invoices as soon as you can."

Next day in the grand jury room of the Geary County courthouse Jonas was being grilled by the county attorney. The prosecutor had already finished with Jennie. "One last question, Mister Brighton. You claim without a word of falsehood, and I remind you, you are under oath, that James Brinkman did not pay you any money beyond the commissions for anything connected with the lot sales. Is that correct?"

"Yes, sir."

"Then why do you suppose he only had two thousand dollars on his person when you shot him?"

"No idea. Maybe he spent it on whiskey and women." Jonas smiled humorously. The jury did not.

"One hundred sixty dollars is a lot of money to spend in what — a week? Don't you think?"

"It would be for me. But I ain't Jim Brinkman. He bought a train ticket, new clothes, and passage on a river boat that I know of. I couldn't say for what was left over."

"Fine. You may step down and wait in the hallway."

Jennie and Jonas sat on a bench outside the grand jury room. "Do you think they'll arrest us?" Jennie said with a grave look on her face and a slight twitch in front of her left ear.

"Nah. They don't have any evidence."

"What if they find out we lied on the stand?"

"We didn't lie. He asked us both if we were paid anything extra *in connection* with the lot sales. We weren't. It was a private matter not *connected* to the lot sales. The only way they find out about it is if he told someone. I don't think he did. He left town pretty fast after he paid us."

Jonas leaned back and lit a cigar. By the time he had smoked it halfway down the bailiff came out and told them the grand jury voted to not indict. Jennie breathed a sigh of relief, but as the first of the jurors filed out none of them looked happy. They glared in disgust at both Jonas and Jennie, which had the effect of paralyzing Jonas. One by one they came by, and he stood watching them with some disgust of his own. What right did they have to judge him and Jennie guilty with no evidence? How do they know Brinkman didn't use some other of his own money to pay the two forty to the Brightons? Finally, the county attorney came out. He stopped in front of Jonas and with a very stern look said, "We know you took the money. We just can't prove it. Best not spend it real soon." He turned on his heel and stomped away.

The two detectives turned in their badges and handed back the letter to Captain Ross. He was courteous but professional. Not friendly like before. They had to wait until the end of the week to be paid by the city. They were paid but not happy. It was not a pleasant time. Everywhere they went they received scornful looks. On the street, in the stores, in the hotel lobby and dining room, even in the saloons people were stand-offish. And to top it off *The Nationalist* newspaper out of Manhattan was hinting around that maybe the Brightons did have the money and were scoundrels themselves. After all, Brighton was just released from prison, where he was incarcerated for grand larceny, and they did skip out on their hotel bill, and wasn't it convenient that Brinkman was killed and couldn't testify, etc. etc. After they were paid, they left town in a rented one-horse buggy for the Younkin Farm. Along the way Jonas began laughing and continued almost uncontrollably.

"What are you laughin' at?" Jennie insisted as she pushed against his side in the buggy.

"Well, ha ha, the city paid us a hundred twenty plus expenses, ha ha, and Brinkman two forty, ha ha." Gradually his hooting subsided and he continued. "That's three sixty total. Not bad for two weeks work, eh?"

"No it ain't. Let's pull off into that field and celebrate. I got a pint of whiskey in my bag and a tingling down under." She nibbled his ear lobe and said breathily, "It ain't the right day but, you're my valentine."

They spread their coats on the ground and sat side by side. After they had a few pulls on the bottle Jonas said with a slight grin, "You are a damn good detective."

"Damn right I am. But, why do you say that?"

"Cuz you guessed my middle name. That's what you were doin', wasn't it?"

Jennie looked puzzled, and then the light went on. "Why sure. I detected the *V* stood for Valentine." She puffed up a little and continued. "Heck. As soon as I knew your date of birth, being born one day after Valentine's Day and all, I knew the *V* was for Valentine. Simple." She snapped her fingers for emphasis.

"Well, simple do what simple is. See if this is simple enough for you," he said as he moved in, pulled her close to him, and lavished kisses on her everywhere.

It was after dark when Jonas pulled up beside the barn. The house was still lit inside, but it would not be for long, and all would be dark for the night. The dog was running around the buggy barking its head off, and Jerry stepped off the back porch with a shotgun. "Who's there?" he shouted.

"It's us, Jerry. Jonas and Virginia. I got to put this horse up, and then we'll be in. Don't wait up for us."

"Oh, all right. Goodnight then, and shut up that damn dog."

CHAPTER THREE
MISSOURI: THE TALBOTT CASE

A few days later, Jonas walked down to J. T. Morgan's Wagon Works and managed to land a job working three days a week, which was fine with him. The other three days he would smith for Younkin. Jennie resumed her helping with household chores, as all the children but Sylvia were still in school. After the census taker came in June and both Jonas and Virginia reported themselves a widow and widower, they decided to tell the Younkins they were married, even though they weren't, and were about to rent a small house on the next farm closer to town. It wouldn't be as far for Jonas to walk to Morgan's, and they could have their privacy. Although they didn't tell Elizabeth or Jerry, Sylvia was becoming impossible with her inquisitiveness. So, they spent the summer in relative bliss in their own home.

In early October, Jennie received a letter from her friend, the town marshal of Maryville, Missouri. There were intimacies in the letter, so she didn't show it to Jonas but told him about it. Over supper at the table she began by saying, "I got another job for us."

"What's that?" Jonas asked and then bit into a fried chicken drumstick.

"There's, or was, a real uppity-up doctor near Maryville, Missoura, named Perry Talbott. What a they call 'em? Real prominent citizen. State legislator, newspaper editor, member of society, and all that gobbly-gook. Highly respected, well known around the state. Well he was murdered on the eighteenth. Coroner's jury couldn't identify any assailant or assailants."

"The eighteenth of last month?"

"Yes."

"Fresh." He forked in a mouthful of mashed potatoes.

"I'm friends with the town marshal. Knew him from detective work before I came out here. He heard about our case on Brinkman and my other one in Junction City. Newspapers I guess. Anyway, same old story. He and the sheriff and the prosecuting attorney think they know who did it, but they can't prove it. They want us to come over and see what we can dig up."

"Who do they think did it?"

133

"Doesn't say."

"Ten bucks a day?"

"Nothing less."

"Might as well. Be good for our business, Hudson and Brighton. No. We are supposed to be married. Brighton and Brighton then." He chomped another piece of chicken. "What do you think?"

"I think so. We'll have to go undercover. Change our names and all. But, if we get an arrest, our real names will come out, and we'll get the credit we deserve and get real well known."

"Got the case closed already, eh?"

They came into Maryville under dark on the last Wabash train of the day. They left their bags at the station and walked right over to the marshal's office. He and the sheriff were there waiting for them. They stood as Jonas held the door for Jennie and she walked in.

"Jonas, this is Sheriff Henry Toel and Marshal Ed Johnson. Gentlemen, this is my husband, Jonas V. Brighton." They shook hands all around, and Jonas noticed an air of disappointment in Johnson and a somewhat ironical look on the sheriff.

"So you went and got yourself hitched, huh, Jennie?" Sheriff Toel said with a broad grin such that his teeth showed under a walrus salt and pepper mustache. Jonas noticed that he extended the grin to the marshal also. The sheriff was about six feet tall, showing a pot belly under his vest, and looked more slouchy than muscular. He was definitely in his last years of service as witnessed by his graying and thinning hair, but his eyes were still sharp and intelligent with a hint of satire coming through.

"Yeah. Figured I needed to make myself a honest woman." She glanced at Marshal Johnson, and Jonas was sure he saw a spark shoot between them. Ironically, Johnson looked a lot like Jonas in a lot of ways — not identical by any means but enough to make one think they might be related. That, too, Jonas took note of.

"All right. Well let's sit and get down to business." The sheriff pulled a wooden ladderback chair around for Jonas, and Johnson brought one around for Jennie. The sheriff took the seat behind the marshal's desk, and the marshal pulled a chair over so he could face the two detectives head on.

"What we got here, like I said in the letter, is the murder of Doctor Talbott. On the night of the eighteenth he just come home from a call on a sick child. He was in his sittin' room readin' a speech when a shot

135

was fired through the window. The bullet went through the doctor's chest and grazed Missus Talbott's calf. Then it stuck in the wall."

"Heavy caliber," Jonas said as he fired up a cigar. "Probably a rifle, huh?"

"We think so," Sheriff Toel said. "Go on, Ed."

"One of their sons, Albert, grabbed a shotgun and ran out to chase the assassin. He fired a shot but says he missed. Said he lost sight of the feller in the dark. But . . ." He paused and looked the detectives directly in the eye. "Here's suspicious thing number one. He and none of his brothers or sisters, eleven of 'em, never chased after the assassin or raised the neighbors to come out and search. Then number two is he died the next day, and while we were interviewin' the family they seemed like they coulda cared less. Showed no sadness or sympathy to their murdered husband and father." He nodded his head up and down slightly to emphasize the fact of his statement.

Sheriff Toel said, "We know the rumors around town how the doc mistreated his wife and children. All the children are wild and undisciplined. They probably resent their father or did, rather. We suspect they conspired and murdered their own father.

Of course, we don't have any evidence. That's where you two come in. What do you think?"

Jonas blew a cloud of cigar smoke to the ceiling and said, "Need a confession. Don't you think so, Jennie?"

"Yes. Any ideas on how we can get undercover with the family?"

"The only weak link we can think of is Belle's, that's Missus Talbott's, brother-in-law Wilford Mitchell. He seemed disturbed by the whole thing," Sheriff Toel said.

"And he ain't the most up and up feller neither. Probably done some thievin'," Marshal Johnson threw in.

"We need to take on false identities, don't we, Jennie?" Jonas looked over to Jennie, who didn't quite sit as close to him as usual.

"Yes. Certainly."

"How about Frank and Virginia Hudson?"

"That gives you a cover, but what about me? That's flat out my real name. Or was." She added the last in quickly with a snap glance at Marshal Ed.

"It's the Brighton name that's got the fame. It has to be covered. Yours should be all right. Don't you think so, Marshal?"

"Sure. It should be all right, Jennie." He smiled just a smidgeon too intimately.

"We can pass you off as my unmarried

137

sister. See if you can lure one of those boys into admittin' guilt." Jonas stole a glance at Jennie and at the marshal, who remained stoic. Jennie, on the other hand, was fidgety.

"All right then. We'll take a buggy ride out thataway tomorrow and see what we can see."

The sheriff described the Talbott house and said, "It's about seven miles south of town in a village called Arkoe."

Jonas stood and ashed his cigar in the spittoon, held the door open for Jennie, tipped his hat, and said, "We will probably go undercover tomorrow, so I don't know when we will be back in touch with you, but we will." He turned to go and stopped, turned back, and said, "Our fee is ten dollars a day plus expenses. Includin' court days. Are you in agreement with that?" he smiled pleasantly.

"Yes, of course. You want it in writing?" Sheriff Toel said.

"Well, now that you mention it, seein' how this case is, maybe we should."

The sheriff wrote out a brief contract, signed it, and handed it to Jonas. "Thanks," he said. "Now can you point us to the best hotel in town?"

"C'mon, Jonas. I know where it is," Jennie said with more than a hint of sarcasm.

■ ■ ■ ■

It was a cool morning the next day as Jonas pulled up in front of the hotel in a rented buggy. He helped Jennie in, and they drove to the far end of town and then turned around and headed south through the residential streets and came back out into the business district. There they stopped for a long while in front of the Nodaway Valley Savings Bank and pretended to be looking it over real careful. Jonas kept a watchful eye for anyone that might be watching them. Leaning against the corner of a café across the street and down two doors, he saw a young man staring at them. Jonas quickly turned his head toward the bank and verbally pointed him out to Jennie. Then he slapped the reins to the horse's back and drove the buggy past the young man, who watched them the whole time as they went by. Jonas kept his head inclined downward but observed out of the corner of his eye. Jennie appeared to notice the fella for the first time as they came abreast of him and smiled at him ever so sweetly. He appeared to be taken aback and pulled off his hat while smiling back at Jennie.

"Bet that's one of the Talbott boys," Jonas

said when they were clear.

"Uh-huh. What makes you think that?"

"Just a hunch."

"Me, too. Have to be the older one."

They drove on down to the village of Arkoe and came to the Talbott house. It was painted dark green with brown trim and looked unkept with a high and weedy lawn, shrubs scraggy, paint peeling. That could mean that Talbott didn't care about his place or didn't want to pay for maintenance. In either case he apparently either couldn't or just didn't make his kids do any chores to keep the place up. Sheriff said they were wild and undisciplined. Oldest was twenty-one. He had to be the ringleader. He said the next one was sixteen with a fertile imagination.

"I got an idea," Jonas said. "Seein' as how they might be a real wild bunch, they just might be interested in outlaws. They might want to be outlaws. We might fake bein' outlaws to get in the family's confidence. What do you think?"

"Sounds as good as anything else." Jennie seemed to be disinterested and distracted, but Jonas said nothing.

They passed the house and went on down the road so as not to draw anybody's attention and cause suspicion. "I see a sign at

140

that drive up ahead. Let's see what it says."
Arriving at the lane leading off the main
road up to a farm, Jonas stopped the buggy
and read the sign, as did Jennie. It was
soliciting farm help and offering a tenant
house. "What luck," Jonas said. "We can
move in nearly right next door to them. Not
more than three hundred yards down the
road."

"You gotta get the job first."

"Well let's go on up and see about it."

The family dog came out running and
barking as Jonas pulled the buggy to a stop
in front of the white farmhouse. It kept
sounding the alarm, running back and forth
on the dirt in the space between the buggy
and the porch steps of the house. A woman
dressed in a plain, olive-green wrapper dress
and a beige full apron appeared in the front
door. She stepped out onto the front porch
and shouted, "Sparky! Hush!" Then she
looked to Jonas and Jennie and said,
"Howdy folks. To what do we owe the
pleasure of your visit?" She was down-to-
earth, hale and hearty. Probably in her thir-
ties. Had a real friendly smile and with a
little color added here and there looked like
she would be real easy on the eyes.

Jonas removed his hat and said, "Howdy.

We saw your sign out front. Came to inquire."

"Well, can't tell you much. My husband's the one you want to talk with. He's out in the field right now. I can tell you the job comes with a tenant house, so we ain't payin' much in wages, but you'd have a roof over your head."

"Much obliged. Name's Frank Hudson, and this is my sister, Jennie."

"Virginia Hudson?" Her smile was replaced by a curious look. "Sounds familiar. You from around here?"

"No. I always go by Jennie. We hale from Kansas," Jennie said just as pleasant as could be. "Our mother and I were livin' in Edgerton. Brother Frank here was workin' in Milford, that's in a few counties to the west of Edgerton. Well . . ." Jennie closed her eyes and bowed her head. "Mother was killed in those awful cyclones of April 18."

"Yes. I believe we heard of that along with all the other deaths from the tornados. I am very sorry for you, my dear."

"Brother Frank was kind enough to fetch me. We are workin' our way back to Terre Haute, where I intend to care for my aged grandmother."

"Oh dear, how sweet of you. Well, I suggest you come back about noon dinner time and my husband can meet with you then."

"Yes, ma'am. But, unless it'd cause a problem I'd like to drive on out to the field and talk with your husband right about now."

"Well, I expect it'd be all right. Alvin's a pretty easygoin' feller. Meanwhile, Miss Hudson and I'll have a cup of tea. My name's Bessy. We're the Grahams. Family's been farmin' here nearly forty years. Alvin's pappy is Amos Graham. Maybe you heard a him. One a the first settlers around these parts. He was the first . . ."

"Yes, ma'am. Sorry to interrupt, but I better get on over to see your husband, uh, Alvin. Jennie, you can get all the history and fill me in later." He smiled with a covert look that said she should do it.

"Sure. You go on ahead. I'll be right here when you're done." She jumped down from the buggy and turned her head to smile again at Bessy Graham. "I bet there is a whole big story of the Grahams' history I would like to hear."

"He's in the corn up thataway." Bessy pointed to the north. Jonas tipped his hat and snapped the reins on the horse's back. He followed a farm alley that split a big field of brown, drying feed corn in the direction she pointed. Along the way he picked up the foul smell of hogs.

When he came clear of the cornfield and transitioned to the fallow ground, he saw at the far end of the cornfield a man he assumed was Alvin Graham. As he came closer, he reined in the buggy horse and saw that the man, dressed in faded denim bib overalls and shirt and a brown felt wide-brimmed hat, was picking corn heads from the ocean of golden-brown stems and piercing the kernels with his thumbnail. Jonas jumped down from the buggy and walked over to the man, approaching, as it was, from his backside. Jonas called out, "They ready to harvest yet?" The man made a little jump and spun around to face the source of the voice.

"Who might you be?" he said as a challenge.

"Frank Hudson. Saw your sign down at the gate. Came to inquire."

"I need farm help. You don't look like much of a farmhand to me. Besides, I just put the sign out this mornin'. There'll be others along."

"I'm a smith and wagon maker by trade. But I am a hard worker, and I can sure help you bring in this crop."

"Smith, eh? Let me see your hands."

Jonas held out his hands, palms up, and

then turned them over. The ground-in black from the forge and the calluses from repetitive tool use were obvious.

"Well, I could use a blacksmith. I got a small forge and some tools. Tried my hand at it. But I ain't much good. All right. You're in luck. Payin' ten bucks a week and providin' meat, produce, flour, dairy, and a tenant house. That set all right with you?"

"Yes, sir. I'll take it."

"Name?"

"Frank Hudson. We was talkin' with your missus up at the house."

"We?"

"My sister is with me. We're workin' our way back to Terre Haute. She'll be takin' care of our grandmother there."

"Uh-huh. Well, you might think about spendin' the winter here after the corn is in, threshed, and sacked. I got a lot a smithin' work needs doin'."

"I'll talk it over with my sister. Can't make any promises though. She's pretty dead set on gettin' to Terre Haute as soon as we can. We almost got enough saved up for train tickets."

"All right. You talk it over with her. Meanwhile, you can move in the house today and be ready to feed the hogs at dawn. I got a hundred and fifty pigs. So you'll need to crack about twelve hundred-pound sacks a corn and pour it out into the troughs. Fill the water tubs, too. You got farm duds? Then we got to get the teeth on the reaper sharpened, cuz in answer to your question we're about ready to cut that grain. I got to go over to Conception tomorrow to meet with a bindin' contractor that's workin' over there. Arrange to get him over here in the next few days. Get that corn cut and sheaved."

"Yes, sir. We'll do that. We don't have but a couple of suitcases. I'll pick up my sister at your house, and we'll be back later this afternoon." The farmer nodded his head and disappeared in the corn. Jonas ran the horse and buggy back up to the house, picked up Jennie, and told her about his meeting.

"Don't much care for the idea of sloppin' a hundred and fifty hogs," Jonas said with a definite tone of disgust in his voice. "But I'm thinkin' maybe we can hitch a ride back here from Maryville with that young man we saw, if he's who we think he is."

Jonas found him in the café eating an early dinner. He sat Jennie at a table not far from him. As she sat down, Jennie glanced over at the fellow. He was staring at her and immediately dropped his gaze when their eyes met. The waitress arrived to take their order. When the food arrived, Jonas said in a voice loud enough to be clearly heard by Talbott, "I just hired on at the Graham farm, and we need to find a ride back down there to move into the tenant house. Would you know of anyone who could help us out?" Before the waitress could even answer the young man was at her side.

"Hello. Couldn't help overhearin'. My name's Albert Talbott. I live right next door to the Grahams. I have a buckboard here in town and could give you a ride down there if you don't mind bouncin' around in a buckboard." He smiled graciously as he looked from Jennie to Jonas with most of his attention on Jennie.

Jonas stood and said, "Well that's mighty nice of you. I am Frank Hudson, and this is my sister, Jennie." With that information Talbott's expression lit up like a bright ray of sunshine. He was a fairly decent-looking young, thin man of about twenty-one years. His face was narrow with low cheekbones and a thin nose under which he sported a small Pennant style mustache of black hair same as his head. He styled a part on the right side of his close-cut hair that was brushed flat on top and straight down the sides so that his head was sort of squarish in appearance. Under a thin brow, his eyes were dark blue and seemed to be perpetually distant even when he smiled.

But, his smile was pleasant enough, and Jennie didn't have any qualms about his appearance. She smiled and held out her hand. "Pleased to make your acquaintance," she said with a flutter of her eyelashes. Jonas could tell the lad was affected by her.

"Do you have bags? I can pick them up for you and bring the buckboard around front."

"Why don't you meet us, say, in an hour in front of the hotel? And thank you again."

The buckboard rattled along and so did Jennie as she prattled on and on about anything and everything. She sat on the seat close enough for her thigh to touch Albert's. And in her prattling, she made sure to be as flirtatious as she could. Albert didn't talk much and sat on the seat pie-eyed, staring mostly at Jennie and paying little attention to the horses. Jonas listened for a while and determined that Albert was smitten with Jennie. Eventually he became bored and dozed as well as he was able, given the jolts of the road. They arrived at the Graham tenant house, and Albert insisted on unloading and carrying in their bags. Once that was done he stood by the door, stared at the floor, and said to Jennie, "There is the big harvest barn dance in Maryville on Saturday night. I was wonderin' if you would like to attend and if I may escort you?" He looked up quickly and searched her face with eager eyes.

"Why I would be delighted to have you escort me. May I call you Albie? Albert sounds so formal, and Al so gauche." His face immediately turned so red it looked like a tomato. Jennie couldn't help herself as she giggled in her handkerchief and fluttered her eyelashes. "Why I'm sorry. I've embarrassed you."

"Oh gee. That's all right. I just never had a girl, uh, give me a nickname is all. Most people just call me Bud."

"You don't like it? Would you rather I call you Bud?" She pursed her lips in a little pout.

"Oh no. I like it just fine."

"All right then. You'll be my Albie."

He flushed all the more and sounded like his throat went dry. All he could do was backpedal through the door onto the porch. Then he kicked his heels and ran to the buckboard.

Saturday night he stood at the door with his

hat in hand, and right off through the screen door Jennie was overpowered by the heavy scent of lavender. His hair was plastered with pomade, and, all in all, he looked freshly scrubbed. He wore a black string tie on a clean white shirt. "Good evening, Jennie. As promised, I am here to escort you to the dance."

"Hello, Albie. Let me grab my wrap, and I'll be right with you," she said like a little baby-cakes.

At the dance, Jennie concentrated all her attention on Albie. Occasionally, someone or another, male and female, came up to Albert for an introduction to Jennie. She did not linger with them and was quick to pull Albert away. Last thing she needed was to run into someone from St. Joseph who knew her and/or her reputation. Finally, she convinced him to leave, and as they were stepping into the doctor's old buggy someone called out to Albert. He turned to see who and said, "It's only my brother, Charles. He's sixteen. I'll introduce you."

"What'cha doin', Bud? Where're you goin'? Who's your friend?"

"Hi, I'm Jennie," she said as she stretched across Albert and held out her hand to Charles. "Bud and I are lovers, and we're goin' on a tryst." She flashed a big smile at him and dipped her head a little.

Charles gulped noticeably and pulled his hat off his head. "What's a tryst?" he asked meekly.

"It's a tête-à-tête."

"What's that?"

"Oh my. You are a child, aren't you? So innocent. Tell him, Albie."

"Aw. He wouldn't understand. He's too young."

"Albie? Ha ha ha." Charles hugged his sides until Albert lunged at him, and he danced away into the dark laughing all the way. Albert slapped the reins to the horse's back and guided him and the buggy around the other buggies parked around the barn. They'd driven about a mile conversing idly about the dance when Albert said, "What's a tate-ah-tate anyway?"

"Well . . . soon as you can pull off the road, I'll show you," she whispered huskily in his ear.

Right about the same time there appeared a big, tall pecan tree about fifty yards off the side of the road. A buggy trail of dual tracks led off the road to a particular spot under the tree. Albert knew it was where couples liked to come for Sunday picnics. He immediately pulled off the road under the tree, and no sooner had the reins tied off than Jennie was on him. She was kissing, licking, squirming. Albert responded in kind, and she permitted him to feel under her dress and explore her body. She purposely did not wear a corset for that very reason. They went on like that for a while, but when he pulled down his pants and tried to make the move on her, she crossed her legs, pulled down her dress, and sat up, smoothing down her clothes. "Not so fast, Albie. We got a ways to go before we take a chance on making a baby together. Don't you think?" she said as sweetly as a pixie blowing magic dust.

Albert groaned and pulled up his pants. "I suppose so," he said and sat back to let himself cool down.

All the next week Albert was at Jennie's door. Jonas was out working on the farm during the day, and Albert was all over Jennie. She always let him go just so far and then held him back to purposely frustrate him. They talked a lot, and he asked many questions of her, seeking her advice on all kinds of subjects. Although he was older than her, it was Jennie who seemed to be the more confident and worldly person in their relationship. And then he started talking about marriage. That's when she said he had to come to supper and get more acquainted with her brother, Frank. Well, Jonas and Jennie were ready for him. They talked with him about all kinds of different things they thought he might have knowledge of, and Jonas poured it on about what a fine fellow he thought Albert was. When Albert told Jennie that he thought Frank was swell and he liked him a lot, they knew they had him hooked. So, Jennie announced that she was putting on a big supper the following Sunday for all the men at the Talbott house. Albert was all for it.

Meanwhile, a few days later, Jonas met with Wilford Mitchell on a dreary, cold morning down in the cornfield and felt him out about the doctor's murder. He determined that Mitchell didn't believe the boy's story, so he told him about himself and that he and Jennie planned to trap the boys into confessing their crime. He wanted Wilford to be there in case he was needed for whatever reason. Wil Mitchell readily agreed, and he told Jonas that earlier that very morning Albert posted a letter to someone in Savannah. Jonas thought he ought to intercept that letter. So, he borrowed a horse from Graham and rode on down to the Savannah post office. He planned to wait for the carrier to show up from Maryville and then see about somehow getting in the mail sack to retrieve Talbott's letter.

It was just about an hour before dinner time when Jonas tied off the horse at the hitching rail in front of the general store across from the post office. He went in the store and bought a sarsaparilla and a small bag of hard candy. Then he went out onto the porch, sat in one of the chairs there, lit a cigar, sipped sarsaparilla, and munched candy while he waited for the postal rider to come in. A little less than an hour and he saw the rider come into town and go around to the back of the post office. Jonas waited five minutes and then tossed his cigar, put the empty sarsaparilla bottle on the porch floor under the chair, stuffed the bag of hard candy in his coat pocket, walked casually across the street to the post office, and went inside. "Hello, sir," he said to the agent at the window. "I would like to buy three first class stamps and an envelope. And if you have paper and pencil I could use I'd be much obliged."

"Yes, sir. I can fix you up." Behind the agent Jonas saw the rider drinking a cup of water with one mailbag on the table in front of him and two more on the floor by the back door. The one bag on the table had the padlock in the hasp of the bag, but it was not locked. The two on the floor were securely padlocked. "Here you go. That'll be nine cents for the stamps and sixteen cents for the paper, pencil, and envelope, for an even two bits."

Jonas set a quarter on the counter, gave his thanks, scooped everything up, and went to a table against the wall across from the bank of individual mailboxes. He heard the postmaster say, "Let's get some dinner at the café before you leave, Burt." The response came back affirmatively, and the postmaster said to Jonas, "When you're done, just drop that letter in the outgoing mail slot right over there." He smiled friendly like, and with a return pleasant smile from Jonas they went out the back door. The open mailbag was still on the table. Jonas waited five minutes, looked through the window up and down the street both ways. Then he quickly stepped through the low swinging door at the counter, removed the lock from the mailbag, and emptied the bag contents onto the table. He spread all the letters out on the table and sorted through them until he found the letter with the *A. Talbott, Arkoe, Missouri,* return address on it. With his pocket knife he managed to separate the sealed flaps so he could re-glue them if need be. There was a bottle of glue on a shelf on the wall. The letter was addressed to someone named Charley Ford. It said:

Dear Charley, we did it. It's all took care of. We don't need your help no more.
Much obliged. Yours truly, Albert.

He hurriedly stuffed the letter in the coat pocket where the bag of candy was and put the other articles in his other coat pocket. Then he carefully stuffed all the letters back into the mailbag and replaced the padlock, but, at that moment, he saw five letters on the floor that must have fallen off the table when he was sorting through them. He started to stoop to pick them up when he heard someone coming. It sounded like women. But, it didn't matter who they were. He couldn't be seen behind the counter. So, he slipped out the back door and rode out of town, headed north for Arkoe.

When the postmaster returned, he said, "Well let's see what you brought me today, Burt." He walked around to the other side of the table and lifted the bag to empty it. As he did, the letters on the floor caught his eye. He looked back to the mailbag and jostled it to make sure the padlock was in

156

the hasp. Then he bent over and picked up the letters. "These letters are all postmarked from Maryville. How'd they get down there?" He looked with puzzlement at Burt. "Somebody's been in this mailbag." He fell silent as he looked to Burt and then to the mailbag and back again. "Who coulda done that?"

"Coulda been anyone. We was gone for purty near a hour."

The postmaster said, "That feller that was in here right before we left coulda done it. You recognize him?"

"No. Never seen him afore," the rider said.

"Guess I better get a holt of the federal marshal."

After Sunday supper, while they still had daylight, they all sat around the front porch talking idly — Jonas, Albert, and Charles, who they called Ed, and Wil Mitchell. Jennie leaned against the door jamb and made google eyes at Albert. Jonas casually blew a ring of cigar smoke through his rounded lips and looked over at the three of them like some sort of sly fox. "What y'all do for a livin'?" he said out of the blue.

They looked at each other once and then turned back to Jonas. "You mean like a job or somethin'?" Albert said.

"Yeah. That's what I mean."

"Guess we don't have jobs. Wil, you used to do farm work when you was married, didn't you?" Mitchell nodded his head *yes.*

"You don't have jobs?" Jonas boomed with a big grin on his face. "Hell, even convicts have jobs."

"How would you know? You been in prison?" Albert sneered.

Jonas's face went cold, and the grin disappeared. "Yes, I have. Was at Andersonville during the war, too." The boys' eyes opened noticeably wider. Mitchell remained stoic.

"Tell us about it," Charles said like a young schoolboy. His eager face was set on a block head of short-cropped black hair. He almost smacked his lips as from under a heavy brow shaped in a *V,* he concentrated his gray eyes on Jonas.

"Sure. I don't mind. Andersonville was a hell-hole death trap. Fifteen thousand Union soldiers died a starvation or disease there. I was lucky. I managed to live 'til we were rescued. Then in seventy-five I was sentenced to five years in the Kansas State Pen for grand larceny. Got out last year in December. Didn't waste no time though. Robbed that little train that runs from Topeka to Manhattan. Then robbed a feller in Manhattan. Then we robbed that bank in

158

Junction City and skedaddled over here so's we don't get caught. And . . ." Jonas stared into each one of their eyes with a look that could freeze a person's blood. He didn't blink as he said in a voice just as icy as his stare, "If you ever tell anyone what I just told you, I'll kill you." He paused for a whole long minute to let it sink in. "Ever kill a man?" he said in a ghostly, almost hypnotic way.

Charles swallowed hard and said, "Maybe."

"Shoot 'em up close so's you can hear the bullet rip through his flesh?"

"Well, no. It was a ways away."

"So, you *have* killed a man." Jonas feigned moderate surprise. "Few months back in Manhattan I shot a man in the head with this here little pistol," Jonas said as he patted his vest pocket. "Killed him. Robbed him of two thousand bucks. You might a read about it."

"Let's see the pistol," Albert said.

Jonas snatched the little pistol from his pocket, held it under his hand on the table, and said, "Can't see it, can you?"

They turned their heads back and forth slowly, and, just as slowly, Jonas palmed the pistol and turned his hand over. The boys stared at it in a minor stupor. Then Albert chimed out, "You killed him with that little thing? How many shots?"

"One shot, well placed. This is a self-cockin' thirty-two caliber cartridge firin' little dandy. You see boys, when you're robbin' people or goin' into a bank or gettin' on a train for robbery, you want to get up close and stay unnoticed. But, if you're swingin' a big ol' forty-five on your hip or carryin' a big pistol in a shoulder holster where the lump can be seen, folks are gonna know you're armed and keep their distance or be suspicious of you. But with this little jewel they got no idea until it's too late and *BAM*!!!" The two boys jerked back from the table in startled reaction to Jonas's shout. "They're dead." He smiled as wickedly as he could. "Now, we're fixin' to put together a gang and hit that Nodaway Valley Savings Bank. You think you might be interested in that?"

"You got the money from that robbery?" Albert said.

"Got what's left of it."

"Let's see it."

Jonas pointed the pistol in the direction of the boys and said as he glowered at them, "I wouldn't try anything if I were you. Jennie's got a derringer in her skirt, too."

"Oh no, no. Didn't mean anything like

that," Albert said as he held his hands up as if to ward off something flying at him. "We're just curious is all. Plus we got to verify your story if we were to join up with you."

Jonas eyed them real good and then stuck his free hand in his pants pocket and pulled out a folded wad of twenties. He fanned the wad, and it certainly did look like a lot of money.

"All right." Albert looked at Charles and motioned with his head for them to pow-wow inside the house. Jonas acted as if he could care less, but covertly he observed closely. They whispered together for a few minutes, and twice Albert glanced over at Jennie. Each time she smiled at him in an admiring way. The third time he held his stare with a pleading look on his face. Jennie let her smile fade and nodded her head as if to say *yes.*

"Well, we decided to partner up with you. But, we want a written contract."

"Whoa now. I told you all about me. Now what about you? How do I know you'd be cut out for robbin' and killin'?"

Albert looked over to Jennie, and she said, "Better tell him everything, Albie. You want to join a gang and be an outlaw like us, you got to prove up yourself."

161

"Well, we killed a man. We planned it, and Ed pulled the trigger," Albert said with hesitation.

"You rob him?"

"No, we didn't."

"Ain't no use to kill a man unless you rob him. What happened?"

"Well, promise you won't tell nobody?"

"Course I do. I just told you my whole criminal doin's. Think I would tell yours and risk you tellin' mine?"

"No. Wilford, are you in this with us?" He nodded his head *yes.* "I want to hear it from your lips," said Albert.

"I stole a few things in my day. I guess I can rob a bank. Hold the horses if nothing else."

"And you swear not to tell anybody what I am about to tell?"

"I do. So help me God," he said with a grin.

"Well, we killed the doctor. He was a bad man and mean and stingy, and he beat our mother, so we killed him. Ed pulled the trigger. Shot him through the window." He looked at each one of them in turn.

"Your pa?" Wil asked in a croaky voice.

"Yep. Our pa, the highly respected Doctor Talbott," Albert sneered.

Nobody said another word until Jonas

said, "Bad men deserve killing. I killed one in prison." The room remained quiet, and the boys held their heads high as if they were heroes. "All right. You draw up the contract, and let's all meet back here tomorrow night at eight. Grahams should be asleep by then."

The next night they all met again in the Hudson house. Albert handed Jonas a contract written in his own hand, dated Monday, October 25, 1880. Crudely written, it was one paragraph of about a hundred words that basically stated the five of them as signers contracted together to rob trains, stages, banks, and safes to obtain booty to share equally; to stay together until death; for any betrayal the punishment would be death; if any one of them resigned it was with a promise of secrecy at the risk of death; and that there was already one traitor that had to be killed first. Jonas read the contract and then let his gun hand rest on his vest over the pistol. "Who's the traitor that needs to be killed?" he asked in a low and even voice with a challenge stare at Albert.

"Henry Wyatt," Albert answered flat out. "He knows what we done, and we think he's gonna turn us in. We'll pay you fifty dollars to kill him." He stared at Jonas with his own challenge.

Jonas relaxed and smiled. "Shouldn't be a problem. Where is he?"

"He's our hired hand. He lives at the house."

"All right. Let me get up a plan for that. In the meantime, you boys sign this contract so's I know you're serious, and we'll sign it when I got a plan to kill Wyatt. Shouldn't be more'n a day or two."

After everyone left and Jonas and Jennie were in bed, they went over the whole scam and laughed and laughed over how easy it was. They kept their voices low though, just in case one of the Talbott boys were snooping around outside.

Early the next morning before dawn, Jonas hitched up two of the plow horses to the wagon, and he and Jennie pulled out for Maryville. He wanted to get past the Talbott house before daylight so nobody would see them. They drove straight to Marshal Johnson's office, arriving as the sun was just coming up. He was sitting at his desk sipping coffee and talking with his deputy. Jonas and Jennie walked through the door casually and greeted Marshal Johnson just as casually.

"Well we got 'em to confess to everything," Jonas said.

"Hot dawg!" Marshal Johnson said as he slapped his thigh. "Let's get the sheriff and the prosecuting attorney here so you don't have to tell it all two or three times. Andy," he said as he nodded to his deputy.

"Hot dog? Where'd you get that from?" Jennie quizzed Johnson with a taunting look.

"Saint Louee. Ain't you ever seen that feller on the streets with his cart sellin' steamed sausages in a bun? I heared some feller call 'em that. So I guess I can, too."

It was a half hour, and everybody was there. Jonas and Jennie went through the whole story, and Jonas handed the contract to the prosecuting attorney.

"Got this letter in Albert's hand, too," Jonas said as he handed the letter and envelope to the prosecuting attorney.

"Envelope's been postmarked. Where'd you get this?" The prosecuting attorney looked curiously at Jonas, who sensed something was wrong.

"Don't care to say. Speaks for itself though, don't it?"

"I suppose so. All right. Good job. Thanks."

The Talbott boys and Henry Wyatt were arrested and incarcerated later that same day by Sheriff Toel. The preliminary hearing was the next day, the twenty-seventh, and again Jonas and Jennie told the whole story along with input from Wilford Mitchell. The three arrestees were held over, and the trial was set for January 13, 1881.

Two days before the start of the trial Jonas and Jennie were glad they decided to move into the hotel for the duration of the trial because people were coming in from near and far. The trial drew so much attention around the county that there was not enough room in the courthouse to contain everyone, so it was moved to Union Hall. About eight hundred people filled the hall. When he was called, Jonas came forward, looking rather natty in his freshly pressed black three-piece suit, new white shirt with a brand new, bright-white linen collar, two and one-half inches high with the points turned down over a very stylish gold imperial silk scarf. It was neatly pressed into his vest, plus he sported linen cuffs with silver cufflinks, shiny black oxford shoes, and well-barbered hair and mustache. He stepped to the witness chair with an air of confident professionalism and look of success about him. Of course, Jennie thought he was overdoing it, but he maintained he needed to set an image. So he did, took the oath, and sat down.

The prosecuting attorney gave him leeway

and asked him to tell his story to the jury, which he did with elaboration and allusions to the successful detective's penchant for gaining his suspect's confidence. Albert made a loud, scoffing cough. Jonas ignored him and finished his testimony. Then he was turned over to the defense attorney for cross-examination. The famous lawyer, Phineas P. Price, did not waste any time and got right to the attack. Sitting at the defense table with the two Talbott boys on his left, he, with steely-gray eyes, stared silently at Jonas for a long couple of minutes. Then he pushed his silver forelock off his forehead, and amid his ruddy complexion he set his mouth in a look of firm resolution. As he hefted himself out of the chair, he looked to be about two hundred fifty pounds in a navy-blue suit, vest, low white collar, and red four-in-hand cravat. He appeared to be a couple of inches shy of six feet tall. Slowly, very slowly he came toward Jonas as if he were stalking him. He held a tablet in his hand, which he consulted before he spoke.

"So, let's see. Mister Jonas V. Brighton is it? Not Frank Hudson. Is that correct?"

"Yes."

"Now Mister Brighton, you've testified that you had a contract with the sheriff to conduct undercover work along with your wife, Virginia, at the rate of ten dollars per day, and that contract the prosecuting attorney has entered into evidence. Is that correct?"

"Yes."

"Mister Brighton, I remind you that you are under oath. So everything I just asked you is true, and you can provide appropriate documents to prove it true. Is that correct?"

Jonas hesitated.

"Mister Brighton?"

"Depends on what you may be asking about. Everything I said is true, but I don't necessarily have documents to back it up."

"What documents do you not have?"

"Virginia and I do not have a marriage certificate."

"Ah ha. So you are not legally married to, let me see, Virginia Hudson. Is that correct?"

"No. That is incorrect."

"I beg your pardon. You stated you are married to one Virginia Hudson, who, by the way, was run out of St. Joseph on morality and chastity grounds. Did you know that?"

"Yes. I knew that. Not the specifics, but I knew she had some trouble in St. Joseph."

"Uh-huh. So since she is a woman of loose

morals you thought you could move her in with you and have your way with her. Is that correct?"

"No. That is incorrect. We are married."

"How can that be when you have no proof of it?"

"Just like Missouri, the state of Kansas allows common-law marriages, and that's us. A common-law marriage. Wouldn't a big lawyer like you know that?"

A murmur went through the gallery accompanied by some gasps and some chuckles. Price stared coldly at Jonas and then paged through his tablet. "Now, Mister Brighton, tell us about your stay in the Kansas State Penitentiary." Another rustling went through the gallery. "You were in prison, weren't you?"

"Yes?"

"What was your crime?"

"Grand larceny."

"Grand larceny?" Price said with alarm. "My goodness. That's rather serious isn't it?" He looked emphatically at the jury. "Were you a detective before you were sentenced to, let me see" — he consulted his tablet — "oh, yes. Five years in prison?"

"No."

"When were you released from prison? Several years past?" A hint of a gleam came into Price's gaze as he stared at Jonas.

"No. I was released early for good behavior in December seventy-nine."

"Uh-huh. So just barely over a year ago." Again, he paused and gave the jury a knowing look.

"So did you learn the nefarious art of detective work in prison?" There were chuckles and grins all around in the gallery such that the judge banged his gavel and ordered quiet.

"No."

"Well, where did you learn it and so quickly?"

Jonas glanced quickly at Jennie and then quickly away. "I guess I just got a knack for it, and I took a correspondence course."

"I see this knack you have for detective work is a help to law enforcement, is it?"

"I like to think so."

"And, therefore, respected in the community?"

"Hopefully."

" 'Hopefully' you say? Hopefully?" he said in a raised voice and glared at the jury. Then he stepped quickly to the defense table and snatched up a sheaf of papers. "Hopefully indeed. But in your case, you appear to have failed in that hope. I hold in my hands no less than twelve affidavits from the good citizens of Junction City and Manhattan, Kansas, testifying to your bad character and questionable means of, and I use the term loosely, investigation."

"Objection!" The prosecuting attorney came to his feet. "Your honor, the state has not been provided the opportunity to examine those affidavits."

"You can examine then now," the judge said. While everything came to a halt the prosecuting attorney did as ordered and then with a deep frown on his forehead handed them back to Price. "You may continue your cross-examination of this witness, Mister Price."

"So now, we've established that you are in a common-law marriage with a woman of ill repute, are an ex-convict, and a shady character in the community at large." He paused and quickly surveyed the jury. "So, it is entirely possible that you and *your wife,* being wicked and immoral, conspired with Sheriff Toel and Marshal Johnson to fabricate a story about an alleged confession by these impressionable young men who simply wanted to impress *you* so they could join your false gang and become outlaws like you led them to believe you were. After all, we still do not know who actually murdered Doctor Talbott —"

"Objection. Mister Price is testifying, your honor."

"Sustained. Get to a question, Mister Price."

"Did you know who murdered Doctor Talbott at the time you wrangled the false confession from these boys?"

"No."

"So you admit it is a false confession?"

"I don't know whether it is false or not. I just told what happened and what was said."

The defense lawyer, Phineas P. Price, kept after Jonas for the rest of the day and half of the next going over the same ground in varied versions. It was obvious that he was trying to convince the jury that Jonas was a despicable man who coerced the innocent young boys to make a false confession. And he didn't stop with Jonas. He went after Jennie with a vengeance. He produced affidavits from St. Joseph and read them in open court in all their lurid detail. He produced alleged evidence to show that Wyatt and Mitchell were the ones who conspired to murder Talbott, did it, and then attempted to shift the blame on the boys through Brighton's false testimony.

The prosecution, on the other hand, had Wyatt, who turned state's witness and testified that several times he was present when the boys were talking about murdering their father. He testified that Charles shot their father, and the bullet had special rifling on it that the brothers carved into all their ammunition. That bullet was pulled from the wall and identified as the one that went through Talbott's body. It had the special rifling on it. They had the testimony of Marshal Johnson, Sheriff Toel, Wilford Mitchell, Jonas, and Jennie.

On January twenty-eighth, Jonas sat in the gallery with Sheriff Toel. Jennie said she had a headache and wasn't up to another day of it all. The jury took two and a half hours to deliberate before they returned a verdict of guilty of first-degree murder. The judge sentenced the brothers to be hanged March 25, 1881.

"Where's Marshal Johnson? I'd think he would've wanted to hear this firsthand," Jonas asked the sheriff as they filed out of the Union Hall along with the crowd.

"Don't know. I ain't his keeper."

"All right then. I'll have a invoice for you this afternoon. We'll probably pull out on the mornin' train." The sheriff and Jonas tipped their hats to each other, and it came through from the sheriff more friendly as it had since the trial. What could he say? They fulfilled their contract. The law seemed happy with that regardless of Jonas's reputation. He walked to the hotel with those thoughts on his mind. When he arrived, he opened the door to their room to see the bed was made. Jennie's bag was gone. He went to the dresser. Her things were gone, and her clothes were not hanging in the closet. He shrugged his shoulders and sat down at the table to make out his invoice.

On his way to the sheriff's office, he stopped at the marshal's office only to find out that Johnson had left town. At the sheriff's office he handed Sheriff Toel his invoice and said, "Ed Johnson left town?"

"Yep."

"Jennie go with him?"

"Yep. They knew each other from St. Joseph. I guess she was quite the hussy but was in love with Ed. He got her out of town when she got in trouble, and he came up here and took the marshal's job. The rest you know, I reckon."

CHAPTER FOUR
A FLY IN THE OINTMENT

Jonas decided to spend the remainder of the winter at the Graham farm working at the forge. It gave him plenty of time to brood about Jennie. He was starting to like her as a common-law wife. They probably could have been real good detectives, too. But she threw it all away for a younger man. That Johnson fellow was probably about twenty-five or so. Jonas just turned thirty-four. Course the sheriff did say they were lovers in St. Joseph. Still, not especially hospitable the way she just up and left behind his back. That deserved a talking-to. Didn't even stay to collect her half of the Nodaway contract money. Maybe in the spring a trip down to St. Joseph to poke around a little would be a good idea. Just see what they were doing. Maybe they needed some money from what she was owed, heavily discounted of course because she skipped out.

■ ■ ■ ■

In May on a clear, warm day with a slight breeze out of the northwest, the morning southbound train pulled into the St. Joseph station with bell clanging, screeching, grinding, and blowing steam. When the train stopped, Jonas tossed his bag to the platform and hopped off. He shook the travel kinks out of his body, fluffed his coat, straightened his tie, popped his derby on his head, and looked up and down the platform just to see what was there. Then he picked up his bag and walked into the station house. The agent was at his window, and Jonas asked for directions to the Pacific House Hotel. He walked south on Main for a short way, then it became Felix Street and turned east. He walked two blocks to Third Street and looked north and south. The street descended gradually to the south, and both sides were lined with storefronts of various businesses in two- and three-story buildings of brick and arched windows. A few of the buildings had pillared porticos with balustraded balconies above. And a few were plastered mostly in white. Heavy cornice work was everywhere present on the building tops. A line of wooden utility poles with crosspieces on which hung telegraph and telephone wires marched down one side of the street. There were globed gaslights regularly spaced on both sides just inside the curbs. The storefronts presented all kinds of businesses offering merchandise he had previously only been able to obtain from the Montgomery Ward mail order catalog. Professionals, too. Dentists, doctors, accountants, insurance agents, and one across the street that particularly caught his eye: a private detective.

Continuous interconnected sidewalks in varying textures and colors of brick and pavers fronted the buildings, busy with people walking here and there, but, oddly enough, there was no overhead porch cover there. The street was covered in gray stone brick pavers, and carriages, coaches, wagons, buggies, surreys, and riders on horses moved up and down the street in both directions. Jonas took it all in. Yelling, people talking, horses snorting and neighing, clip-clopping along, the jangle of harness chains, the creaking noise and rumble of heavily loaded wagons, the odors of manure, bacon frying, and perfume as he occasionally passed a lady with a parasol, properly escorted by a proper gentleman . . . it all assailed his senses. This was his first

177

experience of a city. He had only passed through Kansas City on the train when he was released from prison, so he had no personal experience of that city. He was dressed appropriately in his three-piece suit, so even though he looked around in wide-eyed amazement, he didn't look like a country bumpkin just off the train.

Following the agent's directions, he turned north on Third, and halfway between Felix and Francis he came to the Pacific House. At check-in he asked for and was given a room on the top floor. He refused a bellboy and was advised that the new water works were approved in January and the city would be trenching the streets for pipes starting in a few days. Also, the Pacific House would begin renovations in a week to install inside plumbing. The desk clerk apologized for the expected inconvenience but was quick to assure Jonas that in the end it would be a great amenity, to which Jonas agreed and went upstairs. He unpacked his bag and then went down for dinner in the dining room.

After dinner he went to the lobby, smoked two cigars, read two newspapers, front page to last page, and perused two magazines. While he sat there he also keenly observed persons coming into and leaving the hotel.

He watched the bellboys joshing each other in between rings for portage and the desk clerks busying themselves. By about four o'clock, he decided to go out for a drink. He came out the front door on Third and walked south to Felix and crossed to the saloon he had seen when he walked up Felix. It was called the George A. Sprengel Saloon. Right next door was, interestingly enough, an employment office. Jonas took note of that, just in case.

He had a couple of drinks and played a few hands of poker but couldn't concentrate, so he cashed out and left. He went west on Felix and stopped at the private detective office. In smaller print on the door were stenciled the names Edward Johnson and Virginia Hudson. Jonas scrutinized the stenciling suspiciously and then sucked in his breath as he tried the door knob. It was locked so he peered in through the window but could see nothing but a desk and file cabinet. It was too dark to see anything else. He decided to come back in the morning. He walked back to the hotel, tipping his hat to the ladies he passed on the sidewalk as he went along. After supper he went right up to his room.

In the morning the office door to the detective office was unlocked, and Jonas opened it and stepped through, removing his hat as he did. "Hello. Jonas V. Brighton," he said as he held out his hand to a balding man sitting behind the desk. The man stood and grasped Jonas's hand. He was a little short and rotund in body with a gray walrus mustache and sparkling green eyes set in his round pink face. "Not *the* Jonas V. Brighton from Maryville? Do I have the pleasure of making his acquaintance?"

"Yes. I'm afraid you do."

"Please. Sit down and tell me all about it. Name's Isaiah Elijah Bedford. My pa was a Methodist minister. You no doubt heard the State Supreme Court affirmed the lower court decision, and the Talbott boys are scheduled for execution on June twenty-fourth?"

"Yes. I heard. I've been in Arkoe since the trial. But now I come to the big city. So briefly what happened is me and Jennie Hudson got them to confess."

"So, it *was* Jennie, huh? I wondered about that. Go on."

Jonas went on and told him the story. When he finished, Bedford said, "Well, that didn't take a lot of work, did it? So why are you in town?"

"Thinking about hanging out my shingle."

"I see. Competition, eh?"

"I suppose. Unless we were to partner up."

"Uh-huh. Bring your notoriety to the firm, eh? Become as well known as the Pinkertons, eh? Let me think about it."

"Why are Johnson's and Hudson's names still on the door?"

"Oh, I been after the landlord to get that changed ever since they left town, but he's not real responsive."

"What'd they do anyway?"

"Well, about two years ago now, according to what Ed told me, they thought they would make a big splash by getting evidence the mayor was taking kickbacks and illegal campaign contributions. They used Jennie to entice him with sexual favors. Johnson figured if they couldn't get the kickback evidence, they could blackmail the mayor, because at the time Jennie was only sixteen, and that would not look very good to the public, to say the least. Not to mention the mayor is a married man." He leaned back in his chair and laced his fingers behind his head. "Well, when they made their evidence and threats known to the mayor, things went downhill real fast for them. They started getting unannounced visits from real dangerous-looking men, and more than once there was a dead cat on their doorstep in the morning. That's when they decided to leave town. Ed took the marshal's job in Maryville, and Jennie landed in Junction City. I took over their lease on this place, and that's about the long and the short of it."

"I wonder where they went this time? If you hear from them, I owe Jennie some money."

"An honest fellow, eh? I tell you what. I've thought about it. Let's partner up." He held out his hand.

"Sounds right," Jonas said, and they shook on it.

"I got a few cases I'm workin' on now. Let me fill you in on 'em."

He spent about another hour with Bedford, and then the old detective suggested they get a cup of coffee and piece of pie. Jonas was in the lead as they went out onto the sidewalk. Bedford had his back to him and was bent over locking the door when Jonas stepped quickly back to avoid being knocked over by a large woman charging down the sidewalk. He bumped into Bedford, and that pushed the poor fellow into the door. He let out a grunt as he banged against it. "Sorry," Jonas said. "Are you hurt?"

"No. Thanks, I am fine. What happened?"

"We almost got flattened over by a human

steamroller. See her down the street?" Jake pointed at the woman.

"Uh-huh. You gotta be careful around here. People seem to always be in a hurry."

Jonas spent the next two months working with Bedford on various cases, even assisting the St. Joseph police department. He often frequented the Dobler Brothers Saloon across the street and down half a block south of Sprengel's Saloon. He liked it better at Dobler's. Not as stuffy, and Joshua Dobler had a barber shop right next door. He walked there at the end of the day whenever he was in the office. It should have been an enjoyable walk, but the noise in the street and the bustle of the people always annoyed him. Once, when it was raining he was standing in a doorway of a store to stay dry until the shower passed when a lady with an open umbrella turned from the sidewalk into the store and caught Jonas in the cheek, just under his eye, with one of the pointed arm end caps of the umbrella. It hurt bad and nearly poked out his eye, but she never even paused to apologize.

Another time, one afternoon Jonas stepped out of the door after a shave and a haircut, and as soon as turned to his left on

Felix, he was confronted by a large, boxy man. Jonas stepped aside to press his back against the storefront, expecting the big fellah to move to the other side of the walk and go around him. Well, instead the fellow shot out his forearm, shoved Jonas hard across the chest, and kept right on going without so much as an "excuse me." Jonas flared and yelled, "Hey, jackass. Watch where you're goin'."

The mini-giant stopped in midstream and slowly turned to face him. Jonas tensed his muscles and took up a defensive stance. And then, with surprising speed for a big man, he came at Jonas and caught hold of Jonas before he could evade the charge. The fellow wrapped both his huge hands around Jonas's arms at his biceps. It felt like each arm was being squeezed in a vise, and then he was lifted up so that his shoes cleared the sidewalk. He was carried into the saloon and then back out into the street. That's when Jonas launched wicked kicks once with one foot and then the other into the man's groin. Immediately the grip on Jonas's arms was released, and he dropped to the sidewalk, whereupon he sliced a hard kick with his heel at the man's left knee and then at his right knee. The fellow roared and dropped to his knees. Jonas spun a complete three-sixty and caught his target full on the side of his head with the instep of his right shoe. With a heavy thud, the man fell face-first on the brick, and a little cloud of dust puffed out from underneath him as he landed, out cold.

Jonas pulled down his vest and the sleeves of his coat, straightened himself out, and bent over to pick up his hat. He dusted off the smudged places with the sleeve of his coat, and then the applause began. It came from the men hanging out of the barber shop and the men and women pouring out of the saloon.

"You just knocked out the Steel Knuckles Bomber, Jake Hermann," someone called out.

"Well, the *Steel Knuckles Bomber* needs to learn some manners and common courtesy."

"Where'd you learn to kick like that?"

"None of your business."

"It ain't manly. Men use their bare knuckles."

Jonas sought out the voice and found the speaker. He glared at him, his challenging hard and cold, dark-gray eyes like a narrow beam of light piercing the man's own eyes. "You want to try your knuckles on me?" Jonas growled through his clenched teeth like a junkyard dog. The man stepped out of the crowd and threw off his coat. He took up a boxing stance and held his balled fists up in the manner of the pugilist. He had started to slide step closer to Jonas when a whistle squealed and the man backed off.

"What's goin' on here?" the policeman demanded.

"This fellow here just kicked the hell out of Jake for no good reason. We haven't even had time to check. The Bomber could be dead," someone said. Meanwhile the boxer melted back into the saloon crowd and disappeared, probably through a back door.

"All right. All right. Back up now. Back away!"

Another policeman came running up as a crowd began to build in the street. He began to push them back with his baton.

"Hold 'em back, Bill, while I check on Hermann." He knelt down and rolled the big lug over and listened at his nose. "He's breathin'. Mac, send your boy a runnin' to the station house and tell 'em to send an ambulance." He glared at Jonas and said, "You're comin' with me. Turn around and put your hands behind your back."

As he put the manacles on Jonas's wrists, a fellow Jonas had been playing cards with who was coming out the saloon door when

186

Jonas was being carried in by Hermann said, "George, I saw the whole thing. Hermann shoved this fellow, and he called him out on it. Hermann had him by the arms, raised him up, and was about to throw him in the street and who knows what else. You know how crazy Hermann is. This fellow had no choice. As I see it, he did the only thing he could do and kicked his way out of it. By the way," he said as he turned his attention to Jonas, "that was the prizefighter James Dunne, out of New York, who you almost took on. I don't think you woulda done as good with him. He beat both Jimmy Elliott and Bill Davis, you know."

Jonas remained silent.

"All right. Anybody else see it?"

One fellow from the back of the street crowd piped up and said, "Yes, sir. I was across the street. It happened like this gent said."

"All right, you come with me, too. I'll need statements from both a you. All right, y'all go about your business now. The three a you come with me to the station." The policeman waved his billy club at the crowd.

As they walked away, the saloon crowd booed and hissed. It was directed at Jonas.

"A few minutes ago they were applauding me," Jonas said.

"Hermann was a bully, and that's what they were cheering. But, I think James Dunne soured them when he pointed out your kicking style of fighting rather than bare knuckle," the first witness said. "Where'd you learn that style a kick fighting? I seen it once in Paris, France."

"I learned it from a Frenchman," Jonas said in a perturbed voice. And he didn't tell him it was while he was in prison.

"In France?"

"No."

"Where then?"

"None a your business. Kinda nosey, ain't you?"

"Sorry. I am just the curious type. Word of advice though. I wouldn't go back to Dobler's if I were you. I don't think you are very popular there."

"Thanks. I'll keep that under advisement."

As they all walked in a group toward the station house, a two-horse team and a wagon with a red cross painted on the side with a canopy over the bed skidded to a halt beside the crowd. Two men in white pulled a stretcher from the wagon. They ran over and loaded Hermann, still unconscious, onto the stretcher and lifted it onto the wagon. Then one jumped on the seat and slapped the reins to the horses' backs. Both horses crow-hopped and then dug for traction as their hooves slid on the brick. The wagon was gone in a matter of seconds.

Two days later, Jonas took a furnished apartment on a sublet at Robidoux Row on East Poulin Street, which was on the other side of town from Dobler's. It was in a complex of one-and-a-half-story redbrick buildings and meant he had to walk ten blocks back and forth to the office every day. He didn't mind though, as it was less than a mile one way, and it got him out of the beehive of the city. But he was getting bored. The pennyante cases Bedford was giving him were lackluster to say the least. The surveillance jobs were the worst. He had no idea typical detective work could be so tiresome. Jennie didn't ever say anything about that. Finally, they were engaged on an insurance fraud case, and Bedford sent Jonas to Atchison, Kansas, to gather up some background information on the suspect.

Jonas came into town on the morning Santa Fe and started looking around inside the depot. It was big. It was new. Built just a year ago out of Kansas native limestone, it was impressive, as was the whole Atchison, Topeka, and Santa Fe system. On one of

189

the bulletin boards, there was a notice posted soliciting for railroad detectives to join the AT&SF police force. Now that sounded a lot more interesting than the work he was doing — working undercover on trains to protect against robbers, investigating robberies, chasing down suspects, etc. He immediately wrote down the information on the notice and went to the designated office to apply.

He filled out the forms and handed them to the agent. As he looked them over, he said, "All right. I'll submit this application to the captain. We'll send letters to the sheriffs of the counties of your residence over the last five years for background checks." Then he raised his eyebrows, took off his glasses, nibbled one of the stem ends, and said, "So you are the notorious Jonas V. Brighton out of Nodaway County and the Talbott case, eh?"

"Yes, sir."

"And I see you spent some time in Leavenworth County compliments of the state of Kansas." His voice had an ironic inflection to it. "Don't know what the captain's gonna think about that. All right. You're stayin' at the National. We got your address in St. Joe. Usually takes about a month. We'll be in touch."

"Thank you. I'll check back from time to time if that's all right."

"Your choice."

For the next few days, Jonas went about his business tracking down information. On the third day he returned to his hotel in the early evening and asked for his room key at the desk. He noticed a few men and one couple sitting in the hotel lobby conversing or reading newspapers. While he waited for the clerk to retrieve and hand him his key he felt a presence behind him. He had started to turn and look when a deep male voice said, "Stay where you are, and put your hands behind your back. Jonas V. Brighton, you're under arrest." And he felt the familiar cold steel on his wrists as the cuffs were snapped in place. Hands gripped his shoulders, and he was turned to face the arresting officer, who said, "Deputy United States Marshal Allen. I have a federal warrant for your arrest."

"What's the charge?" Jonas demanded.

"Tamperin' with U.S. mail in Savannah, Missouri."

"What? There must be some mistake. That was evidence in a murder trial."

"Uh-huh. I have an arrest warrant and am takin' you to Kansas City."

"Who's the affiant?"

"Don't know. My guess is the U.S. attorney for the Western District of Missouri in Kansas City. Let's go."

"How'd you know I was here in Atchison?"

"Just happened to come by the AT and SF police office. The desk clerk mentioned that you had applied for a detective job with the Santa Fe. Now let's go. We got a train to catch."

Jonas stood with his attorney in front of the judge, who said, "Mister Brighton, you have pled not guilty to the charge of mail tampering. Gentlemen, please." He gestured to the prosecutor and Jonas's attorney.

"Your honor, the defense requests a continuation of the trial until after the first of the year to take into account the Christmas holidays and allow us sufficient time to prepare a proper and comprehensive defense."

The judge looked at the prosecutor.

"No objection, your honor."

"Bail?" the judge inquired.

"We do not see the defendant as a flight risk. However, to offer assurance perhaps a bail is appropriate."

"It is a minor case. Five hundred dollars bail." He banged his gavel. "Next case."

The Grahams, some friends of theirs, and Sheriff Toel were in the gallery and ponied up two hundred dollars of the bail money. Jonas paid the rest.

"Thank you so much for traveling here and paying my bail. I'll repay you just as soon as I can," Jonas said to the Maryville group. "Very good of you to come."

"Least we could do for what you did for us," Sheriff Toel said.

"Not to mention a lot of smith work you did for us, too," Alex Graham said with a grin.

"Sorry about Jennie," Sheriff Toel said. "She probably wouldn't a been any good for you anyhow."

Jake dropped his gaze to the floor and bobbed his head up and down. Then he raised his head and with a smile said, "Let me buy you dinner before you head back north," Like a family, they all walked out of the courthouse over to a nearby restaurant.

In a week, he was on the late-night train east. He hopped off in Illinois and was not heard of for a year before the federal marshals caught him and brought him back to Kansas City.

Jonas sat with his arms folded across his chest and glared through the bars at his attorney. "Why are they dogging me like this? It's not like I stole anything. The letter was used as evidence that helped convict those Talbott boys."

The attorney held up his hands in futility and said, "I know. I know. I can't figure it out. But I wish you hadn't skipped out. Obviously, that only makes the case harder."

"I could tell they'd turned on me. Threw me out like dishwater. I'm sick of jail time. So I left. And I paid back all the folks who put up my bail. Probably how they caught me. On a return address or somethin'." His brow was pressed into a dark *V* shape, and his jaw was so tight it looked like he was grinding his teeth.

"Well, we'll do the best we can. I have to leave now."

Jonas was returned to the general jail population and a cell with three other men. He rolled onto his bunk, folded his hands across his chest, and tried to banish all thought from his mind. It wasn't working. That afternoon, however, things changed when he was hauled off to the U.S. attorney's office. He was a stern-looking man with a dark-brown Van Dyke beard and mustache, short hair plastered down with a prominent part on the left side, and serious blue eyes. "Please take off the handcuffs.

No need for that," he said. "Mister Brighton, I am Donald G. Lincoln, no relation. This is John C. Montgomery, the Daviess County, Missouri, prosecuting attorney."

Montgomery also looked very stiff and formal. He wore rimless glasses, parted his brown, medium-length hair just an inch to the right of center, and had Slavic features about him on a clean-shaven, pale face. He wore a high, straight collar with a black cravat and pearl stickpin. His suit was dark gray. He held his hand out for a shake. It was limp and damp.

"Pleased to meet you, Mister Brighton."

Jonas said nothing.

"Well, let's get right down to it. Please sit down." Lincoln sat behind his desk and Jonas and Montgomery across from him in leather client chairs. "Mister Brighton, you may be aware that the notorious outlaw Frank James turned himself in to Governor Crittenden just this past October. He is now awaiting trial in Gallatin for murder in the robbery of the Rock Island Railroad train just outside of Winston last July, eighty-one. Mister Montgomery here is the prosecutor on the case."

"Mister Brighton," Montgomery said. His voice was calm and quiet but firm, just on the verge of reedy. "It is our belief that, in

195

spite of the evidence in hand, because of the sympathies of the general populace, Frank James will be acquitted by a jury of his peers. That would be a travesty, and we want you to help us prevent it from happening."

"Me? What can I do?"

"You can take the deal we're gonna offer you and act on it," Lincoln said.

"What's the deal?"

"If you will work undercover in the Gallatin jail in an attempt to obtain incriminating evidence from Frank James, I'll drop the mail tampering charge against you."

Jonas sat there a little stunned. He said nothing.

"The Nodaway County prosecutor is a colleague and friend of mine. He let me read his case notes," Montgomery said. "I am impressed with your ability to obtain a confession from the Talbott brothers without them ever thinking it was being done. I wonder if you could do the same with James?"

"You want me to be a jailhouse snitch on Frank James?" Jonas was just a bit incredulous.

"Informant would be a better word," Montgomery said. "Wouldn't you be able to ingratiate yourself with James like you did with the Talbotts and get him talking?"

"I don't know. I suspect Frank James and the Talbott boys are two different animals."

"Mail tampering draws a maximum five-year sentence. You wouldn't want to do that again, would you?" Lincoln chimed in.

"No, sir. I would not. But, there's a lot to consider here. If I have to testify in open court or even submit an affidavit, word will get out, and I'll be a marked man, by the James gang no less. That is not good."

"No. I suppose it isn't. You would have to change your identity and leave the state. We would send you in under an assumed name."

"How long you planning on letting the charade go on?"

"The trial is set for March. I would say that if you're not making any headway by the end of January then there won't be much hope. We would have to curtail the operation. But if you are successful, then we would continue right up to the trial date if we have to."

"You don't sound real sure about this."

"A few months' undercover work in exchange for a five-year term in prison?" Lincoln raised his eyebrows and held out his hands to his side, palms up. "Sounds like a pretty good deal to me, especially since you don't even have to produce. Course, we'll have the guards watching you to make sure you're doing the job."

"You sound more sure about the prison term. I have to be found guilty in a court of law by a jury of my peers before I'd be doin' any prison time. There are mitigating circumstances in my case."

"You didn't get a search warrant and blatantly broke federal law by opening the mail, to which you have already confessed in open court. Really don't see how you would be found not guilty."

"Maybe I'd get sympathy like Frank James. Those boys did murder their own father, you know."

"Not likely. I already talked to the district judge about this, and he assured me he would pull jurors from the south end of the district and maybe even direct a verdict of guilty." Lincoln sat back and eyed Jonas with a steady gaze.

"Sounds like the deck is stacked against me."

"Not really," Montgomery said. "You're free of course to make any decision you want, Mister Jaggers. Orville Jaggers. That's the name of your new identity. Do you accept?"

"I'd like to see my two boys for Christmas."

"Sorry. That won't be possible. We hope you'll be chummy with James by then. When he is visited by his family for Christmas, it will be a good time to maybe overhear some damaging testimony."

"I'll want the whole deal in writin' and signed by the judge."

"We can do that, can't we, Don?"

"Yes, of course."

"Welcome to the prosecutorial team, Orville," Montgomery said as he held out his hand. Jonas reluctantly took it for a shake. His grip seemed firmer this time and his palm drier. "We will have papers on you for a robbery arrest in Coffeysburg. You can make up your own story from there."

A deputy sheriff from Gallatin rode in front of Jonas. He wasn't the talkative type and steadfastly refused to ride abreast of Jonas. After two or three attempts to pull up alongside of the deputy only to be rebuffed by a touch of the deputy's heels to the side of his horse, Jonas gave it up and followed along behind. It was snowing with a wind at their backs. Wearing his heavy overcoat and a gray wool blanket wrapped around him and over his head, Jonas huddled himself in the saddle but nevertheless shivered the whole seventy-five miles from Kansas City to Gallatin. He was thankful for the two night stops because he could at least warm up in a jail cell that was out of the weather. In the cell, once the manacles were off, he stamped his boots to bring his feet back to life and blew his breath into his hands to warm them. After several minutes, the shivers ceased, and he could relax. At least he was given hot coffee and a hot supper, which he gobbled because he was near starving. There was no stopping for food on the road with this deputy.

The deputy was dauntless. He would not stop to let the storm blow over. They were on the road before sunup each morning. The horses could only be walked in the wind-driven snow, and so it took them three days to get to Gallatin. By the time they did get there, the snow had stopped falling, but the wind was still piling up drifts everywhere. A man was shoveling snow off the sidewalk and entrance to the redbrick two-story courthouse. Smoke blew sideways from all three chimneys of the courthouse, and the snow was piled up almost to the top of the handrails of the weather side of the walk-around on the large cupola. Jonas saw all the snow but didn't think anything of it. The deputy passed in front of the courthouse and then pulled up across the street in front of a stout building, also constructed of redbrick. It had very small windows with bars on them.

The deputy pulled Jonas out of the saddle and shoved him in the direction of the vestibule door. Inside the vestibule the deputy called out, "Yo the jail. Unlock the door and let me in."

"Who be hollerin' out there?" a man's gruff voice came from inside.

"It's Larson. Now let us in."

A speakeasy door opened, and a bearded man peered out. "Oh, howdy, Buck. Hold on a minute. I'll get the key."

Inside the front office of the jailhouse, a small black cast-iron three-burner cookstove radiated against one wall, and it was warm, at last. A couple of tables and chairs were in the room, along with one roll-up desk, a rack of rifles and shotguns on one wall, and a big ring of keys hanging on a peg next to a thick wood door that also had a barred speakeasy door in it. The door stood wide open. On a row of pegs next to the door they came in were heavy coats and hats.

"Signin' in Orville Jaggers. Transfer from Coffeysburg. Waitin' trial on a robbery charge."

"All right now," the jailer said. "Any personal belongin's?"

"Yeah. Here's a sack a things."

"All right. Just set it on that table there. I'll make an inventory later." The jailer was an older fellow with a bald head, full, close-cropped white beard on a ruddy round face and head, and twinkling blue eyes. He wore no shirt, just his gray union suit under braces that held up his black pants, which were tucked into the tops of his brown, flat-heeled boots. He had a little paunch, and a wide scar ran across his right cheek up to the crown of his head.

"All right, Jaggers. Let's git them irons off you. And git you settled in your new home." Jonas was staring at the scar on his head.

"You like that?" the jailer queried sarcastically. "Yankee tried to bayonet me in the head at Westport, but I run him through with my saber, and that was the end of that. You ain't a Yankee, are you?"

"Up yours, old man. I was in Andersonville. So don't go about braggin' around me of your feats of war." Jonas glared at him hard. He hoped the talk was passing through to the jail so James would hear. He wanted to impress him with his toughness because James was tough.

"Git on in there!" Larson pushed Jonas

hard toward the door to the cells, but Jonas kept his feet and stood straight when the jailer opened the door to the cells with an evil grin on his face.

In the lockup itself there were four cells in a row along a corridor. Each cell had iron bars and doors in front and bars in between the cells. The barred cages looked to be about eight foot by ten foot, and each contained two bunk beds with lumpy tick mattresses filled with straw and pillows of the same, and a slop bucket for human waste. Two cells were occupied, with one fellow in one of the end cells lying with his face to the wall, covered in a gray blanket, and the other on the other end standing against the bars like some kind of spectator.

"All right. You git on in this one right here. That's good. Now I hope you're comfy in your own little apartment here, ha ha," the jailer said as he put Jonas in the cell next to Frank James, slammed the cell door, and turned the lockset with the big key, making a distinct clang as the bolt slid home.

"What's your name, sir?" Jonas said as he turned to face the jailer.

"Johnny. Johnny Reb. And I betcha your real name is Billy Yank. Ain't it?" He sneered at Jonas, who turned his back on him and then sat on the edge of his bunk. He was satisfied that it would be hard for anyone to suspect that he and the jailer were in cahoots together.

It was cold in the cell, as the only heat was that which came through the open door to the front office where the cookstove burnt up the coal shoved in regularly by the jailer. "Of course, you won't refuse the rebel beans or bacon I cook up for you. And you might be eatin' some good old Confederate pan bread. Mightn't you, Billy?"

"Yeah, and you'll be emptyin' my slop bucket filled with Yankee shit every day, won't you, Johnny Reb?"

The jailer spun on his heel and stomped out of the lockup, saying as he went, "Yeah, and I might just run you out in the snow in your union suit to the privy."

"His name is Albert Smith." The voice came from the fellow in the bunk in the cell next to Jonas's. He assumed it to be Frank James.

"The jailer?" Jonas queried.

"Yeah."

"Thanks." James had talked to him first. That was a good sign that maybe Jonas could befriend him.

"From Coffeysburg, huh, Jaggers?" the other fellow said.

"Ain't from Coffeysburg. I was just passin'

through. Besides, ain't no business a yours anyway, big ears."

"What a you mean, big ears?"

"Snoopin' on the talk in the office about me."

"Would y'all kindly quiet down?" James shouted with an air of authority to his voice.

Two hours later, Jonas was flat on his back in his bunk staring at the bottom of the bunk above him. He was trying to formulate strategies for the task at hand. About that time, the fragrance of coffee brewing and food cooking drifted back into the lockup. Jonas felt his stomach rumble, and he realized he was hungry. In another fifteen minutes, Smith came in with a pot of coffee and three cups. "You gonna have coffee, Frank, or are you just gonna lie there until mornin'?" James rolled over and sat up with his stocking feet on the cell floor. That's when Jonas got his first good look at Frank James. He was a thin man. Not large by any measure but not a small man, either. He looked to be about the same age and height as Jonas. Maybe a couple of years older. He wore a full beard of medium length. His hair was dark brown to black, parted on the left side, short but full on top and on the sides under which his large ears protruded noticeably. His face and head were elongated, and his sad-looking dark eyes were set close together under an unremarkable low brow. His nose was small and his skin white. He was a somber looking fellow. Probably very closed lip.

"Suppertime," Smith called out as he balanced two tin plates on one hand and arm and a third in his other hand. That one he slid under James's door, and the other two he shoved under the door where Jonas and the other prisoner were in their own cells. "Bone appatee," he said as he went out the door.

"Same as last night!" the other prisoner yelled after Smith. "Can't you do anything but beans, bacon, and biscuits?"

Smith stuck his head back in the door and said sarcastically, "What would monsure prefer? Perhaps a nice juicy beefsteak? Oh, but forsooth. Monsure is in jail. Too bad. He ain't got no choice. Now shut up and get that grub down afore I take it away from you." Then he popped back through the door.

"Ain't that bad to me," Jonas said just loud enough for James to hear. There was no answer. "What about you?"

James didn't answer and didn't look up. Jonas decided to let it pass.

Next morning there was a biting chill in the lockup even with the stove radiating away out in the front office. During the freezing night, there just wasn't enough heat from the stove to reach the lockup and overcome the cold that seeped through the brick walls. Jonas stayed in his bunk wrapped in two blankets. He had to relieve himself real bad but held it back so he didn't have to get out of bed.

"Hey! Yer got any hot coffee out there? It's freezing in here," the other prisoner called out.

"Keep yer britches on. We're in the middle a changin' the guard here. I'll bring yer some coffee in just a minute," Smith yelled back.

"Always get this cold in here?" Jonas asked James. The man just looked at him once and then looked away.

After the breakfast tins were cleared away, it started to warm up a little as the storm had passed. It was a bright, sunny day outside. Jonas asked James, "They got any cards in here? Wanna play some cards? Maybe some gin rummy? Hey, Albert," Jonas called out. "Got any playing cards we can use?"

Albert brought in a deck of cards and handed them through the bars to Jonas. "Now don't bend 'em all up. Onliest deck I got."

"Of course not. We'll take real good care of them. And, don't want to be a bother, but could we have a small table between the cell bars and a stool for each of us?" Jonas looked at Albert with a meek-looking plea expressed on his face.

"What a yer think this is? The Taj Mahal?"

"The Taj Mahal is a tomb," James said as he sat on the edge of his bunk.

"Huh?"

"If you want to compare to a fine hotel, you can't do better than the Planter House Hotel in St. Louis."

Jonas stared curiously at James. He hadn't realized James was an educated man.

"Fiddlesticks. I'll git yer a table and stools."

"You didn't say if you wanted to play some cards," Jonas said through the bars.

James looked up at Jonas, shrugged his shoulders, and said, "Guess that'd be all right."

"Good. Good. You like to gamble? We could play for beans or something." Jonas chuckled. James did not.

"Ain't a gambling man."

"But, you like fine hotels, huh?" James said nothing. "Where'd you get your learning?" Jonas continued the query.

"Read a lot."

"What do you read?"

"Anything. Mostly Shakespeare these days. You heard a him?"

"Can't say I have."

"Figures. You have to be a philosophical thinking man if you're going to read and understand Shakespeare. And you are?"

"Like to think so."

Smith brought a small table and stool and put them in Jonas's cell and then set down a stool in James's cell. "That suit your highness?" he asked Jonas.

"Yes, thank you, Mister Smith."

Jonas arranged the table at the bars between the cells and set his stool next to it. He shuffled the cards, and they played for about two hours until James said he was bored and wanted to read. He stood up and went to his bunk, pulled out an old-looking book from under his mattress, sat on the bunk, and leaned against his pillow to read.

"Whatcha readin'?" Jonas asked.

"Like I told you. Shakespeare, and I don't like being bothered when I am reading."

■ ■ ■ ■

It went on like that just about every day for two weeks. The other prisoner had been released, and it was just Jonas and James in the jail. Jonas bided his time but never really felt like he was gaining ground with James. He couldn't find a crack. So one day at cards, he just started talking.

"I've robbed four stores and a card shark. Ain't been caught but one time. This last time because I didn't follow my system." He expected James to ask about his system, but he never even blinked an eye. So, he went on. "First, I pick stores in small towns that didn't have a marshal. I checked the town over real good just to double check and make sure there weren't no law around. Makes sense, yeah?" No response. "I ain't greedy, so a small take to carry me over is just fine. That's why I am happy with a small store. Second, I case the store out for a week or two to figure out when it might have the most cash on hand. That's the day I hit it, when it has the most cash right before closing time. Usually that's right after the end of the month when everybody's been paid and comes to buy at the store. Are you with me so far?" No response.

210

"Third, I always wear a mask. Got to keep from bein' even close to identified. Fourth, I always use a pistol to scare folks with, but it's unloaded. I don't want to hurt nobody."

James glanced up at him with a look of disdain. Jonas recovered quickly. "A course I keep a loaded pistol in my waistband. A Smith and Wesson double action, short-barrel thirty-eight. In case I have any trouble I gotta shoot my way out of. How 'bout you?" Didn't even look up. "Fifth, always keep a fast horse tied up out front to get away on. Sixth, don't stop runnin' away for at least twenty miles and make a cold camp. No smoke. Then go on to the next job. What a you think of that system?"

James threw a card down, looked up, and stared at Jonas for a minute, then asked in a flat tone like some kind of stoic philosopher, "How'd you get caught this time?"

"Didn't check the town as careful as I should. Didn't know it, but there was a deputy sheriff passin' through town. He was in the café eatin' his supper. A woman in the store I was robbin' screamed, and I hightailed it outta there. The deputy took out after me. His horse was faster than mine, and he just run me down."

"Why didn't you shoot him?" That he said with a cold, hard stare into Jonas's eyes with enough intensity to penetrate his skull if that were possible.

"Well, I didn't want that on my record. Would you have if it were you?" Jonas thought this was the moment he might break through, but James stood, dropped his cards on the table, and looked down at Jonas sitting on his stool.

" 'You speak an infinite deal of nothing.' William Shakespeare. *The Merchant of Venice.*" He stepped over to his bunk and flopped down with his book. Jonas stared at his cards blankly for a minute and then dealt himself a solitaire hand.

A week later they were playing cards again, and Jonas said, "Anybody coming to visit you for Christmas?"

Without looking up from his cards James said, "Anybody coming to visit you?"

"Nope."

"Me neither. Don't want my family risking the winter weather just to come wish me well. 'These violent delights have violent ends and in their triumph die, like fire and powder which, as they kiss, consume.' William Shakespeare. *Romeo and Juliet.*"

"Uh-huh."

After the first of the year, Jonas decided to

give it another try. Smith had just returned James to his cell after he visited with his lawyer. "How'd it go?" Jonas asked.

"Usual."

Jonas waited twenty minutes until they both were on their backs in their bunks, and then he said, "You recall when I was tellin' you about that deputy that caught me, and you asked me why I didn't shoot him?" No answer. "Well, I've been thinkin' about it, and I guess the real reason was I didn't want to have that on my conscience. It's bad enough gettin' caught and facin' prison but then to carry around that load a guilt on top of it. I just don't know. I think that's what held me back. What do you think?"

" 'Conscience doth make cowards of us all.' William Shakespeare. *Hamlet.*"

"Now what the hell is that supposed to mean? You think it's some kinda bravery to shoot a man?" Jonas jumped out of his bunk and stood stiffly at the bars between the cells. He had about had it with this Shakespeare-quoting murderer. His voice rose, and he felt the old blind anger well up in him. "I killed plenty a men in the war and another in prison in Kansas, but none of them were out and out murder. Killin' a deputy when fleein' a crime is flat-out murder. And of a lawman to boot. But you,

you holier than thou Shakespeare-quotin' blackheart, are a murderer. Aren't you?" Jonas's knuckles turned more white by the second as he gripped the bars and stood rigid, blazing mad and glaring hotly at Frank James.

Still on his bunk, James turned his head to look at Jonas and said, " 'Your brother too must die; consent you, Lepidus?' William Shakespeare. *Julius Caesar.*"

"There you go again with the Shakespeare horse shit. You're a hypocrite."

James slowly rose up from his bunk and walked toward Jonas. "I've been readin' William Shakespeare's works from my father's library since I could first read, and I can assure, sir, it is not horse shit. The play, *Julius Caesar,* is about treachery and betrayal. In the quote I just gave you, Lepidus agrees to betray his brother and gives the okay for his murder. Just like you Mister whatever-your-name-is." He launched himself at Jonas, caught his shirtfront between the bars, and, pulling, slammed Jonas against the bars. "You're the hypocrite," he snarled. "I know you're a plant."

"What're you talkin' about? I ain't no plant. What a you mean by that anyhow?"

"I mean you been tryin' to cozy up to me and get me to confess. It ain't gonna work.

You ain't had any visit from a lawyer since you been here. And Smith left you here in this cell next to me when Robertson was released. He always separates the prisoners. But not this time, eh?"

"That's crazy. I ain't gonna do no such thing. And as far as cozyin' up to you I think I'd rather cozy up to a rattlesnake. You ain't very friendly at all." Jonas seized Frank James's wrist in his right hand, his smithy's hand, and twisted James's hand loose from his shirt. He squeezed hard, and he could see the pain register in James's eyes. "I ain't sure whether you're a bad man or not. Cuz if I thought you were a bad man I'd kill you right here and now." He pushed hard on James's arm and sent him flying across his cell to land on his bunk, butt first.

When January thirty-first came around Jonas was released, a free man with no warrants out on him. He headed for Independence to see his boys.

At the supper table the first night at his sister-in-law's house, Jonas gazed admiringly at his boys. Harry was thirteen years old and Edgar eleven. He held up his glass of sweet tea toward them and said, "A fine pair of young men here. I am proud of you boys." He smiled like the proud papa he was. Both the boys smiled back but with reservation. They seemed unsure, and Jonas picked up on it. But what could be expected? They hadn't even hardly seen him for the last seven years. Then he turned to Mary and said, "And I can't thank you enough, Mary." He beamed an appreciative smile at her and then added, "and you, too, Johnathan. I am very much obliged."

"Well, we're glad to be of help. How about a cigar in the parlor if you're finished with your supper?"

"Sounds good."

After they lit up Johnathan said, "What you been up to these last few years?"

Jonas ran through a narrative of his adventures that consumed a half hour, and when he finished Johnathan asked, "So what now?"

Jonas shrugged his shoulders and said, "Haven't given it much thought."

"You know there's a handbill just came in down on the bulletin board in the post office. You might want to take a look at it. Some fellow in Texas is looking for detectives to chase down cattle rustlers."

"That might be interesting. I wonder what it's all about?"

The next morning Jonas was in the post office copying down the telegram information in his little notebook. Then he went to the telegraph office and sent a wire per the instructions in the notice. A week later he received a letter of explanation and a blank application form. He filled out the application and sent it off. Another week and he received a letter that set out an interview time and place.

While time passed, he took Harry and Edgar to Baden's dry goods store and told them they each had twenty dollars to spend on whatever they wanted. It was fun for Jonas to watch them take their time inspecting all kinds of products that attracted their fancies. He took them snow sledding and even rented a mule to pull them along on their sleds. Before Jonas came, they were restricted to fishing the pond outside of town. It was iced over on the edges, so Jonas said they needed to fish the river, where they caught some big fish and were all the more excited for it. But, it all came to an end when the appointment letter arrived. Two days later he was on the train headed south to Texas.

Chapter Five
Texas: Learning the Ropes

As the train approached the Decatur station, Jonas wiped the fog off the window with his sleeve and peered out to get his first look at the town. There was not much to look at compared to Kansas City or even Independence for that matter. It was not much different from the many Texas towns he came through on the train from Independence. Decatur was the end of the line, and he was looking out the window to see if he could espy the stage depot and any kind of way house to lodge for the night. The stage was scheduled to leave the next day at seven in the morning for points west through to Seymour. It stopped the first night in Jacksboro, and then he only had fifteen more miles to his destination at Jermyn.

The morning was gray and icy, frosted over by the cold wind that came out of the north. By six-thirty, Jonas was already huddled in the post office by the wood stove, rubbing his hands together. He wore a long, black, wool Ulster coat over his navy-blue three-piece suit. Even with his heavy-duty union suit on, he was still cold and almost shivering. The postmaster was at his desk bundling the last of the mail for the stage to take west. He put it in a canvas bag and looked up when the train station agent burst in.

"Got a couple of late ones," the agent called out.

"Where to?" the postmaster replied. Jonas stepped over and shut the door left open by the station agent.

"One to Loving at Jermyn as usual, and one for a feller I don't recognize in Graham."

"All right. Let me have 'em." He put each telegram in a separate yellow envelope, set one aside, and stuffed the other into one of the mail pouches he was working on. Then he picked up three pouches, went outside, and set them down beside the door. He rushed back inside and stopped by the stove next to Jonas and the train agent to warm his hands along with them.

"This is a wicked storm comin' down from the north. I ain't ever seen it this cold, and I been here in this part of the country for nigh onto fifty years now," the postmaster declared.

"What's normal this time of year?"

"Well, we can freeze sure enough but not this cold, and hardly ever with snow like this."

"Guess we just got to buck up against it. Me, I'm pretty used to it, being from Kansas. Couldn't help but overhear you have a telegram for James Loving?" Jonas queried.

"That's right, mister. Why do you ask?" the postmaster said with a hint of suspicion in his voice.

"Name is Jonas V. Brighton. I am a detective, and I have an appointment with Mister Loving. I can deliver that telegram to him if you would like."

"Brighton, huh?" the telegraph agent said. "Yeah, I've seen that name come across the wire in the last few weeks. He's probably tellin' the truth, Bert." The agent spoke assuredly.

"That's well and good, but we have a contract with Will Blakely at the general store in Lost Valley to collect the mail bag from the stage. So, we'll just leave it at that."

"Just tryin' to be helpful." Jonas flashed a winsome smile at them.

"Blakely can decide what he wants to do at his end. Obliged just the same. 'Bout time to board now. Stage is comin' in," the postmaster said as he nodded toward the door.

Jonas hefted his valise and stepped out to the boardwalk. The driver had the six-horse team at a trot, and as he came closer he slowed them to a walk. When the team was abreast of the post office door he yelled out, "WHOA, YER HOSSES" and pulled back severely on the reins while stomping the brake lever on the right side of the driver's box. The horses stiffened their legs and slid to a stop while the coach slid toward the boardwalk and stopped just as the wheels touched the outer edge of the boardwalk directly in front of the door. Jets of vapor blew from the horses' nostrils in audible blasts as they snorted and breathed heavily from their labor. They chomped their bits and tossed their heads to and fro, causing the chains of the harness to jangle noisily. Steam rose from their wet backs, and they were covered in snow and mud from their chests, around their shoulders, and down their flanks to their hind ends. They stomped their hooves in the frozen slush and broke through it, sending splashes onto the boardwalk. One horse whinnied and reared once in his traces, which caused the driver to race out of the box down to the front wheel and grab the bridle of the rearing horse. He spoke calmly to the horse and stroked his muzzle. That calmed the big boy, and the bulging whites of his eyes relaxed back to normal.

Jonas admired the driver's handling of the horse and the team in general. And he had to smile as the driver slid around the front pair of horses with a rope in hand. His beard, mustache, eyebrows, and front of his hat were thick with frost. But he didn't seem to mind as he spat tobacco juice at the icy slush in the road and wiped his mouth with a gloved hand. He tied one end of the thick rope around the big hitching rail and loosely looped it around the necks of the front pair and returned the end to the rail, where he tied it off. "Five minutes," he hollered. "Stoppin' for five minutes. If you have to use the privy now's the time to do it. We ain't stoppin' agin for four hours until we git to the way station. Change out the horses there." He had cupped his hands to his mouth and called out into the wind like he had done two hundred times before. It was obviously routine. And then he went around back to the outhouse.

Brighton was looking at the coach. It was dark green with what he could barely tell were gold wheel rims and spokes. The wheels and the coach body halfway up were covered in snowmelt mud like the horses. It wasn't the appearance of the coach Jonas was interested in. He looked all around to make sure all the leather window flaps were tied down good. It was going to be breezy enough without a flap coming loose and a hurricane blowing through the coach.

The driver came out onto the boardwalk and said to Jonas, "Yer the only passenger. Got yer ticket? Alrighty. If'n yer don't object we can git started right away. Never know what might be out there blockin' the road." He winked at Jonas and motioned for him to board the stage. "They's plenty a wool blankets for yer to use. Hep yerself." Then he went to the hitching rail and untied the tether.

Jonas laid a gray wool blanket over his legs and wrapped it underneath them. Then he draped another blanket over his shoulders and retrieved a cigar from his inside coat pocket.

The driver threw the mail bags up to his box and then climbed up the front wheel to the box, arranged the bags under his seat, got himself situated, picked up the reins, kicked off the brake, and said loudly but calmly, "Okay, boys, let's giddy up slow and easy now." He lightly slapped the reins on the backs of the horses, and they lurched in place as they lost traction on the ice. But they caught themselves quickly, regained their footing, and slowly pulled the stage away from the boardwalk. The stage rolled out of town headed west with the wind quartering from the north. The snow had stopped, which made it easier for the driver to make time. But it didn't make it easier for Jonas as the coach bounced along the road and tossed him to and fro from one side to the other and from front to back. And when they hit the deeper potholes he was nearly thrown off the seat. Cautiously, stiffly, and with a sore back, he stepped off the coach at Jacksboro. He was very glad he only had fifteen miles more to go from there to his destination.

It was early afternoon, and black clouds were over Jermyn, so Jonas hurried in a stiff-legged walk to the house he was directed to. It was sure enough icy rain a coming. He carried a medium size carpetbag that contained his only possessions, amounting to mostly clothes and the family bible. Arriving at the two-story house, painted dark green with cream-colored trim, he climbed the steps to the front porch and twisted the knob on the brass rotary doorbell. He removed his hat and waited a minute or less before the door opened, and he was greeted by a middle-aged, ordinary-looking woman who flashed a contagious smile at him.

"Yes, sir? You must be Jonas Brighton," she said. "We've been expecting you. I am Mary Loving." She held out her hand, which Jonas grasped, and she gave him three strong pumps. Her chestnut hair was piled on top of her head, and she wore a white silk waist blouse tucked into a blue pin-striped cotton walking skirt with a flounce bottom. "Please come in," she said as she held the door open for him. He wiped his boots vigorously on the thick bristle mat and raised each foot to double check and make sure there was no lingering mud. "Get in out of the cold. My, it must be below zero out there. Mister Loving is in his office. You can wait here in the parlor, and I'll announce you. Hang your hat and coat here on this tree. Please have a seat."

The smell of wood smoke was about the house, and Jonas guessed there was a stove going somewhere. The odor was different from any wood smoke he was familiar with. He took a seat in a green velvet armchair and glanced back at the Persian rug he had just come across. No tracks, so he thought he was good. He looked around the room, taking notice of the white lace curtains in the windows, the elegant wallpaper on the walls, and the other fine Victorian furniture arranged throughout the parlor. He heard a door open and close, then a man's footsteps coming toward him from the hall. James Loving appeared dressed in Levi blue jeans with the cuffs turned up so they wouldn't drag and catch the heels of the brown cowboy boots he wore. He had on an oxblood-colored shirt plaited in white stripes and made of what looked like Madras cloth. Over the shirt he wore a plain brown leather vest and no collar. Jonas guessed him to be a little over six feet tall, of average build, strong through the shoulders, flat stomach. His hands showed the wear of manual labor. His hair was dark, flecked with gray, as was the thick mustache riding over a mouth set firm. His nose was a little hawkish between high cheekbones, and he had a thick brow over hazel eyes set in a weathered face. He came toward Jonas and with a stoic look offered his hand.

"Mister Brighton. Jim Loving."

"Nice to meet you, Mister Loving."

"Call me Jim, and I'll call you Jake, if that's all right with you. We don't carry formal handles out here on the range. More inclined to nicknames." He smiled with a show of teeth. Right off, Loving's lazy Texas drawl in a baritone voice and friendly smile put Brighton at ease.

"Well, that's what they called me in the army, so I don't mind. In fact, I prefer it. It was my wife who called me Jonas all the time. I just went along with it."

"You married?"

"Widower."

"Uh-huh."

"I want to learn all I can and fit in real fast. So, right off, may I ask what kind of wood are you burnin' in the stove that has such a sweet and spicy odor?"

"Wal, that's mesquite. We ain't real happy with it. It's tryin' to swallow up all the grassland. So we burn it every chance we git. I would like to burn it off the land, but that would probably start a huge range fire. So better not, if you git my drift. Let's git started with the interview. Come on into my office."

They walked down the hall a few steps, and Jim opened a door to a room. He motioned for Jake to enter, and he followed, then closed the door behind him. "Have to keep the door closed. Mary can't stand the fragrance of cigar smoke in the house." He smiled. Jake returned his smile. "Here, have a seat." He motioned to one of two black leather club chairs on either side of a lamp table upon which stood a lamp with a wood base and cream-colored shade backed by a window with rust-colored drapes. Jake set his valise on the wood floor to the outboard side of the chair and sat comfortably in the buttery Cordova leather. Otherwise, the office was plain enough except for the big oak desk opposite the door over which hung a huge set of longhorn steer horns, matched by another set on the wall behind the desk. On the wall opposite Jake hung a head mount of a whitetail deer with a magnificent rack of antlers. Under it along the wall was a bureau type bookcase. The walls themselves were plastered and painted a cream color. Jim was at the bureau.

"Whiskey? Cigar?" he asked with his back to Jake as he poured from a decanter into two glasses.

"Don't mind if I do. Since it's my birthday. Thanks."

"Wal now, happy birthday and on behalf of the Stock-Raisers' Association of North-West Texas, welcome to the great state of Texas." He handed a whiskey to Jake and raised his own in a salute. "Here's how," he said and clinked Jake's glass. "How old are you now?"

"Thirty-six. Oh, and here." Jake reached into his inside coat pocket and pulled out the telegram and some other mail. "Mister Blakely gave them to me to carry to you when I asked directions to your house." Jim held a round humidor of cigars out to Jake for him to select one and took the correspondence in his other hand. He gave Jake a match and went to his desk, where he dropped the mail on the desktop and slit open the telegram envelope. He read the wire quickly and let out a grunt. "Xavier Calhoun up at Comanche Creek says he's lost another fifty head to rustlers and wants a stock detective yesterday. Harumph. Wonder what's goin' on up there? He's got a line rider named Johnny Rayner that is a dead shot who's supposedly keepin' rustlers away from the Flying XC. That's his brand. He might get lucky, though I got Wes Wilson workin' the Dodge City Trail out of Seymour. I —" He cut off his statement as if he were about to say something he thought better of.

After sitting in the other black leather chair and lighting his cigar, Jim said, "Tell me more about your background and why you want to be a stock detective."

Jake sipped a little whiskey and puffed his cigar. "As I said in my letter, I don't have any range experience, don't know cattle, and don't know ranchin', but I am a fast learner. I am an expert marksman from my days in the army, and I can ride. What I do know is criminals and undercover detective work. My last case was for the Daviess County prosecutin' attorney in Missourah. I was workin' undercover in the same jail they had Frank James locked up. They paid me to attempt to befriend him and obtain evidence on him regardin' his upcomin' trial." Jake pulled on his cigar and sipped some whiskey.

"And?" Jim queried.

"He is an interestin' man. Tight-lipped. He said he sniffed me out from the beginnin'. I didn't get anything, and the prosecutin' attorney gave it up. So, I decided to take a little time off and headed down to Independence to visit my boys."

"You have family?"

"My wife died in seventy-six. Cyclone in Kansas. My daughter, too. But my brother and his wife took in my boys. He died, but she wanted to keep the boys, and they wanted to stay with her. She's remarried now to the postmaster. That's where I saw your handbill. Sounded different and interestin' to me. Thought maybe I could put my detective skills to use here. So, here I am." Jake smiled friendly-like.

"Generally, I discourage family men from

becomin' stock detectives. It's dangerous work and not much time spent at home."

"Well, I am not burdened that way."

"In five years I've lost two men. Naturally, I don't want to lose anymore."

"Of course."

"Ever kill a man?" Jim looked keenly at Jake over the rim of his glass as he sipped his whiskey.

Jake swallowed the whiskey he was swilling in his mouth and held back a cough. As a detective, being an astute observer of human behavior, Jake knew he himself had flinched when the question was out, and that Jim had seen it. Now he had to decide. How far would he go in the explanation that would surely be asked of him? He puffed his cigar and blew a cloud of smoke to the ceiling. Looking Jim straight in the eye he said, "Yes. One in prison and one on the job in Manhattan."

"Were you an inmate?"

"Yes, I was. Another inmate was attemptin' to assault me, and I defended myself."

"What were you in prison for?"

"Grand larceny. I stole two mules."

Now Jim blew a cloud of smoke to the ceiling and gazed upward as if he were contemplating the shape of the smoke cloud. He returned his gaze to Jake and said, "Good that you answered honestly and forthrightly. I already checked into your back trail. Just got the report yesterday in the mail. You've only been out a few years. Any problems since then?"

Jonas V. Brighton now aka Jake Brighton thought that one over real hard. He could lie and try and skate through, but there were newspaper articles on the matter. Loving already declared that he checked Jake's background, and he seemed to appreciate honesty. Maybe he was setting a trap. Better be honest.

"Yes. What got me there was a dumb mistake. I am not a thief and sure not a cattle rustler." Jake smiled at his little joke. Jim did not. "Ever hear of the Doctor Talbott case in Missourah?"

"Read about it."

"That was my case."

"Yeah. I place the name now. Congratulations."

"Havin' spent time with criminals, I understand how their minds work and the language, etcetera, that allows me to get among them without suspicion. That is what I am offerin' here." The two men held each other's stare as they contemplated the situation.

"What were the other problems?"

"I opened a letter written by a suspect I was investigatin'. I turned the letter in as part of my evidence, and the prosecutin' attorney used it in his case. Afterwards, a U.S. marshal arrested me for openin' the letter and took me to Kansas City, where I was bailed out by prominent citizens of Nodaway County, where the Talbott boys were hanged based on my evidence." Jake was breathing a little heavy so he took a gulp of whiskey to settle himself down. He felt a little riled as he re-hashed the affair. "Well, I felt like I was betrayed, and I left the state of Missourah and went to Illinois. I was upset, too, because I had planned to spend Christmas with my boys. Then a year later I was arrested by marshals for the alleged mail offense. They took me back to Kansas City and offered me a deal to drop the charges if I would work undercover in the prison where they were holdin' Frank James. I already told you about that. Still irks me."

"I thought you said they paid you for the undercover work."

"They did. They gave me my freedom. I didn't mean money."

"Yeah, well, I think you are basically honest. You see, I know Deputy U.S. Marshal Allen. He used to be in Fort Worth before he transferred to Kansas City. I checked with him, and he pretty much confirms all you've said. Apparently, they respect your undercover work, eh?"

"I don't know. I'd like to think so."

"Yeah. That's kind of what I had in mind. Stayed away from hirin' men with criminal records, but, in this case, I think I will make an exception just to try out this undercover idea." He smiled assurance at Jake like it was all done. "Pays seventy-five a month, expense reimbursement, one dollar per head of recovered stolen cattle, five dollars per captured or killed rustler, and half the reward money of any wanted person. I say 'person' because we got some real female varmints ridin' the range nowadays. You no doubt heard of Belle Starr. She comes across the Red River from Indian Territory, rustles cattle, and runs 'em up north to sell. I don't know where she is or what she's up to now. Haven't heard much about her lately. Submit a expense report and voucher for extra pay every month. So, are you interested?"

"Yes, sir. Very much."

"All right then." Jim stood and with a big grin held out his hand, and Jake stood and clasped it firmly. "Welcome to the posse, stock detective.

"The association has a petition before the legislature to obtain peace officer status for our stock detectives," he added. "It is movin' slowly. Someday, though, it'll pass and become law. In the meantime though, you are just a citizen doing a job for the association, which is pretty powerful. So, any arrests or recovery of stolen cattle will legally be as a private citizen. But, like I said, the association is behind you one hundred percent, and there are a lot of big guns in the association. But there are those rogue judges out there. Crazy zealots. They don't get re-elected. But, just make sure everything you do is aboveboard and legal, and you'll be all right. If you get in a bind, the association will provide legal representation."

"Thank you, sir. I'll give it my best."

"Good. Let's finish our cigars while I lay out my plan for you and pick out a horse and saddle. Then we'll have supper. We'll put you up in the bunkhouse. You can leave that pocket pistol you're carryin' in your vest in your bag. Nobody'll bother with it in the bunkhouse."

"My pleasure." Jake smiled. He liked observant people such as himself.

They sat back down, and Jim said, "Like I said, I have detective Wes Wilson working out of Seymour. Damn fine man and real good with brands and range tactics. Seymour is about fifty miles west a here." He pointed in a westerly direction. "It's next to where the trail crosses the Brazos, but there ain't any herds this time of year. So I was thinkin' I'll send you over to spend a couple of months with Wes to learn the ropes. Here." He handed Jake a book. Jake turned it over in his hands and read the title, *The Stockmen's Guide and Handbook* by none other than James C. Loving. Then he looked up at Jim, smiled, and said, "I'll study it real hard. What's the trail?"

"The Dodge City Trail that cattlemen use to drive their cattle to market. Like a Chisholm Trail only further west. There are more than six hundred brands in that book. The more you can memorize the better you'll be." Jim gave Jake a look of exaggerated confidence. "Once Wes says you are ready, I am gonna send you up to the Flying XC. I'll arrange with Xavier Calhoun, he's the owner, to sign you on to his crew. Damn fine man. Known him a long time. Family's Texian. One of Stephen Austin's old three hundred families. You heard a them? No? No matter. They came west from the Tennessee River country in Alabama and grew from there. One a the biggest operations in

Texas now. You can work undercover as a hand on the ranch. You'll meet Walt Guthrie. He's the cow boss. I'll send Wes up there, too. He can work out of Vernon. Any questions?"

"Nope. I am sure I'll have many as time goes by."

Jim gave Jake a comical once-over look and said, "Gotta git you out of those city duds. You're gonna need boots, spurs, britches, chaps, shirts, vest, bandana, coat, and hat. Blakely can fix you up over at the store. If you don't have the money, I can pay him out of your salary."

"I have a coat hanging out there on your hall tree, and I have money, but I would rather use yours." Jake grinned with a slightly sly look in his eyes.

"Ha ha. Businessman, too, I see. That'll be fine. Okay. Let's get you a horse and saddle. I'll lend you both as long as you like, as long as you are an association detective. Then I expect you to turn 'em back in to me unless, of course, you ever want to buy 'em." Jim grinned big and chuckled just a bit. "I'm a businessman, too," he said feigning seriousness. "Finish your whiskey? Okay, let's go down to the barn. Johnny Tosahwi is my wrangler. He's Comanche and a real nice feller. Educated on the reservation

237

from the time he was a little sprout. Nobody knows horses like Johnny. He can coax the devil right out of any wild stallion. Bring your bag. We'll drop it off at the bunkhouse. Get your hat and coat. I'll get mine on the way out back."

Jim led Jake down the hall to the kitchen and then out to the screened back porch, where he grabbed his hat and coat off a peg on the wall. "Damn! Looks like it's fixin' to let go with a big one. We better get a move on."

They crunched across the frozen grass behind the porch and under the big cotton-woods, then out onto the hard-packed dirt and over to the barn and corrals, which were both painted brown. Corrals with a few horses milling around in them were arranged on both sides of the barn, and the big double doors were closed. Jim opened the small door for them, and they stepped into the dark barn. It was cool inside but still much warmer than outside. Typical in its layout were stalls down both sides, a tack room, feed storage room, and other storage spaces at the ends, with a farrier shop in the far corner. Not typical, however, was the lack of odor from horse urine and droppings. It mostly smelled of fresh straw and other inoffensive odors. They took a minute to allow their eyes to adjust as Jim closed the door.

"I like a clean barn," Jim said. "The cowboys are out checkin' the cows. Calvin's gonna start pretty soon, and we want to try to keep the pregnant ones together. I'm raisin' up a herd of shorthorns. Less injury all around than longhorns and more beef. Johnny should be around here somewhere. Johnny?!" he called out. "Johnny!!" he yelled again.

"Over here, boss," Johnny called back as he came through the small door of the barn at the farrier shop end. "Was out in the corral." He walked up to them, shrugging off the cold as he came. "Colder'n a witch's tit out there."

"You ain't wrong there. This here is Jake Brighton. He's our new stock detective. He needs a horse, saddle, and tack. I want him to have a good cow pony that's fast with plenty of endurance. I'm thinkin' Jasper. What do you think?"

Johnny sort of looked Jake up and down and said, "Jasper? I guess. Maybe that bronc'll take to him and maybe he won't. And if he don't, well you know how that can go, boss." Johnny glanced amusedly at Jake.

"Well, let's see how it goes. Where is he?"

"Out in the corral with the others."

"Jasper is a good strong stock horse. Six-year-old gelding. Black and white paint. He can run like the wind forever. But, he's got a mind of his own, and he don't take kindly to many people. There was one hand we had though a year back or so who Jasper really took to, and they made a great team. Maybe you can work that magic," Jim said to Jake with a sparkle in his eye.

"Maybe," Jake said speculatively. "I'm pretty good around livestock, especially mules and horses. Let's have a look at him."

"This way," Johnny said with a nod of his head in the direction of a side door in the barn wall between stalls. He opened the door, and clustered around it on the outside were about eight horses of the Loving remuda. Johnny pushed them back and said, "It's comin' near on to feedin' time. They are all thinkin' they're gonna come in and get fed. Ha!"

Among the group of horses stood a big feller distinguished by large tobiano black and white splotches of color and a golden tail and mane. Probably stood about sixteen and a half to seventeen hands. He looked to be well muscled and more alert than the other horses. His ears were pricked forward, and he stared critically at the group of humans who had just entered the corral as if he were questioning what they were up to. Jake liked him immediately and began to slowly walk up to Jasper. The horse did not move and watched Jake intently.

As Jake approached close enough to get a good look into his eyes, he saw intelligence, which he liked even more. Slowly, but not too slow, closer he came, talking gently to Jasper. He stood next to him and rubbed his neck with one hand, and the other he slipped into his coat pocket and pulled out a piece of hard candy, which he slipped to Jasper's lips. Jasper sniffed the candy and then nibbled it off Jake's palm. He wasted no time crunching the sweet with his molars, swallowing it, and nickering for more. Jake gave him another piece and then walked away from Jasper, who followed him into the barn, where Jake gave him a last piece. He stroked his neck and said, "That's enough for today, boy. Tomorrow there will be more, but only once a day. You want me to put him in a stall?" Jake called out to Johnny.

"Sure. That one right behind you is fine."

"I can feed him, too."

"All right. Might as well get right to it. I reckon he's about twelve hundred pounds, and he ain't doin' nothin' much these days since it's winter and all, so I been feedin' him about twelve pounds a hay and a couple handfuls of oats. Fed him this mornin', so you can give him a fork of hay and a handful of oats."

"Up in the loft?"

"Yep."

Jim watched all the getting-acquainted doings with Jake and Jasper while he leaned against a post and chewed a piece of straw. Seemed like Jake knew what he was doing, and he was quick enough up and down the loft ladder, which meant he was probably strong enough to endure the range, even though he was on the higher side of the age Jim preferred for his detectives. A ball of hay came down the chute, and Jake came back down the ladder, then went into the feed storeroom and came out with a small sack of oats. He did right by giving the oats to Jasper first and right out of his hand. Then he fluffed up the hay in the fodder rack in the stall, stroked Jasper's neck a few times more, and then backed slowly out of the stall, shutting the gate behind him. He went over to the inside well and pulled up a bucket of water, poured the water into another bucket and set it on a stand outside Jasper's stall where he could reach it to drink but not kick it over.

"I think we will get along just fine. We both got a sweet tooth," Jake said as he glanced with a smile at Jim first and then Johnny. Jim nodded his head in agreement, and Johnny shrugged his shoulders and said, "I'll let you know after you get up on his back and we see what happens." He chuckled friendly-like. "Jasper's been known to throw more than a few cowpokes. But I'll probably keep them all in tomorrow until the storm blows over."

"I'll help you keep the barn clean tomorrow," Jake said with a serious and friendly look.

"Much obliged. I can always use some help around here. More than a body can do in a day."

He glanced slyly at Jim, who tossed away his straw chew and waved his hand at Johnny saying, "You're just slowing down, is all. And I hear the dinner bell a ringin', so you better get a move on."

"I can help feed," Jake said.

"No. Mary's expecting us for dinner. And we don't want to cross Mary, do we Johnny?"

"No, sir." They both chuckled.

Next morning, Jake listened to Will Blakely go down the list of items piled on the counter beside him. "Two pair a denim pants, two flannel shirts, two cotton shirts, boots, spurs. You want regular Texan or Mexican? I got these fancy Mexican with jingle bobs in case you want to be heard coming." He grinned. "Or these plain Buermann's, or . . ."

"I'll take the Buermann's and the plain leather straps and buckles," Jake said. "Mexican spurs are too noisy with their big rowels and jingle bobs and all."

"Alrighty. Stetson Big Four, belly nutria is the only color I got, leather vest, blue bandana." He went on and on and then came to the weaponry.

"So, what shootin' irons do you want? Come on over here to the case and see what I have."

"Do you have the Winchester Repeater in forty-four caliber with octagon barrel?"

"Right here," Blakely said as he pulled the rifle off the rack. "Only twelve-fifty. But since you are damn near buyin' out the whole store, I'll give it to you for twelve bucks." He grinned big. Jake smiled and picked up the rifle with his right hand. He felt it for weight, and it felt right. Then he laid the fore stock in his left hand and pulled the lever down with his right. He looked into the ejection port to be sure the rifle was unloaded, levered the bolt closed, and pulled the trigger. He dry-fired the weapon three times and was satisfied with the action. Then he brought the butt to his shoulder and sighted through the sights. "It'll do," he said flatly, then turned his attention back to the gun display,

"I see you have the Colt Double Action Army revolver," he said.

"Yes, sir. You can see I have a big selection. What's your preference?"

"I'll take a forty-four short barrel."

"Sure you don't want a forty-five in a seven-and-a-half-inch barrel? More impact power. More accuracy at longer range?"

"No, five and a half is fine for me. I ain't any kind of gunman, so I need a short barrel to clear the leather faster. Besides, any shot more than say fifteen paces and I'll use the rifle. Forty-four is plenty enough punch, and I can interchange ammo with the pistol and the rifle. I'll need a holster and two cartridge belts and one of those toad stickers with a sheath you have over there."

"Yes, sir, coming right up. Try this pistol for feel." He handed him one of the guns, and Jake worked it in his right hand, checked the action, and looked down the barrel. All seemed good, well-greased and brand new. He again dry-fired three times, testing the smoothness and ease of double-action firing. It was just a hair tight, but he figured it would loosen up after he put a few rounds through it.

"Can you take out the lanyard pin in the butt? It bothers me."

"I think I can do that. Got a pair a pliers in the back."

"Good. Thanks. Now I need three boxes of cartridges and a coil of that cow rope, fifty foot ought to be good. And three of those piggin' strings. And the best drover's whip you have there. And these saddlebags and that scabbard. And one of those medium-size black slickers. And a canvas tarp, say four by eight. And one of these heavy wool blankets," he said as he picked up a folded gray blanket and dropped it on the countertop. "And maybe, yeah, another tarp. Same size."

"You need a loop, too, for roping."

"I can't lasso any good, so no sense wasting my money. I'll use the whip to get them cows to go where I want 'em to go."

"Well, you don't always have to throw. You might need to pull a cow outta the mud or get one untangled from the brush, and you can just loop it around their horns. I'd get one if I were you if you're gonna be working with cattle."

"Okay. Throw it in with a pair of those leather gloves. And last but not least, a bag of hard candies. What's it all come to?"

"Just a minute. Let me finish addin' it all up. Let's see. Twenty-six bucks for the weapons." He mumbled to himself and wrote down his list on the bill at the same time. "All told it comes to ninety-two dollars and fifty-eight cents."

"All right. Jim said the association would cover the bill outta my salary."

"Yes, sir. I'll send the bill over to him."

"Well, here's ten bucks down payment. Do you have a place I can change into my new range duds?" Jake asked as he retrieved two five-dollar gold coins from his vest pocket and tossed them on the counter. Blakely slapped them down flat before they spun off the counter and swept them into his free hand.

"Very well." He made an entry on the bill with his brown pencil, underscored it, and removed the two pieces of carbon paper from the pad. "Total due is eighty-two dollars and fifty-eight cents." He tore off the original copy of the bill and handed it to Jake. "You can change right behind that curtain over there."

Jake came out dressed in the denim pants, boots, blue flannel shirt, buckskin leather vest, blue bandana, and the wide-brimmed Stetson felt hat with the six-inch crown. He picked up the coat gifted to him by the state of Kansas, put it on, and shrugged on the slicker over it. He tested the ensemble for fit and flexibility and was satisfied. "Whew, getting hot in all these clothes. Think I will be warm and dry out there on the range?"

"Yes, sir. I think you'll be just fine."

Jake pulled off the slicker and coat and said, "Let me try on the belts and holster. Here, let me fill the cartridge belts with bullets first." He set up the cut-away holster on the belt for a left to right cross-draw and slid the knife scabbard to the other side. Then he strapped on the other belt and the holstered belt over the top of it and across it so that the off-holster side was higher than the other side. Had there been another holster it would have looked like a regular two-gun rig. He picked up the pistol from the countertop and slid it into the holster, then pulled it out as fast as he could. It was a smooth action with no grab from the holster. He did that three times. "Need some oil for the holster to keep it slick."

"Got some Frank Miller right over here. It's only a dime. Since we already got the bill all made up I'll throw it in for nothing."

"Much obliged. Will it be all right for me

to leave all this gear here until the storm breaks? Don't want to get it all wet carrying it over to the ranch HQ."

"That'll be fine," Blakely said with a good-natured servant's smile. "I'll put it all right here in this corner behind the counter. But, I don't think it would get much wet until you got it all back inside and the freezing rain melted off. That's a regular Texas whopper of an ice storm going on out there."

Jake turned and looked out the window through which he saw the rain flying horizontal and sticking to everything in sight, immediately turning to ice. It was already about a half-inch thick on the roof posts of the covered boardwalk in front of the store. "Sure is," Jake said. "But I got to get back to the barn, so I better get to it." He shrugged into his coat and slicker, clamped his hat on his head, tied his bandana around his face, picked up the rope, loop, and whip and said, "Thanks, Blakely. I'll be back when the storm breaks." And with a wave to the storeowner he launched himself through the door and slid across the board-walk to the dirt in front.

He turned in the direction of the ranch. That put the wind at his back, for which he was thankful. Trudging fast, head down, he came to the barn and burst through the small door that slammed shut behind him. His slicker was stiff with ice, and his hat was covered, too, but he cracked it off by slapping the hat against his leg. As he was pulling the slicker off, he looked up to see all the stalls occupied by horses and Johnny at the other end of the barn by the farrier shop. Jake trotted up to him hoping that he had the little forge going so he could get warm by it. He was in luck. One of the buckskins was tied outside the stall and Jake could see that the old shoes were already off.

"Sizing shoes for re-shoddin'?" Jake asked as he immediately began rubbing his gloved hands together over the forge. "Glad of it for the heat."

"Yeah we're real cozy here in the barn. Feel sorry for them cowboys. They're probably holed up in the south line shack with no fire, no coffee, eating jerky and hardtack. That's why I went to wranglin' instead a punchin' cows." He pulled out a red-hot horseshoe with a set of tongs, turned it on edge on the anvil, and pounded it with a hammer a few times, then dipped it in a bucket of water. The water sizzled, and steam rose up until the shoe was cooled and he pulled it out. Holding the shoe up to the light of the forge he said, "That should do."

"Mind if I practice lassoin' down the center of the barn here?"

"Go right on ahead. We ain't goin' nowhere. Just don't throw on any of the horses. They don't ever like it, especially here in the barn. And Jasper hates it the most."

Jake was already heading for Jasper's stall. Hanging his head out over the stall gate, the horse's ears went forward, and his head stayed real still as he nickered while he focused on Jake. He walked past Jasper to the barn door and picked up his rope and loop and his whip. Jasper rumbled louder. Jake came up to the stall and stroked his neck while Jasper nosed around Jake's coat pocket. "What're you after, boy?" Jake cooed. He pulled a piece of candy from his pocket and slipped it to Jasper. Then he stepped back several paces and uncoiled the whip. He lashed out with it beyond the stall next to Jasper's and snapped it so that it popped loudly. Jasper never missed a crunch of his molars on the candy and smacked his lips contentedly to savor the sweetness. All of the other horses also took no notice.

"They're all cow ponies," Johnny called out. "They're used to that sound. Been on plenty a drives."

Jake nodded his head in agreement and waved off to Johnny. He was satisfied the whip pop wouldn't bother Jasper. So he rolled a barrel over to the middle of the center aisle and lifted it up to stand on end. Then he picked up his rope and loop and stepped off thirteen paces away from the barrel. He opened the loop and let some rope out, twirled the loop around his head and tossed it to the barrel. It fell short. He pulled in the slack, let the loop out, and tossed again. It fell to the right. And then again to the left, and short again.

"Here, let me give you a hand," Johnny said as he stepped up behind Jake. He showed him how to hold the loop down from the honda, swing the lariat like a wheel going around horizontally overhead, and how to use his arm and wrist to cast the loop forward. "Once you get the hang of that, you can practice how hard to throw the loop to reach your target. Here — try it."

Jake threw the loop, and it hit the barrel, almost looping around it. "Try again," Johnny said in a calm and teacher-like voice. "The trick is in the wrist."

Jake threw again, and the loop glided over and dropped down around the barrel. He smiled. Johnny slapped him on the back and said, "Now you got it. Keep practicin' just like that. You want to get to where you can throw the loop a lot faster. It's easy to drop a loop around a barrel that ain't movin'. A calf that's runnin' around or a gallopin' horse ain't as easy. But, you got all afternoon, ha ha."

And Jake did practice all afternoon, stopping only from time to time to scoop up hooey dropped by the horses and exchange wet straw in the stalls for dry. Gradually he was lassoing faster and faster with most of the loops catching around the barrel. Again, Johnny sauntered up behind him and said, "Gettin' better, by jingo. But, now it's feedin' time. Supper'll be ready in less than an hour. I am ready for a cup a hot coffee. How about you?"

"Sure. I've been ready all day," Jake said as he climbed up the ladder to the loft. He started carving out pitchforks of hay off the stack and tossing them down the chutes. Then he jumped down and filled a bucket with oats from the sacks in the feed storeroom. While Johnny put away tools, shut down the forge, and cleaned up the farrier shop, Jake slipped another piece of hard candy to Jasper before he distributed all the feed.

"All done?" Johnny called out.

"Yep."

The next morning the freezing rain turned to snow, so after feeding the horses and cleaning out the stalls, Jake spent most of the day in the bunkhouse reading Loving's *The Stockmen's Guide and Handbook.* He went over early before the evening feeding and practiced some more lassoing. Then he and Johnny cleaned the barn, fed the horses, and were about to go to supper when amid thundering hooves and whoops the cowboys barreled into the corral with the lean-to shelter. Johnny opened the door to the corral, and they saw seven of them, their horses packed with snow up to their shoulder points, as were the cowboys' boots and chaps. Snow and slushy mud flew from their hooves as the horses jockeyed for position. They whinnied and nickered loudly as they saw and smelled the barn. All the cowboys had their hats cinched down tight and noses and mouths covered with bandanas. As they pulled the horses to a halt they swung out of the saddles and ran a few steps with the horses before they stopped.

"Wild as the west Texas wind," Johnny said not too loud. "But a good crew. Jack Carson is the cow boss. That's him in the black hat and blue bandana."

As they were tying off their horses to the hitching rail Johnny called out, "Little cold out there, boys?" He grinned big and ducked as a snowball went flying over his head.

"Johnny, we need blankets for these hosses. And don't bother yerself none. We'll feed 'em," Carson hollered.

"C'mon," Johnny said. "Let's get 'em some horse blankets."

They came back with armfuls of blankets, and as they passed a cowboy carrying his saddle into the tack room the cowboy asked, "Got a new stable boy, Johnny?"

"Not since you, Billy, ha ha. But we'll go ahead and blanket your hoss for you. You can feed and water him yourself though. We ain't carryin' no feed or water for y'all."

"Since when did yer ever feed and water my hoss?"

"Since you got kicked in the head that time that made you as loco as you are, and I had to take care of him." In saying that, Johnny took off running to the corral, laughing all the way. "Lucky he's so tired or we would surely have had a wrestlin' match," he said laughing. "You wouldn't know it, but we are best pards."

The cowboys came in with saddles, tack,

and wet blankets and went out with feed-
bags full of oats and buckets of water they
pulled from the well inside the barn. Each
of them cared for their own horse as Johnny
and Jake wrapped and cinched fresh blankets around all the horses. Then the cowboys
led their horses to their stalls and forked in
hay for them. When they were finished, Jack
Carson pulled Johnny aside and asked,
"Who's the tenderfoot?"

"Oh. That's Jake Brighton. He's the boss's
new stock detective."

Jack looked at Jake and then back at
Johnny with a quizzical look on his range-
worn face.

"Waitin' for the storm to break so he can
ride out on Jasper."

Jack grinned at Johnny, and he grinned
back at Jack. "Guess we'll see 'bout that,
eh?" Jack said as he spat a stream of tobacco
juice into the snow. "Boss here?"

"Yeah. Reckon he's up at the house."

"Better go report in." They hunkered
down and started walking to the house. "He
ain't gonna be happy. We lost a few cows in
that ice storm. Soon as it started snowin'
we corralled up as many as we could out by
the south shack and then hightailed it for
the barn. Ain't had a hot meal in three days.
Gonna have to haul out some hay in the

mornin'. We'll get it from the stack in the south field."

"Good. Cuz I can't spare any remuda hay."

"Uh-huh." Jack looked hard at Johnny as if to remind him who was the cow boss.

The storm passed in the night, and the morning broke bright and sunny but freezing cold in still air. Jake woke up with the rest of the crew and had a hot breakfast. Soon as he could he spoke to Jack, who came over from his little foreman's house.

"Mr. Carson, I hear you are plannin' to take out a wagon to haul some hay today."

"That's right," Jack said with just a hint of curiosity in his voice.

"Well, I don't have anything to do yet, and I am a right good mule skinner. I can drive for you, and I can pitch hay with the best of 'em. Be glad to help."

"All right. 'Cept we'll be usin' horses. Ain't got any mules. Four-horse team should do it."

"I can drive horses, too."

"All right. That'll give me another man to round up cows instead of drivin' the wagon out. Obliged. Johnny should have the rig hitched up. You can follow our trail in the snow."

Jake arrived at the south corral about an hour after the cowboys. It was late afternoon, and he wasn't expecting to overnight at the line shack, but there was no changing it now. He reined in the team at the shack, and Jack stepped out. "You made it, huh. Any trouble?"

"No trouble."

"All right. Billy, you and Jake can start forkin' hay into that wagon and then spread it to the cows in the corral. Okay. Git to it now."

Billy climbed up beside Jake, and, when he was set, Jake uncoiled the bull whip and snapped it twice over the horses' heads while slapping the reins to their backs at the same time. The wagon lurched forward, and Jake guided the team over to the haystack in the middle of what looked like probably a meadow below the corrals about five hundred yards off.

"You're a pretty good skinner," Billy said. "Good with that whip."

"I have some experience. Let's get loaded up."

Cowboys kept pushing cows into the corrals all afternoon. Jack watched them as he forked hay up into the wagon. He was trying to take note of their technique and was learning a good amount about punching cows. "All cows? No steers?" he said to Billy from the top of the stack in the wagon.

"Yeah. Steers ain't got no calves in 'em. They have to get by as best they can on their own. These shorthorns ain't like the Texas longhorn though. They ain't as tough. I dunno if they're gonna make it through the winter. We still got a couple hundred head of longhorn left. Guess the boss knows what he's doin' though."

By nightfall they had loaded and spread three wagonloads of hay. Jack said they should get three more out in the morning before they headed back to the barn. The temperature was heading up, and the cows should be good with that much hay to feed on. So when morning came they got the loads off and then headed back to the barn through the slush. That evening Jake was exhausted and hit his bunk about an hour after supper. The rest of the crew sat on the bunkhouse porch, drank coffee, smoked, and told lies while they stared at the Milky Way on a clear and crisp night. Billy commented on what a good wagon driver Jake was. Good with the whip, he said.

Before dawn, Jake crunched out to the barn under a cloudless sky and sidled up to Jasper. He gave him his hard candy and fed him some oats and hay. Jasper ate, and Jake talked to him low and calm while he brushed him out. He set a bucket of water by the crib. Then he went and helped Johnny feed and water the rest of the horses, including the ones out in the corral under the lean-to. "You have a saddle and tack ready for me, Johnny?" Jake asked while they were fluffing hay.

"Sure I do. Good one, too. Double hitch. Boss said to give you a good one. He likes to have his detectives well equipped. You'll like it."

"Okay. I am going to saddle Jasper today and walk him around. Maybe I'll get up, and maybe I won't. Just depends on how he acts."

"You sound like you know something about horses."

"Well, it just makes sense. I don't have any experience like you do in breakin' and trainin' horses. But, it's clear as glass from the way you all are actin' that Jasper is somewhat of an ornery horse. So, I intend to take my time and befriend him as best I can. I guess that Mister Loving suggested him for me because, in spite of his orneriness, he is a real good range horse. Would I be correct there?"

"Oh, he is that. And it is true. We think we might get a laugh when you try to mount him. But maybe we won't. As for me, I am rootin' for the horse, ha ha. Just kiddin'. I'm hopin' you two get along real good. One thing is for sure. If Jasper takes to you, it'll be you and only you. Ain't nobody else gonna ride him."

Jake smiled and said, "Sounds fine to me. Now can I see that saddle?"

He slipped the bridle over Jasper's head and the bit into his mouth, talking calmly to him all the time. Then he smoothed the blanket on Jasper's back and gently lifted the saddle up on top of the blanket. Before pulling the cinches tight on the double rig, he gave Jasper a piece of hard candy to distract him so he wouldn't blow out his belly, making it hard to get the cinches properly tightened. He smoothed the hair under the cinches and tightened them just enough so the saddle wouldn't spin, while not making it too tight on Jasper. He connected the two cinches and was satisfied that Jasper could buck all he wanted but the saddle would stay put.

He led him out to the corral and into the frozen mud. He buttoned his coat and tied his bandana around his mouth. In no time he could see his breath coming through the bandana and Jasper's breath blowing out of his nostrils. "I know it's cold, boy, but we gotta git this done," he said softly into Jasper's ear and patted his neck. He led him around the corral at a walk for about twenty minutes. Jasper nosed his coat pocket and nickered all the while begging for candy. Jake knew that most horsemen looked down on giving horses sugar because the horses usually became a big nuisance, always begging for sugar, and some of them got downright hostile about it. But, he needed to befriend Jasper quickly, and candy was the best way to do it. Still, he waited until he finished leading Jasper around the corral before he gave him any candy. By that time the sun was up, and the corral was completely bathed in warm sunlight, which caused the ground to thaw rapidly. In no time mud was slushing under Jake's boots with every step he took.

He gave Jasper a candy and then eased to Jasper's side and gently stepped up into the stirrup. He then splashed down and then up and down again several times. Jasper didn't seem to mind, so the last time he swung up into the saddle. The big paint stood still for about fifteen seconds as if he were making his mind up about whether or not he wanted to throw his candy supplier off his back. He lowered his head, and Jake immediately jumped off the saddle and pulled firmly on the bridle so Jasper's head was close to his. He said, "No, Jasper. No. Don't do that."

He dug out a piece of candy and held it away at arm's length from Jasper's nose. Then he put the candy back in his pocket and jumped into the saddle. Jasper bucked, and Jake jumped out of the saddle again and did the same thing with the candy. It went around that way three times, until on the fourth mounting Jasper remained still. So, Jake slowly dismounted, caressed Jasper's nose, and slipped him a piece of hard candy. The morning went by with Jake and Jasper working together, trotting and loping around the corral. As the various ranch hands walked by, from time to time Jake pulled off his hat and waved it at them with a big grin spread across his face. They guffawed and snorted, but he could tell they were impressed. Jake discriminately gave Jasper candy at the right times, and the horse soon learned that good behavior brought reward. "Good boy, Jasper. You showed 'em you're a darn smart horse."

Then Jake rode him out of the corral and kicked him into a gallop. He ran like a thoroughbred with the wind splaying his mane as if it were a flag at high mast in a gale. Smooth and sure was his gait as Jake gave him his head and marveled at just how fast he was for a big quarter horse. He let him go for a mile and then reined him in to a trot and then a walk. Jasper was barely breathing hard. "You're good, strong, and fast," he said into Jasper's ear.

Jake found a place to tie Jasper to a mesquite bush out away from the ranch HQ. He left him there on about a ten-foot lead. He pulled the rifle from its scabbard and walked about ten paces from Jasper. He levered a cartridge into the breech, pointed the muzzle away from him and Jasper, and pulled the trigger. The rifle bucked in his hands and belched a flame from the muzzle, but he took no notice because he was watching Jasper the whole time. The big paint snapped his head up and glared at Jake, but he didn't try to run. "So you are used to that, eh, Jasper? I suspect Loving knew that. Well, that's good. Yes, sir. That is good."

There was a good-sized boulder about fifty yards out from Jake. It had a black spot on it that looked like it was about a foot in diameter. There was no mesquite or sage blocking the line of sight over the snow-covered range grass, so he found a flat rock that was dry and set it down on the snow for a seat. He sat on it, raised his legs so his knees were bent, and braced his elbows on the insides of his bent legs. He pressed the butt of the rifle tight into his shoulder, levered a cartridge into the breech, cradled the rifle in his left hand at the forestock, wrapped his right hand around the stock right behind the hammer, and gently placed his index finger on the trigger. He inhaled and held his breath, sighted in on the center of the black spot, and squeezed the trigger. He took five shots and then walked out to look at the target. "Pullin' about two inches to the left," he said to himself. He walked back to his seat, sat down, and took aim again, this time just a tad to the right. He fired five more rounds and checked the target again. The center of the black spot had a gouged-out ring in the stone about four inches in diameter. "Not bad," he said. "I can live with that. Have to get a gunsmith to adjust the sights if I can ever find one out here. Meantime I'll be aimin' a tad to the right."

Next, he dug out a bunch of rocks about six inches in diameter, arranged them on a boulder to his left and walked about ten paces away. Quickly, he spun around, pulling the Colt at the same time, crouched, turned his upper body to the left, held his right arm straight out, aimed, and fired six shots in quick succession in fluid double action with each trigger pull. Five of the six rocks were blown off the boulder. "Mmmm," he said, set up six more rocks, and performed the same maneuver. Six out of six. "Better," he said. "Need more practice though."

He went back to Jasper and slipped him a piece of candy. "Good boy," he cooed as he rubbed Jasper's neck. He spent the rest of the day in the saddle just roaming around looking at the countryside, resting the gelding once with no candy. That would come when they were back in the barn. Everything was mostly white, but he could see the many changes in the elevation in some places, what with mesas and ravines and the seemingly endless ocean of grassland off in another direction dotted here and there by clumps of mesquite. And then in another direction the land was almost covered solid with mesquite and other scrub brush of the northwest Texas plain. This was wide open country a lot like he was used to in Kansas, except Kansas was all farms and more rolling. This was wild range not yet groomed for crops. And you could see a lot further out here on the range, especially if you got a little elevation. The sky just seemed bigger, too. Jake took it all in visually and breathed in big gulps of the air. He thought he was going to like it.

Well before dawn Jake rolled out of his bunk and stoked the fire in the stove, adding wood a little at time till he had a good fire going. Then he did the same thing on the cookstove. The crew was out at the line shack with the cows, and the cook had the day off. Johnny slept in the barn, so Jake had the bunkhouse to himself. He crawled back in underneath his blankets and waited for the stove to warm up the bunkhouse. It took about twenty minutes to be warm enough for him to venture out again. He put a pot of water on the stove and then pulled on his boots and ran out to the privy. He rushed back in the bunkhouse slapping his arms around his body and making *brrr* sounds. He put a set of clean long johns on his bunk and his toothbrush and powder. Then he packed all his stuff in his valise. He dipped his finger in the pot of water and found it warm enough, so he stripped off his union suit and did his washup. He dried himself and put on the clean union suit and the rest of his clothes. Last came the boots. Once done, he went into the kitchen and fixed up a pot of coffee and waited for it to boil. Then he fried up some eggs and slabs of bacon with a few slices of Cookie's tasty bread. Coffee was ready, and he had himself a little morning feast. He brushed his teeth and then threw the dirty wash water out the door of the bunkhouse. Time to pack up and head out.

At daybreak Jake had Jasper all fed and curried and was tying his satchel behind the bedroll on the saddle when Jim Loving walked up. "Mornin'," he said. "Another clear day. Good for you. Reckon you'll be headin' west?"

"Yes, sir. I am anxious to get on the trail."

"Hear Jasper is workin' out real good, long as you keep givin' him candy." Jim smiled and looked sideways at Jake. "He's a good horse. He'll do you real good. Here's your letter of introduction to Wes. I posted a letter to him, but what with this weather he may not get it, so this is just in case. You should go to the Madison Boardinghouse in Seymour, and if Wes is not in town you can inquire there. That is where he is staying. You might want to get a room yourself. There is a way station about a day's ride from here. Just follow the stage road. You can get supper there and bunk in the stables. Then you got about another twenty miles to Seymour." He paused and looked seriously into Jake's eyes. "As the old Roman legionnaires were fond of saying, 'Courage and honor,' detective." Jim held out his hand. Jake took it, and they shook hands, looking eye to eye.

Jake shrugged into his black slicker, took up the reins, and stepped up into the saddle. He turned Jasper and trotted him past the barn, where he saw Johnny standing in the door. Jake tipped his hat to him. Johnny waved.

CHAPTER SIX
MORE ROPE LEARNING

A little past noon on a clear but breezy and cold day, Jake trotted Jasper into Seymour on Main Street and then slowed him to a walk as he looked around at the buildings standing here and there, plus all the structures under construction even at this time of the year. Jake had heard that the railroad was coming and thought that was probably the reason for the growth that seemed to be going on. He made note of the two saloons across the street from the livery stables at the edge of town and the post office on Main Street just north of Morris Street.

Just across from it on Main was a fairly new looking hotel built of stone. He came to a low, and weathered, structure of vertical boards with the gaps covered with strips of wood. Over the entrance, there was a sign saying it was the county courthouse. He stopped at the hitching rail in front of the courthouse, tied off Jasper, and went up the steps to the front door. He entered a small lobby, looked around, and quickly located what he was looking for. Taking a quick glance left, right, and behind to make sure he wasn't being watched, he eased over to the bulletin board and looked at the wanted posters. Three were for rustlers and had multiple copies tacked to the board, so he pulled a copy for each one. He folded the posters and put them in his coat pocket. Then he stepped away quickly, not wanting anyone to take notice of him.

Jake came out, and, taking up Jasper's reins, he walked with him back to the post office. At the post office he also checked the wanted posters. They were the same ones as at the courthouse, so he ignored them and got directions to the Madison Boarding-house.

As luck would have it, the Madison was located at the corner of Morris and Tackitt, and the stables were two blocks over and two blocks up at the corner of Main and Oregon Street. He rode over to the board-inghouse first. It was a large, white two-story with a dark pitched roof and no porch over the door in the gable end. The muddy street in front of it was shaded from the afternoon sun by the house itself, and Jake felt the coolness as he rode up. There was a hitching post with a ring off to the side of the front door, so Jake tied off Jasper's reins there. Three wooden steps led up to the door. He went up and looked for a doorbell. There was none. He knocked on the door and waited. No answer. He knocked again, harder. The door opened outward, and Jake was swept off the steps, almost falling in the mud. "Yes?" demanded a very stern looking woman with black hair piled high on her head in a large bun and dressed in a just-as-black dress. She glared at Jake from where she stood in the doorway.

Jake removed his hat and said, "Sorry to bother you, ma'am, but I understand this to be the Madison Boardinghouse."

"It is."

"Well, I am lookin' for a room. Do you have any available?"

"Perhaps."

"I am also supposed to meet Wesley Wilson, who I believe is boardin' here."

"He never said anything about meetin' anyone here."

"I have a letter of introduction from James Loving." He fished the letter from his inside coat pocket and handed it to her. She looked it over, and Jake wondered if she could read, because it did not look like she was reading it.

"I suppose this is good enough reference. I don't take any boarders without references. But stock detectives workin' for Jim Loving are welcome no matter what. Room, breakfast, and supper are fifty cents a day. Do your own laundry. Wash shack is out the back door along with the privy. A bucket of hot water'll be outside your door every morning by five thirty. Breakfast at six. I give a little leeway for breakfast time but not much. So don't take advantage. Supper at five thirty sharp. If you miss it, you miss it. No exceptions. Grab your bag, and scrape your boots real good before you come in. Wes ought to be in for supper." She did not smile.

"Would it be all right if I just left my bag and bedroll here while I put my horse up at the livery?"

"Reckon so."

"Whew. Real pleasant lady, huh, Jasper?" He rode around to the stables and dismounted at the barn door. As he did, he glanced at the two saloons side by side across the street. One had a sign over the porch that read Brazos Saloon, and the other one had a sign that read Aces Wild Saloon and Gambling Parlor. He would visit them starting tomorrow night to get a feel for the potential for information gathering.

Clientele should be fairly heavy now that things were slow out on the range. Or at least he thought they must be slow what with the weather and all. He didn't really know. But then, Jim said his cows would be calving soon. So maybe there wouldn't be much action at the saloons.

"Hallo the barn," he called out as he stepped inside the livery. "Anybody here?"

"Yo. Back here," came a man's voice from the opposite end of the barn.

Jake led Jasper into the barn and found the stable man.

"Howdy," Jake said. "I need to stable my horse for the night. Be takin' him out most every mornin' and bringin' him back at night."

"Howdy to yer, too. Name's Quincy Brown. This here's my livery. Best stables in three counties." His voice was croaky like he was on the verge of laryngitis.

"Only three?"

"OK. Make it four." He grinned a smile that showed a few missing teeth under a nose that was decidedly hawkish and sprouting a crop of black hair poking out of his nostrils. His roundish head was mostly bald, and what sandy-colored hair he had was cut short. But, his gray-blue eyes were sharp and keen. He was about Jake's height, a little thinner though, probably a little older than Jake, but he still seemed to be full of vigor. And Jake took due note of the pistol tucked into his waistband. He held out his hand to Jake for a shake. "What can I do for yer and this fine lookin' paint yer got here?" he asked as he ran a hand down Jasper's neck.

"Nice to meet you, Mister Brown," Jake said as he shook Brown's hand. "Name's Jonas, er, Jake Brighton. Like I said, I need to stable my boy here."

"All righty. We can do that. Be ten cents a day includin' hay. If yer want oats it'll be another two cents a day." He smiled so very congenially.

Jake busted out laughing. He couldn't hold it back. He found this Quincy Brown quite comical, but in a good way. Brown was a natural salesman. Maybe he missed his calling, but then Jake did take note of how deft he was with Jasper and how the paint seemed to take to him. So maybe not.

"Well, that sounds fine to me," Jake said while attempting to stifle further laughs.

"What's so funny?" Quincy said, still smiling, but not as broad.

"Well, ah, I was just marvelin' at your sales pitch. Not something you normally see from a livery owner," Jake said with a direct stare into Quincy's gray-blue eyes. He wasn't sure where this was going to go, and he was taking precautions as he lifted his right hand to his gun belt and hooked his thumb over the top of it just left of center.

"Oh! Well, no offense taken. Guess nobody never took note of it before. Can't seem to lose my old ways. Used to be a horse trader back in Fort Worth many years ago. And I can recognize good horse flesh like yer paint here. What's his rations?"

"Well, he's gonna be real busy out there on the range every day, so I think he better have two forks of hay and a pound of oats twice a day. What do you think?"

"Sounds about right. Oh, I forgot to tell yer. Groomin' is another two cents a day, and saddle and tack storage is a penny a day. So if yer want all the shoot it'll cost yer fifteen cents a day." He grinned big now, knowing that Jake had him all figured out.

"I'll feed and brush him myself. So I guess we are settled at thirteen cents a day. Or is there a discount for me doin' my own feedin' and curryin'?"

"Ain't no discounts in this here establishment."

"Maybe I'll just take my business somewhere else," Jake said with play bravado.

"Go ahead if'n yer want. Course yer'd

have a ways to go since the nearest livery is in Wichita Falls. Might get one of the ranches close by to put yer up. Course then yer'd have to walk back and forth to town. Or . . ."

"All right. All right." Jake held his hands over his head as if he were being robbed. "You got me. Thirteen cents. Agreed?"

"Agreed."

"Now where's a feller git a shave and a bath around here?"

"For that yer gotta go back down Main here and turn left on McLain. A block up to the barber shop. Or . . . yer can go right across the way there to the Brazos. They got some soiled doves there that'll give yer a real nice bath and a shave and more if'n yer want it." He bounced his eyebrows up and down and smiled slyly.

"Well, I ain't walkin' all the way back there in the mud, so I guess it's the Brazos." He smiled and then said with a more serious look, "But I only want a shave and a bath. Damn whores cost too much for anything else. What stall you want me to put Jasper in?"

"Right over there. Number five'll be fine. Yer can put yer saddle and tack on an empty tree in the tack room. Yer gonna feed and brush him before yer baaaath? Wouldn't wanna git all smelly agin' would yer?"

"Yeah I'll do it now." Jake finished his stable chores, gave Jasper a piece of hard candy, picked up his rifle from where he had leaned it against the stable wall, and started out the door.

"Yer might ask for Gracie over there at the Brazos. She's a real looker. Young and pretty," Quincy called to Jake as he cleared the barn door. Jake just waved his hand over his head.

Jake got a little more than a bath and a shave from Gracie at no extra cost. Not much more, but still he cursed himself as he walked out of the saloon. "Damnation and tarnation! Now I got another sin to add to my list. Probably ain't a priest around here anywhere." But, Gracie did give him a nice bath, good shave, and trimmed his mustache nice and neat.

He came to the door of the Madison and scraped the red-brown mud off his boots on the inverted U-shaped scraper and then finished them off real good on the stiff-bristled scrub brush nailed upside down to the bottom step. He opened the door and stepped inside. Sitting in one of the parlor chairs reading a newspaper was a man dressed like a cowboy in a faded black shirt. At the sound of Jake's entry, he lowered the paper and gave Jake a real big once-over. Then he raised the newspaper back up to hide his face. Jake looked to where he left his bag and bedroll. They were gone. He had started for the hallway to the back of the house when the man behind the newspaper said in a serious tone, "The proprietor here don't cotton to whoremongers."

Jake stopped in his tracks and turned to face the incognito man. "Are you addressin' me, sir?" Involuntarily, he raised the barrel of his rifle and moved his left hand to the forestock.

"I am."

"And just what is your meanin'?"

"My meanin' is to josh yer, detective." The man lowered the newspaper and beamed out a big grin to Jake. "Wes Wilson," he said as he stood and held out his hand. "Quincy ratted yer out."

Quickly, Jake understood and said, "Well, I'll have words with that sum-buck. But, good to meet you, Wilson." Jake looked into his eyes as he took his hand and noted his firm grip and muscular build. He couldn't help but stare for a few seconds at the big blonde handlebar mustache that swept across his bronze face, weather worn by many years on the range.

"Call me Wes. Yeah, I know I need to git

over to the barber shop," he said with a grin and the bravado of the perpetual adventurer shining in the glint of his hazel eyes.

"Let's sit down and jaw a bit. Missus Madison took yer gear upstairs. I been out at the L Bar Ranch. Got back yesterday after sunset, so I didn't git Jim's letter until today. I been busy all day with brand registrations, so I didn't git a chance to warn Missus Madison of yer comin'." As they moved to sit in the parlor chairs Jake saw that Wes seemed to float carelessly with an air of self-confidence and capability for action.

"Does she get any friendlier?"

"Missus Madison? Not much. She's had a tough go of it. She and her husband were early settlers out west here. She lost her husband and two daughters to Comanches back in seventy-one. Only she and her son survived. I guess they weren't there when it happened. I think they were in Decatur. I guess when the hotel was built about three years ago she sold her land to the L Bar and put up this here buildin', figurin' she could compete for long-stay guests like us. The town was startin' to grow. Settlers started comin' in from Oregon last year. Mostly farmers. She has business savvy and is tough as nails. But, she ain't very friendly, ha ha."

Wes suddenly averted his gaze to his right and his smile immediately disappeared. Jake followed his gaze and saw Mrs. Madison standing in the doorway to the dining room with her hands on her hips and a facial expression as dark as a northwest Texas thunder cloud. She glared at Wes and announced, "Supper is served" and then spun on her heels to turn her back on them. She stomped back into the kitchen. Wes looked back at Jake and feigned a sheepish look. Then they got up and went to the dining room. On the table there was a tureen of piping hot chicken and dumplings and a platter full of fresh-baked biscuits, a bowl of boiled carrots, and a pot of coffee. The two detectives helped themselves to the vittles, and as they were eating three more boarders came in. A man by himself and a man and woman who appeared to be espoused. She was an attractive brunette, and Jake had to force himself to keep his eyes off her. They kept to themselves and responded to Jake's casual questions with one-word answers. He gave up trying to be social.

After supper the detectives retired to the parlor and lit up a couple of cigars. "Missus Madison don't mind cigar smoke, but she forbids spirits," Wes said with a wink. The couple finished their supper and started to come into the parlor, but the woman covered her nose with her hanky, and they changed direction for the hallway to the rooms. Just as well because that put Jake more at ease with the distraction gone.

"They ain't real social folks," Wes said matter-of-factly. "Wal, I figure we'll work on brands startin' tomorrow. Take the day to go through Loving's book on brands of the ranches hereabouts while we ride on over to the L Bar. Once we get up to the Flying XC, which ain't very far, mind yer, we don't need to be concerned with much more than a flying X ridin' over a big C. Purty brand. I like it. Biggest outfit here south of Seymour is the Hashknife. Rustlers like to steal their steers and drive 'em north to sell to the buyers in Dodge City. But they's got to have a buyer who'll ignore the brand, so they's usually go even farther north of Dodge City. If they's get the calves before they's are branded, then they's fatten 'em up and drive up to Dodge City under some phony brand. I'm tellin' yer all this to show how hard it is to change the Hashknife brand. But we'll git to all that tomorrow. Right now, why don't we git to know each other? I'll tell yer all about me, and then yer kin tell me about yerself. How's that sound?"

Wes's history was unremarkable. Born in Texas. Son of a cow boss. Cowboy for years. Good friend of Jim Loving. Started with him from the beginning of the organization of the stock detectives. Since he had already told it all to Loving, Jake decided to tell all to Wes. He seemed to take it all in without any objection, and then he shocked Jake when he admitted to rustling a few head when he was young. "Since we been thieves ourselves we know how they think, eh?" He laughed. "But, they's a few cowboy rules yer oughta know jest so as yer kin git along out on the range and in town, too. Never pass anyone on the trail without sayin' 'Howdy.' If yer come up on somebody from behind, give a loud halloo before yer git inside pistol shot range. Don't wave at a man on a horse. It might spook the horse, and the man will think you're an idiot. A nod is just fine. After yer pass someone on the trail, don't look back at him. He might think yer don't trust him."

He paused, took a few drags off his cigar, leaned in toward Jake, frowned, pulled his lips tight, showing his clenched teeth, drilled his hazel-eyed stare into Jake's eyes, and said, "Ridin' another man's horse without his say-so is nearly as bad as makin' love to his wife. Never even bother another man's horse. Never shoot a man who ain't armed. Never, ever, shoot a woman. A cowboy is steady and easygoin' even when out of sorts. Complainin' is what quitters do, and cowboys hate quitters."

He eased back in his chair and took on a more pleasant expression as he puffed his cigar. Jake smoked and listened. He made no comment or indicated any persuasion one way or the other.

"A cowboy always helps someone needin' a hand, even a enemy," Wes continued. "When cowboys leave town after a few days of carousin', it's all right for them to shoot their six-guns into the air, whoop like crazy, and ride they's horses as fast as they can. It's called 'hurrahin'' a town."

"You do that?" Jake asked.

"Used to. No reason to anymore." Wes grinned. He continued, "A horse thief can be hung with no judge or jury." He pointed his finger at Jake as if he were giving an order. "If'n yer know he's a horse thief and yer catch him out on the range, hang the son of a bitch. 'Less a course he has a reward on his head. Then, naturally, you want to bring him in for the reward." He sat back and smiled as he said, "Never try on another man's hat. Don't even touch his hat. Never wake a feller by shakin' or touchin' him. He might wake up fast and shoot yer. Real cowboys don't brag. A braggart who is all gurgle and no guts ain't got no place on the range. A cowboy don't talk much. He saves his breath for breathin'. No matter how sore and tired and hungry yer are after a long day in the saddle, always tend to what yer horse needs before yer own, and git yer horse some feed before yer eat. Cuss all yer want, but only around men, horses, and cows. That's 'bout all I can think up right now. Kin yer remember it all?"

"Yeah. I think so. Guess we'll find out." Jake grinned. "Let's head over to the Brazos. I'll buy you a drink."

"Yup. I need it after that speech. There's one more thing. It's particular to our line a work. It's an old vaquero sayin'." Again he leaned in and held Jake eye to eye. "There is a fine line between catchin' an outlaw and becomin' one." He nodded his head once as if to confirm what he said. "Yer git the gist a that?"

"Yes, I do. I have experience in that way. It's a hard thing. You know the outlaw is guilty of the crime you are investigatin', but you just can't quite get the evidence to prove it. So you fudge a little. Break a little law that you think will be forgiven when the whole case pans out." He stopped there and studied Wes for a quarter of a minute. He decided to leave it there and go no further. "Yeah. It's a game I don't want to play. Always try to keep the law on my side."

"That's the ideer." They grabbed their hats and coats off the pegs at the door, sat the hats on their heads, put on their coats, and went out into the dusk as the sun had just dropped below the horizon. There were some clouds gathered in the west, which gave a spectacular red-orange glow to the whole western sky. "What a yer think of our northwest Texas sunset?"

Jake looked at the sky and said, "Same as Kansas. Same all over the world probably. Magnificent as usual. Depends on the cloud cover."

Wes kicked a dirt clod and jammed his hands in his coat pockets.

They came to the Brazos and stepped up onto the porch and stamped the mud off their boots. Wes opened the closed saloon doors and went through first. Jake closed the doors behind them. Immediately he nonchalantly searched the room through the tobacco smoke for Gracie. Lamps were already lit, but he couldn't quite see every corner, and she seemed to be nowhere in sight. He calculated the days and figured it was Thursday, so maybe she didn't work Thursday nights. Or maybe she was working in the back or upstairs.

They stepped up to the bar, and each ordered whiskies. While Wes tossed his down in one slug, Jake watched the mirror on the back bar. Wes said, "Want another? My turn to buy."

"Thanks, but I'll just take my time with this one."

"Suit yerself. Me, I like a couple of jolts, and then I take it easy. Alex!" he called down the bar and motioned with the glass in his hand for another shot. The bartender came with the bottle and filled Wes's glass, then looked at Jake, who made a slight wave-off of his hand next to his glass. Wes gulped the shot and said, "One more and I'll walk it down instead of takin' it at a gallop. Ha ha!"

"Let's sit down over at that table." Jake nodded toward a table in the corner that allowed a clear view of the whole saloon. There was a table in the opposite corner with six men at it playing poker. Two were cowboys, two were some kind of other laborers wearing bib overalls, and two were dressed in suits, so they were gamblers or professionals of some sort. Three more tables filled the space between the poker game and the bar, and three tables were between Jake and Wes and the bar. To their left was a group of tables covered in red and white oilcloth. Two cowboys were sitting at one of the tables with mugs of beer and wolfing down steaks and potatoes, so Jake rightly figured a feller could get a meal here. A pair of sporting ladies hovered around the poker table, close but not too close. One of them started for Jake and Wes. Jake said, "You in the mood?"

"Nah. Not tonight."

Jake held up his hand discreetly to stop the dove's progress. She gave him a pouty look, tossed her head, and went to the bar, where she pressed up against one of the five men there.

"Any suspected rustlers in here tonight?" Jake asked.

"Just Charlie Dalton over there at the poker table . . . the one in the black cowboy hat. He's a hothead, too. Thinks he's a gunman. Used to be a hand at the Millett Brothers down on Miller Creek before the Hashknife bought 'em out just last year. Milletts had a reputation of hirin' on outlaws. Seems like cattle and he disappear regularly at the same time, and then he shows up back in town at the poker table with money to play. Tried to follow him a couple of times, but he made me both times. Reckon he knows who I am. Ain't never talked to him though. I hear tell he killed a feller up in Dodge City."

Jake pulled the wanted posters from his coat pocket and looked around the room to make comparisons. He didn't see any that looked like any of the wanted subjects.

Wes leaned over to gander at the posters. "Those are old posters. Those fellers all been arrested and jailed," he said with an air of finality.

Jake stuffed the posters back in his coat pocket. He would study them later to try and memorize the likenesses just in case. You never knew what could happen. Meanwhile he studied Charlie Dalton and took note of the pistol in a cut-away holster on a cartridge belt strapped around his waist with a big silver buckle. The pistol was a nickel-plated and pearl-handled standard single-action Colt. Judging by the size of the cylinder it was probably a forty-five caliber with a long barrel. He was right-handed. Looked to be about average height and build. Black hair. He was wearing canvas braces over a green shirt tucked into brown britches. His spurs were flashy with

289

big Mexican rowels and jingle bobs attached to wide leather straps and silver buckles.

"Maybe we keep an eye on him since he's here in town, eh?"

"Wal, when we can. We got a lot a work to do out of town. I got a lot to show yer. And since our specialty is catchin' cattle rustlers yer got to learn about cows and rustlers." He faked like he had made a really profound statement.

"Yeah. Understood. I think I'll see if I can get in that game. Play a little poker and conduct a little suspect assessment."

"Huh? Oh yeah. Sure. Go ahead."

"How about you?"

"Nah. I'll have another one and then head back to the barn. See yer at breakfast. Bring yer bedroll. We'll be gone a few days."

Jake sidled over to the poker table and stood back until the hand was finished. Happened to be Charlie Dalton who raked in the pot. Jake said, "Any chance to get in the game?"

Dalton looked him up one side and then the other, front and back. "Ten dollar buy-in. Yer got a sawbuck, tenderfoot?" he said with an arrogant sneer.

Jake again wished his new clothes were a little more wore in so he didn't stand out so much. Nevertheless, he took an immediate dislike to the man. He could smell Dalton all the way across the table, and it wasn't just sweat smell. That annoyed Jake after he himself had just had a bath and all. He couldn't abide people who smelled worse than most.

Instead of returning an insult, he grinned big and said, "Sure I got ten bucks. Can I get in?"

The other cowboy said, "Sure. C'mon sit yerself right down here in this empty chair."

Three hands passed, and Jake folded each one of them. Dalton asked in a surly tone, "Yer gonna play like a big boy, tenderfoot, or just keep foldin' every hand?" He wasn't smiling, and Jake felt his ire rising. He fought it down.

Even still he looked steadily into Dalton's eyes and saw evil dancing around in them. With a smile at the devil he said, "I'll play when I get the cards to win."

"So yer ain't a gambler."

"No. Only bet a sure thing. And I don't think this table has any luck for me, so I'm cashin' out. Figure I got nine bucks in." Jake calculated a tactical retreat was best at this time before he was provoked into doing something regrettable.

"I knowed yer was a tenderfoot, tenderfoot. Ha ha."

Jake ignored him and went to the bar to settle up. And from the back room out came Gracie. She glanced around the saloon, spied Jake, and sashayed right over to him. He saw her coming, and, when she was right up close, she squeezed in next to him. She was a little doll with blonde, curly hair and shiny, deep-blue eyes. There was a span of light-orange freckles across the bridge of her nose and under her eyes over her rosy-red cheeks. She had a deep cleavage that was proudly displayed by the low-cut dress of lacy red and white calico she wore. "How yer doin', Jake? Back for more, honey?"

"Hi, Gracie." He couldn't hold back a friendly smile because he really liked her. "Not tonight, honey. But tell me about that varmint at the poker table in the green shirt."

She turned to see who he was talking about and then turned away, watching in the mirror. "That's Charlie Dalton. He ain't worth spit. Damn rattlesnake he is. Mean, stinkin' dirty, foul-mouthed braggart. Bad to the girls. I won't let him near me. We all hate his guts. Surprised he hasn't cursed us out yet. He will, the more whiskey he gets down his gullet. In fact, I think I'll take the rest of the night off just to be clear of him. You can come up to my room if you want."

"Thanks, Gracie. I'll take a rain check. I been in the saddle the last two days and spent last night in a stable, so I am spent. That bath helped a lot though." They both smiled knowingly. "I have to be up and on the trail early. Thanks for the information." He winked at her, and she turned to prance up the stairs. All she said confirmed what Jake thought about Charlie Dalton, and when he looked at him in the mirror he saw him watching Gracie go up the stairs. He was practically drooling.

Well before sunup Jake and Wes walked through the small door of the barn. Quincy already had the lamps lit. Jake grabbed a bucket of water and was letting Jasper drink when Wes came by and said, "Well, I'll be! Is that ol' Jasper?"

"In the flesh."

"He's a fine horse, one a the best all-around range horses. Knows how to handle stock real good. So I'm told. Jim offered him up to me a few years ago, but he throwed me, and I said that was it. I'll git my own horse. He throwed yer yet?"

"Nah. We got an understandin'. We work real good together. You'll see. What are you ridin'?"

Wes went over and backed a large copper-red bay quarter horse gelding out of his stall and paraded him around by the halter so Jake could get a full profile view. The horse was gifted with deep black points all the way around — forelock, mane, tail, stockings. He was the same size as Jasper, standing about seventeen hands, well-muscled, with a shallow belly. But he was not happy about being pulled away from his feed and water as he tossed his head up and down in protest.

"Look at this handsome boy," Wes said. "All right, all right. Here you go." He walked him back into the stall. "He's real good with stock and has a lot of endurance like Jasper. But he is gentle as a baby. I raised him from a colt."

"What's his name?"

"Wal, I read somethin' once 'bout a noble steed, and I said that's my boy, so I named him Noble."

"Hmmm. Sounds good. So we got a pair to draw to. Noble and Jasper."

"Yup."

After taking care of their horses, they were first at the breakfast buffet in the morning. Jake served himself up some scrambled eggs, bacon, a biscuit with gravy, and coffee. They were finished and out the door just as the other boarders came in for breakfast. Back at the stables, they saddled their horses, tied their bedrolls, sacks of oats, and slickers on the back of the saddle and rope, loop, and canteens of water on the front of the saddle, and sheathed their rifles in the scabbards, stock facing forward. Lastly Jake lashed his bullwhip to his saddle up front.

As they led the horses to the door Wes called out, "Quincy!"

He appeared from the feed room. "What?" he called back. "Y'all tryin' to start a stampede in here? Yellin' around like that." He shook a finger at them as he walked up. "What d'yer want?"

"We're gonna be gone a few days. Just wanted to let yer know so yer don't give away our stalls."

"Yer pay for 'em, and I ain't gonna give 'em to nobody else. But if'n yer don't I kain't gurantee nuthin'."

"We're payin' for 'em. Don't fret 'bout it."

"Ain't frettn'. Jest let'n yer know what's what."

"Thanks."

They rode out under a bright morning sun in the face of a stiff breeze, turned left on Oregon Street, and headed west. They trailed the north side of the Brazos on the upper ridge until the river started to get snaky, so they left it and rode a straight line toward the L Bar Ranch. Along the way, Wes talked incessantly about brands. He showed Jake all kinds of tracking methods and signs. The ground was drying out, and there were tracks along the way that Wes could point to. Every once in a while, they would cut a trail made by a cow or steer or a horse with rider. Wes showed Jake the mark of a shod hoof and other sign, and how to pick out the direction of travel of the track maker.

When they came upon a bunch of cows or steers, Wes would have Jake practice roping them and then pull them in close so they could examine the brands.

"Yer want to be real careful when yer ropin' a big steer or heifer or cow. Gotta always keep the rope tight. If they start comin' at yer, yer got two choices. Drop the rope, turn, and run away from it or, if yer got a good stock horse, turn yer horse, keep the rope tight, and pull that critter in a circle until he is so dizzy he gives up, ha ha! But, never rope a bull unless he's stuck in the mud or somethin'. They's a lot stronger than yer horse, and they's mean. That's what that bullwhip you carry is for. They'll run from the pop of the whip. Bet yer didn't know that, did yer?" He grinned at Jake.

"I knew it. Remember I told you I used to drive freight wagons in Kansas before I got into trouble. Same idea. Drivin' mules. Drivin' oxen." He smiled a gotcha-there smile at Wes.

The further west they rode, they came across more and more cattle on the range. They were all branded with a big *S* on the side of the neck and a big *L* on the left side of the body.

"That way the L Bar brand is easy to see a long way off, and it takes a lot a work to disguise with a runnin' iron," Wes explained to Jake. "The location of the brand is almost as important as the brand itself."

He showed Jake how he could recognize a burn from a running iron versus a straight branding iron. "Yer should check every brand yer don't recognize against the brands in Jim's book. If it ain't in the book it's probably a phony rustler's brand. These critters are all loafin' about where they should be, so I ain't concerned. That's another thing. If you run across some cows out on the range where they shouldn't be, they's probably strays. Cowboys always drive strays back to where they belong, and so do we." He went on like that for nearly the whole way and only stopped talking when they stopped to eat, take naps, and rest the horses. Finally, just before sunset, they arrived at the L Bar headquarters located about midway between the Wichita River on the north and the Brazos River to the south. Lots of tents and one corral. That was it.

"They's just startin' out. I been kinda helpin' 'em along," Wes said.

Next day, under a gray sky, they watched the crew spread hay to keep the cows in close to the headquarters and then cut out the heavies. Wes explained the heavies were the cows about ready to give birth. Jake marveled at the work the horses did in working the heavies, who were constantly attempting to return to the herd. The cowboy's horses pulled the heavies by rope into an area where the cowboys kept them so they could assist the birth if need be. They watched a few cows calve and the cowboys watching over everything, taking steps as necessary to save as many compromised calves as possible. Wes explained that normally they let the cows calve naturally, but when there were problems, the cowboys often have to reach in and pull the calves out. He also bragged on the L Bar as a progressive ranch that rounded up the cows during calving time. Other ranches were letting the cows and calves fend for themselves and then go round up the calves in the spring for branding and turn them out to the range again. He estimated they lost up to twenty percent of the calves that way. At thirty bucks per head when driven to market, a thousand head herd loses about six thousand dollars right out the chute from a loss of twenty percent of the calves.

The next morning broke with huge patches of puffy clouds floating in the clear, blue sky. It was a little cooler but well above freezing. "I reckon it's Sunday morning," Jake said as they were saddling up the boys. "Don't suppose there's any services around here."

"Wal, there is, but not this early, and we got to git goin'."

"How about down the trail a ways?"

"Nothin' but grass, mesquite, and rocks, and, oh yeah, cows, ha ha!" Wes, standing beside his horse, looked across the top of his saddle at Jake, who was already saddled and facing Wes with Jasper's reins in his hand. "Yer a church-goin' man?" Wes asked.

"When I can. How about you?"

"Wal, I was born in Denton County and baptized in a Methodist Church, but I ain't seen the inside of a church building in a long time. How about yer? Yer been baptized?"

"Yep. Catholic. I guess there's still hope for us, eh?"

"Reckon so, if the Almighty can furgive all my sins, ha ha," he said with a big grin as he stepped up into the saddle.

The two detectives were on the trail by sunup headed southwest. All the snow was melted off, and the ground was drying out real fast. "Where exactly are we goin' today?" Jake asked as he and Wes walked their horses side by side.

"South. Down to the Circle Bar B Ranch. It's part of the Bayliss Land and Cattle operation started up by Don Bayliss. He's a real savvy banker outta Dallas. Started up around Waco about fifty-two I reckon. He's buyin' up railroad and school land and hired Ole Olsson as his manager. He's a Swede. Been around a long time. Got some real good-lookin' Hereford bulls. Where we're goin' is the headquarters. There's two other spreads in the operation. One more in Throckmorton County and another in parts of three counties southwest a here. They all run the brand of a *B* with a bar through it in a circle. Call it the Circle Bar B. It's in Loving's book. There's somethin' I want yer

to see there. That's why we are headed thataway."

"What's that?"

"Thorny fence."

"Barbed wire?"

"Yup. Bayliss is one of the first stockmen
to start fencin' off his land out here in
northwest Texas. And the cattlemen who
ain't ownin' any range are gettin' real ornery
about bein' fenced outta range they's used
to grazin'. And then if there ain't any way
to git to range that is still open or even a
water well . . . if yer see what I'm sayin'?"

"Well, do the big ranches own the land
they are fencin' off?"

"Most do. Some don't. I fear there's a lot
a bad blood buildin'. Surprised Jim didn't
mention somethin' 'bout it to yer. Part a
the reason why the Milletts sold to the
Hashknife. Farmer settlers were puttin' in
fence to protect their crops, and the Milletts didn't like it. Said it was cuttin' them
off from graze, so they were cuttin' the
fences. Finally, they got disgusted and sold
to the Hashknife."

"No, he didn't say anything. But, what
the hell. If a man owns land and he wants
to preserve his range by fencin' it off, I say
that is perfectly right and should be law."

"So do I. But I still think we should investeegate just for our ownselves in case we need to know someday."

"Need to know what?"

"All about fencin'." He looked at Jake with a creased brow as if Jake should see the obvious. "And both sides of the story."

"Oh yeah. I see what you are sayin'." Even though he didn't. Fencing is fencing. Where's the complication in that?

"Grass is startin' to stand up more. But it ain't startin' to turn color just yet," Wes said as they trotted the horses side by side. "We got to head a little southwest a here 'bout fifteen miles. There's a island and some shoals in the river. It runs pretty shallow at that spot this time of year, and the horses won't shy from crossin' it. They won't swim in the cold water. Can't blame 'em, eh?"

"No. Can't say as I do."

"Cross the river and stay east of it headin' south. We can cross at Seymour on the way back. That's another reason why there ain't much rustlin' activity this time of year. Water crossin's are just too dern cold. Cows are dumb but not that dumb. They won't cross cold water neither."

They passed through grassland spotted here and there by the underlying rosy-red dirt surrounding the L Bar ranch headquarters and beyond for a few miles, then came to a large section of a red washboard of shallow canyons and ridges tightly covered in patches by groves of mesquite, shinnery oak, juniper, and chokecherry that looked like giant green serpents crawling on the land. It was quiet except for the cooing of the doves and the whistling quail all around. Wes picked his way up and down ridges through the scrub, and Jake followed. The brush tugged at their chaps as they pushed through it, but Wes was careful to avoid mesquite bushes. "Yer gotta stay away from them devil bushes. Like these here. They's thorns is poisonous. Get an infection from them real fast. Poison the horses, too," Wes said.

Jake leaned way over and could see that Jasper's forelegs were getting scratched up. He was beginning to take a disliking to mesquite. A big whitetail buck jumped out of the brush as they neared his day bed and bounded off out of sight over the next ridge. He only had one horn. "Kind of late to still be sheddin' his antlers," Jake said.

"You hunt deer?"

"Of course. I ain't always been a city slicker." Jake grinned at Wes.

Jake unbuttoned his coat and let it stay open as the day was warming up. From the tops of the ridges they saw antelope off in the distance on the grassland. A large red-tailed hawk soared overhead, dipping high and low against the white backdrop of the clouds. Flocks of brown-headed cowbirds flitted through and around the trees squawking all the while. "Them birds are called cowbirds. They'll be lookin' for a herd a cattle as soon as they can. They pick up bugs and stuff that the cattle kick up when they are grazin' and movin'. Go through the cow pies, too, to find seeds and stuff. Whenever you see them in the spring, summer, and fall, there is usually a cow around somewhere." Jake nodded his head in acknowledgement.

"That's another thing. Any other time but winter and right after a big storm this here country is dustier'n hell. And there ain't no way cattle can be moved without raising a dust cloud. So we always check every dust cloud we see. Rustlers like to keep the critters in the canyons and low country so they cain't be seen. That's why we ride the ridges and git our spyglasses out. Yeah?"

"Makes sense to me," Jake said as he looked out over the plain.

They came down the southwest side of the canyon shelf and back out onto grassland. In another five miles Wes announced, "There's the river. And there's our island."

He pointed up river to a spot about two hundred yards off where there was a small island with shoals around it at a bend in the middle of the red-brown water. "See it? There's a wide and shallow crossin' down-river about four hunnert yards. That's where we'll cross."

"Yup. You think we better rest the horses and eat somethin' before we cross?"

"Reckon it's 'bout that time."

They led Noble and Jasper over to a grassy patch that looked relatively dry, hobbled them, loosened their cinches, and slipped off their bridles, hanging them on the saddle horns. They dug some jerky and hardtack from their saddlebags, unslung their canteens from the saddles, and turned the horses out to the grass. Then they went over to a dry rock, sat down, ate, and, pulling their hat brims down over their eyes, laid back for a little siesta. So far Jake was enjoying himself in Texas. Course it had only been ten days, and who knew what the future held? He thought about his boys. They were getting up there now. Wouldn't be long and they'd be fending for themselves? Then he dozed off.

"Time to git back on the trail," Wes said as he kicked the bottoms of Jake's boots. Jake sat straight up and his hand involuntarily went for his pistol. The holster was empty.

"Ha ha ha. Member what I told yer about touchin' a sleepin' man? He might wake up fast and shoot yer? Ha ha. Wal, yer sure did prove that one out, didn't yer? Ha ha. That's why I pulled yer pistol while yer were sleepin'."

Jake grinned at the sight of Wes in stitches and at himself for responding like he did. "All right, all right, Mister Jokester. Let's round up the horses."

They watered Noble and Jasper in a small creek that emptied into the Brazos. "Why don't we just let 'em drink from the Brazos?" Jake asked.

"The river is powerful salty. Don't let Noble drink from it. Yer shouldn't neither. 'N fact most a the rivers here in the northwest are salty. The Brazos, the Wichita, the Red. Guess livestock can drink from 'em. Yer gotta watch 'em for horses though. Lotta the creeks are seepin' salt, too. Run into the rivers. Most a the salt in the Brazos comes from Croton Creek west a here in Stonehill County. Just gotta be careful is all."

They walked the boys parallel to the river's edge of muddy brown water about fifty yards off and came to the wide, shallow place where Wes wanted to cross. It was a place in the river filled with coarse sand and fine gravel shoals from side to side in a span about one hundred to two hundred-fifty feet across. The river broke up into dozens of shallow little rivulets that ran through the shoals.

"I guess yer know a river ain't nothin' to take lightly. They gotta be studied a little every time yer want to cross. I ain't been down this way in over two weeks, and things can change in that time, 'specially after the storm we had." He pulled his telescope up and scanned both sides of the river, the brown water, and the shoals that still looked gravelly, which was good. "Okay. Yer see that flat spot on the other side? That's where we're headed. We'll start right down here at this flat spot on this side. Reckon the water's less'n a foot deep here with a good gravel bottom. So we can run the boys through it before they realize what's happenin'. Jest so yer know though, usually don't never run a horse through a river. Never know what's on the bottom. But here I know what we got. And watch out for shoals like these here. Yer gotta make sure they ain't quick-sand afore yer go out on 'em. I know these ones are all right. Whatever you do, don't stop. Keep spurrin' him 'cuz yer'll never git him goin' agin' in this cold water. I'll lead off. We'll lope down to the river, and when we git 'bout ten yards from the water we'll spur them into a gallop and git across real fast. Stay 'bout five yards off to the side of me. Horses don't like to git splashed in the face." He pushed his hat down and pulled the stampede drawstring tight under his chin. Jake followed his example. "Yer ready?" Jake nodded his head *yes,* and they nudged Noble and Jasper into a lope.

When they came to the spot Wes wanted, he let out a "Yahooo!" and spurred Noble into a full gallop. Jake spurred Jasper, and he lunged forward about two feet into a flat-out run. They hit the water with Wes and Noble in a slight lead and Jake and Jasper about five yards back on the left. As they galloped across the river the brown water sprayed out to the sides from every plunge of the horses' hooves. Jake raked Jasper's flanks with his spurs in a constant out and back motion but not too hard and with the spurs turned out so they didn't puncture him. He could feel the power of the animal under him and the wind in his face blowing the front brim of his hat back. Jasper was gaining on Noble, and suddenly Jake realized they were racing, so he yelled, "Yahoo! Yahooo! Yahooo! Go, Jasper! Go!"

Wes looked over his shoulder and turned his head to follow Jasper as Jasper pulled ahead of them and gained the shore before Noble. He pulled off his hat and let out another series of whoops with a big grin slashed across his face. It was contagious, and Jake did likewise as he pulled back on the reins. They spurred and reined the horses in circles and whooped and slapped their hats on their thighs. Then Wes rode off to the southeast, and Jake followed, laughing and grinning big.

There was no trail. They were riding Noble and Jasper at a trot through the brushy grassland, navigating by Wes's sense of direction. "I ain't crossed a river like that in a long time. Where I am from they got bridges everywhere," Jake said to Wes with a beaming expression on his face. "That was a real good ride. I think I'm likin' this cowboy stuff, and I guess old Jasper showed himself to be top hand, eh?"

"Wal, he won that one all right. But I ain't willin' to say he can beat Noble 'less he beats him on dirt and Noble knows he's racin'. I think Jasper snuck up on him this time." Wes wouldn't look at Jake.

"Oh. Uh-huh."

The further south they rode, the better the grass condition they came across. Winter was being chased back north where it came from by a pregnant spring. It could strike back, but Wes thought they had seen the worst of it for the season. About halfway to their destination, they stopped for the night at a grassy meadow with big mesquite trees by a creek. Wes located the ashen campfire ring under the tree he had used before, which was good because they wouldn't have to build a ring of stones. They pulled the bedrolls, saddlebags, and saddles off the horses and dropped them by the fire ring. Then they led Noble and Jasper to the creek for a good long drink. After that they led the boys to the edge of the grass, hobbled them, and slipped off their bridles. Each of them held a pile of oats in their hats up to the boys, and they dug in, nickering as they munched. They gathered dry wood where they could find it and built a fire. By sundown Wes had the coffee grounds boiling in a pot. The aroma was pleasing to their range-weary senses.

"Here's a little somethin' I got from the cook at the L Bar," he said as he pulled a small package from his saddlebag that was wrapped in butcher paper. He opened the package to reveal a slab of beef brisket. "Huh? What're yer think a that? And looky here. More from the cook." He opened a small sack and reached in to pull out a fresh baked biscuit. "More where that came from." Lastly, he opened a tin of already cooked pinto beans. He set the beans on a stone close but not too close to the fire so they would warm nicely. "Now. How about that? We are gonna have a feast. Ol' Wes is takin' pretty good care a yer, wouldn't yer say?"

"I sure would, honey. Did yer bring any sugar for my coffee?"

"Why, whatta yer know? I sure did. Ain't that sweet a me?"

With that, they guffawed and drank their coffee as the meat hung on a stick over the fire sizzling away. The sky was clear. It was a crisp night with still air. An almost-full moon was increasing in light as it rose above the eastern horizon, and already the coyotes were singing.

Next day about a half hour before sundown, they trotted Noble and Jasper through the gateposts under the span of a beam from which a large rusted steel Circle Bar B swayed gently in the breeze. "This is the headquarters," Wes said. "Big spread. Eighty sections. Straddles the Salt Fork and the Double Mountain Fork a the Brazos. Probably fifteen thousand head. Mostly longhorn. But, like I said, they's bringin' in

Hereford. That's the big house over there on that little rise. Bunkhouse over there." He nodded toward a long, low-rise adobe with a covered porch along its entire length. The barn and lots were to the left of the bunkhouse. Between the bunkhouse and the big house were two small adobe houses. Out a ways from the bunkhouse and main house, a wooden windmill tower stood in place already erected. The wooden wheel of vanes with its tail was on the ground resting upside down next to the tower, and next to it lay the sucker rod and flywheel mechanism.

"That's a new invention Ole and Bayliss are puttin' in. It's called a windmill. It uses wind power to pump water outta the ground. Ain't that somethin'?" Wes said as they trotted by the windmill tower.

Jake gave him a sarcastic look and said, "I seen them all over Illinois last year."

"Oh. I forgot. Yer a civilizee." He grinned.

Over between the house and bunkhouse by the other two houses was a windlass set over a well with a watering trough next to it. Off to another side, there was a large pile of fence posts stacked neatly side by side and another stack of rolls of barbed wire. Looked like it was a very busy place, and there should be more men out and about, but, late in the day as it was, the hands they saw were putting tools away, feeding the horses, and washing up for supper.

Wes slowed Noble to a walk and headed to the bunkhouse. "See if Bill Smith is here. He's the cow boss," he said to Jake as he searched the area for a sign of Bill Smith.

"Thought you said Ole Olsson was the foreman."

"He's the manager for all the Bayliss operations combined. That's the way a lot of these big outfits do it. Every ranch has a cow boss who works for the manager who works for the owner. Some big outfits like the Flying XC have a cow boss, and a range boss and a trail boss who work for the cow boss. See that fencing material over there." He nodded his head toward the fence supplies.

"Uh-huh."

"Hey, Shorty! Howdy!" Wes called out to a man walking from the lots toward the bunkhouse. Wes sidled Noble up closer to the bunkhouse. Jake nudged Jasper to follow.

Shorty raised his hand and waved it over his head. As he came closer he said, "Howdy yerself, Wesley. Making the rounds, are yer?"

"Yeah. Is Bill here?"

"Nah. He's out west with the cows. We

got them high grade Hereford shorthorns, yer know. Wal, he's workin' with the heavies. Got 'em gathered up in a draw. Says he ain't gonna lose a single calf. Ha!"

"How come yer ain't out there with 'em?"

"I ain't feelin' so good today, so Bill told me to stay in the bunk for the day."

"How come yer out walkin' 'round then?"

"Can't stay in the bunk all day. I'd go loco. Had to get some fresh air."

"Uh-huh. I can ride that horse. Where yer got them Hereford bulls holed up?"

"They're down on the south range."

"How fer is that?"

" 'Bout two mile."

"Uh-huh. How about Ole? He around?"

"He's up at the house with Don. They's schemin' somethin' up."

"All right if we camp here for the night? Drop our saddles and borrow some a yer hay? Put the horses in the lots?"

"Wal, I ain't the boss, but seein' as how he's not here and four a the hands are with him, there's room for yer in the bunkhouse. Don't see how it'd hurt for yer to stay a night."

"Thanks, Shorty. We'll take care a the horses and then have a talk with Ole."

Shorty waved his hand again, and Wes and Jake moved closer to the bunkhouse, tied off the boys at the rail, stepped off, and dropped their saddles and gear. Then they walked the horses over to the stock trough for a drink, then back to the corral, where they slipped their tack and turned them in with the other horses. Fresh hay was scattered about the lot. "Better watch 'em a minute. Make sure they git along okay," Wes said. "Don't wanna raise no sand."

"Huh?"

"Start trouble."

"Oh."

"Looks like they's all right. Let's wash up."

"Hey, Ves!" They turned to see Ole Olsson calling to Wes, waving him over from the front of the big house porch, where another man stood beside him. So, the detectives changed direction and headed for the house instead of the bunkhouse.

"Howdy, Ole. This here is Jake Brighton. He's a new stock detective. We're breakin' him in, so I am showin' him around."

"Pleased to meet you, Mister Brighton. Ves, I don't think you ever met Don Bayliss, the owner of the Circle Bar B," he said as he gestured toward Bayliss. He was a tall man with a full, well-barbered beard that was slightly darker than his sandy hair that was parted in the middle with a slight wave on both sides. He was thin, and his face was lean and manly. He appeared to be experienced and looked out on the world with a steady and confident gaze with his astute, hazel eyes.

"Wes?" Bayliss queried for a last name.

"Wilson."

"Good to meet you, Mister Wilson and Mister Brighton. You are stock detectives for the Stock-Raisers' Association?"

"We sure are."

"Well, that is good. Why don't you join Ole and me for supper? We were just going to the wash-up trough."

"Thank yer kindly, but we been on the trail a few days, and we ain't exactly fit for supper. Maybe we best et in the bunkhouse," Wes said as hospitably as he knew how.

"Nonsense. This is a cattle ranch after all. Distinguished visitors should dine in the main house." Bayliss smiled and frowned at the same time. Wes looked quizzically at Jake, and Jake shrugged his shoulders.

"All right then. We thank yer."

"Fine. Let's wash up and have a drink before supper."

Ole held the door of the house open for everyone as they trooped in. There was a parlor of moderate opulence on one side of the front hall and a similar dining room on the other side. Both had dark wood floors with southwest style rugs covering the majority of the floor. A potbellied stove on a low stone platform was against the far wall of the parlor purring away. It was nice and toasty in the house, and both Jake and Wes removed their coats and hung them with their hats on a fairly large hat tree. "Mind if we remove this hardware?" Wes asked as he patted his gun belt.

"No. Please make yourselves comfortable."

The kitchen was accessed through a door on the side by the dining table. They all stood in the parlor in a semicircle, and Bayliss offered cigars around from a humidor box. "Cuban," he said. Each man helped themselves, and Wes had started to bite the end off of his cigar when Jake gave him a sharp poke to the ribs with his elbow. At first Wes reacted with a flare of anger until within the same two seconds he saw Jake's discreet sign of *No-no.* He nonchalantly glanced around and saw Ole clipping his cigar end with the cutter Bayliss had handed him and then pass it to Jake. Then he understood. His turn came, and he inspected the cutter quickly, figured it out, and clipped off the end of his cigar.

"Wal, that beats bitin' and spittin', don't

it?" Wes declared as Jake cringed. Wes dug into his vest pocket and pulled out a stick match, but Bayliss came by again and offered a candle for him to light his cigar. Wes hid the match by cupping it in his hand and took the candle. "Why, thank yer," he said. Then Ole poured vodka from a cream-colored stoneware decanter into four tumbler glasses and handed one to each man.

"Wal, what yer got here? White lightnin'?" asked Wes. Jake looked inquiringly at Ole for the answer as well. He, too, was not familiar with vodka.

Ole laughed heartily and said, "No, Ves. It is Svedish vodka. Made from vinter veet."

"Winter wheat? Not sour mash?"

"Yup," Ole said.

Wes stared at the clear liquid in the glass, sniffed it, but, before he took a drink from his glass, he waited to see how Jake would do it. Bayliss was just finishing lighting his cigar, and when it was going good he nodded to Ole.

"Vell, here's to meeting each other. Let's enjoy it. Skoll!" Ole declared as he held his glass high. "Skoll!" came the joint response from the three other men. And then Wes said, "Here's how," and he clinked his glass to Jake's and then the others.

He forgot all about following Jake's example and tossed the liquor back, swallowed, exhaled audibly, and said, "By gosh, that is smooth. I could fall in love with that, ha ha."

Everyone smiled appropriately, and Wes, looking around, noticed they were sipping their drinks rather than taking it like a slug of whiskey in a saloon. "Guess I kinda put the spurs to that one," he said a little sheepishly. "Not the way yer supposed to do it, huh?"

"I find it more enjoyable to take it slow and easy, kind of like sipping fine Kentucky bourbon. But plenty of my friends in Dallas like to toss back shots. So have at it however you desire." Bayliss was quite gregarious and genuine in his conversation.

"Wal, I'll have another, but I'll pull back on the reins and sip it along with the rest of yer. I ain't ever had any vodka afore. Yer Jake?" He shot a curious look at Jake.

"No never. Very tasty though. Like you said, nice and smooth." He smiled real friendly like. "You are from Dallas, Mister Bayliss?"

"Well good. Glad you enjoy it," Bayliss said. "Yes. Please call me Don. I am just out here making the regular inspection and coordinating plans with Ole. I spend most of my time in Dallas. I have banking interests there. But, it's good to get out of the city. I enjoy it out here on the range. Tell me, though, are you keeping the rustlers at bay, or is that not a fair question?"

"Oh, fair to middlin' I reckon," Wes answered with a smile. "Thieves are pretty much leavin' your critters alone. Brand is too hard to change with a runnin' iron. Everybody knows they come off the Circle Bar B, so none a the buyers'll touch 'em without a bona fide bill a sale or some proof of a drive by Bar B hands. The buyers are a pretty savvy bunch, and they ain't lookin' to cause themselves any extra trouble. Yer rustlers around this part a the range are mainly stealing from the Hashknife and drivin' the beeves past Dodge into the Dakotas and Montana." Wes spoke like one who was sure of everything he said as kind of an expert.

"Well, that is good news. I always thought we have a good brand," Bayliss said with a proud smile. "I don't mean to put anything over on the Hashknife, but it is good for us, eh, Ole?"

"Yes, sir. Course you got a couple of detectives working out of Abilene, too, don't you, Ves?"

"Yup. Curly Benson and Will Caldwell ride outta Abilene. Couple a damn fine stock detectives."

"Well, Mister Brighton, you're very quiet. Wes always do all the talking?"

"Pretty much for now," Jake said as he gave Wes a sideways glance. "I am officially in trainin' right now, so I wouldn't want to say anything about what I don't know from experience or schoolin' I guess."

"You look like a man of means. You must have some specialty."

Jake sipped his drink and puffed his cigar, blowing the smoke up into the air. The tip glowed orange as he glanced at Wes, who ever so slightly shrugged his shoulders.

"Yes, I do. I am a detective hailing out of Missourah. You may have heard of the Doctor Talbott patricide case. That was my investigation."

"Ah, yes." Bayliss raised his eyebrows and bounced on his toes about a half inch, twice. "I read about it in the paper, and, now that you mention it, I do remember your name being reported as the man who obtained the evidence that convicted the culprits."

"Yes. It was an undercover investigation. I had to make myself out as a criminal to gain their confidence and join their ranks so they would brag about what they did. I mainly do undercover work, and that is the idea Jim Loving has in hirin' me. As soon as I finish my apprenticeship on the range under the tutelage of the legendary Wes Wilson" — he said tongue in cheek and could not suppress a little smile as he caught Wes out of the corner of his eye pretending like he was not impressed — "I will attempt to infiltrate various bands of rustlers, arrest them, and haul them off to jail, if not kill them." He said the last part like a hardened man who meant business. Wes was pretending like he was busy with his drink and studying his cigar.

"Mighty fine cigar, Don. I thank yer agin' kindly," Wes said in a clear attempt to change the subject.

"My pleasure, Wes. I must say I am impressed, Jake. May I ask . . . you are talking about Jim Loving?"

"He's our boss," Wes said firmly. "Secretary and general foreman of the Stock-Raisers' Association of North-West Texas. Damn fine man, too. Yer not a member of the association?"

"Oh yes, of course. Yes, we are members."

"Excuse me, Don, but I am curious. By the looks of your supplies on hand you intend to fence your property?" Jake queried.

"Yes. That is correct. We will fence all the ranches. We have fifty thousand acres here at the headquarters, and we own all the land, as we do on the other spreads."

"Excuse me again. I don't mean to be nosy, and if I overstep please tell me, but, again, I am curious from whom did you acquire such vast holdings of land?"

"Oh, I don't mind your asking as long as you don't start asking about money." He smiled an artificial smile, and his eyes revealed a hardness. "We primarily scooped up land from the state school lots. I put together an investor group, and year after year we bought the school sections and whatever else we could find. Gradually, we kept building up the herd and the acreage. Soon as the railroads figured out they don't need all that land they get from the government and start selling, we will buy it up, too. And that is how we acquired legal ownership of such vast holdings, as you call them."

"I see. Very interesting," Jake said genuinely, or at least seemingly genuinely. He was not about to enter into a discussion on the privilege of the rich, and he didn't really hold it against them. If anything, he was a little jealous. "Forgive me. I am ignorant on the matter. Other than keepin' the public, so to speak, off your property, what does fencin' achieve? And, mind you, I am not against it. Just part of my range education." He chuckled and took another drag off his cigar and a sip of vodka.

"Oh, no. I understand. For years the public and railroad land has been open range and sort of claimed, not legally of course, by whoever used it on a regular basis. There was no range management. Small ranchers with no land of their own to speak of would run their cattle out onto the open range in the spring, gather a certain number for market in late spring and summer and leave the rest on the range to grow their herd. The result is simply overgrazing. The grass is losing to the mesquite, and we are losing rangeland. Since we own our land, we don't intend to let that happen, so we have to restrict access. Just like every other cattleman, we want to build our herd, and we need our range to do that. It is no longer free grazing range. And I suppose one could say it is sad, yet it is the way of American commerce. This is the wave of the future. Big investment firms are beginning to buy up the large ranches like ours. We want to turn a profit, of course, and stockholders are ruthless, if you follow my meaning. Whew, you got me going. That was a speech. But, I see Ruby is serving supper. Shall we?"

"Any chance we can take a gander at the fence you are puttin' in?" Wes asked as they moved toward the table.

"Am I under investigation?"

Wes and Jake almost dropped their cigars and drinks but covered it up nicely. "Why heck, no!" Wes declared. "Whatever give yer that kinda ideer?"

"We are just tryin' to add to our knowledge of the changin' range you talked about so we can better serve the Stock-Raisers' Association. Besides, what possible crime could there be to investigate? I don't think Texas has any laws on fencin'," Jake said and spread his arms a little to add emphasis.

"Ha ha! Sorry. It was just a knee-jerk reaction to a couple a detectives asking to look at something. We are fencing on the north line. Where are you heading?"

"We're workin' outta Seymour and headed back thataway," Wes said.

"Well, you are in luck. You'll go right up to the fence then."

"Any gates so's we can get through?"

"Sorry no. You'll have to go down to where the crew is currently working at the east end," Ole said. "Tom Jonesboro is the hand in charge. I'll give you a note so there won't be any problems. Now, let's enjoy this supper. What do vee have tonight, Ruby?"

"Venison tenderloin. The fence crew shot him about a week ago. I've been hanging it to cure ever since. Should be real good. I fixed it my special way."

"Excellent. Nothing better than Ruby's special venison."

As they walked to the bunkhouse tent after brandy and finishing their cigars at the house Jake said, "Did yer know about my undercover mission from Jim?"

"Who, me?"

"Yes, yer."

"Wal, let me say this. Yer see, me and Jim been pards a long time. He purty much tells me everthing that concerns me. Yeah, I knew, so's I can figure out what to show yer. Makes sense, don't it?"

"I suppose. Just wish you would have told me."

"I was gonna when I thought the time was right."

"All right. No hard feelings." Jake held out his hand for Wes to shake.

They rode out at sunrise with not a cloud in sight. The day was warming up fast. In four hours they came to the fence. The terrain there was rolling, golden-brown grassland with mesquite in the cuts and creeping up over the swells. They reined in the boys and looked left and then right. The fence was up against a long band of mesquite and scrub. For as far as they could see in both directions, a line of posts marched one right after the other, endlessly fastened by five strands of barbed wire.

"Wal, what a yer think a this?" Wes asked.

"I think it looks like it'll do the job."

"Yup. Shore will. It's steel wire. On this side is Circle Bar B. On ta other side is free range, but it is all scrub and no good grass. So there's no more graze for the small rancher."

Jake shrugged his shoulders and said, "There's such a thing as property rights."

"Yeah, I know. But, out here it's always been open range ever since the white man came and pushed the Injuns out. How's that for what-a-they-call-it?"

"Irony."

"Yeah. Irony. Now the white man is gettin' pushed out by his own kind. Ha ha! Anyway, old habits die hard, is all I'm a sayin'."

"Yeah. Have to see how it plays out." Jake bent down from the saddle and looked closely at one of the brace assemblies. It was two stout juniper posts about five feet high stuck in the ground with a beefy cross-support between them about three quarters of the way up the posts parallel to the fence. One post had the wire ends wrapped around it and pulled tight down the fence line. It was braced by the crossbar and the other post. The five strands of barbed wire fence ran down the fence line with posts about every ten feet and much thinner mesquite stays stapled to the strands of wire.

"This is where it all begins," Jake said. "Probably the same set up at the corners. The stays down the fence line keep the strands from twistin' on each other. Think it'll hold a herd back?"

"Depends. If the critters are just walkin' along, they'd probably turn and follow the fence. But, if they's runnin' or stampedin,' I don't think it would hold 'em. What it will do is cut down a lot on the strays, and like you said keep the unwanted out."

"Yup."

Jake reined Jasper to the right and walked him east along the fence line. Wes and Noble followed. They spurred the boys up to a trot, and in two miles a white-top chuck wagon with a single good-sized tent next to it came into view another half mile out. As they trotted up to the camp they saw that the crew was in for chuck. Before they were on the camp, two cowboys separated from the crew and came out with rifles hanging in their hands.

"Halloo, the camp!" Wes called out. "We come from Ole Olsson. Lookin' for Tom Jonesboro."

"That'd be me," one of the cowboys said, squinting against the sun as he looked up at Wes.

"Howdy. Wes Wilson. I'm a detective for the Stock-Raisers' Association. Ole gave us passage around the fence. I have a note from him."

"Let's see it."

Wes nudged Noble forward and leaned down to hand the note to Jonesboro. Jake watched him take it and look at it as if he were reading it. He could see the cowboy couldn't read.

"All righty," Jonesboro said with a smile. "Y'all et yet? Got plenty a chuck here if you want some."

"Thanky. We could use some dinner. Got any water around here for the horses?"

"There's a creek about a half mile northeast. We been haulin' water up from it."

"On ta other side a the fence?"

"Yup."

"All right. Had any trouble from anyone while yer been buildin' this here fence?"

"Nope. Yer plannin' on bringin' some?" Jonesboro said in an open tone of challenge.

329

Wes stepped out of the saddle and walked deliberately over to Jonesboro, got up real close, and stared down at him. "I told you," he said low and terse, "I'm a detective. The only trouble I bring is fer rustlers. Yer a rustler, Mister Jonesboro?" Then he smiled, tipped his hat, and remounted Noble. "C'mon, Jake. Les ride. I ain't likin' the company here. Let's git back on up to Seymour and more hospitable folks."

They loped Noble and Jasper to the east down the fence line, went around the end, and then turned northeast. They came to the creek, watered the boys, and sat down for a cold dinner of hardtack, jerky, and canteen water. "Tell me," Jake said, "what was wrong with the company back at the fence buildin' camp?"

"Aw, I didn't like that little smart-ass Jonesboro. He was tryin' to start trouble. He's a rustler. I could smell it on him. How'd I know, yer ask? When yer been around these sons-a-bitches long enough, yer can tell. They's all the same. I seen it in his eyes. He wanted to kill me." He spat a piece of gristle, cut off another piece of jerky with his knife, and slid it into his mouth. "Normally, I'da et with 'em and started talkin'. Let 'em talk, too. Trap 'em into admittin' somethin'. But, I wasn't in the mood, and we got a long ride to the Hashknife headquarters. So I said let's mosey."

"So you're sayin' he works for the Circle Bar B and is stealin' their cows at the same time?"

"Yup. And mavericks and cattle from other ranches, too. Used to be cattlemen'd let their top hands build up their own herds by givin' 'em a few head as wages and lettin' 'em keep what mavericks they could find, catch, and brand with their own brand."

"What's a maverick?"

"Oh, yeah. Sorry. It's a calf that gits away from the herd without a brand. So with fencin' goin' in they's less mavericks, open range is goin' away so a cowboy ain't got anywhere to graze a herd even if he could build one. And the ranchers don't need as many cowboys to tend the herd because it's all behind the wire. Am I makin' sense to yer?"

"Yup. Like yer said before. Old habits die hard. But profit lives on forever. They that profit, live on. Those that don't, die, so to speak."

" 'Xactly."

"But shouldn't you inform Ole Olsson about Jonesboro?"

"Ain't got no hard evidence."

"Well, at least that you suspect him."

"Right now, it's just a hunch. Boss doesn't like accusin' cowboys just on a hunch." Wes shrugged his shoulders. "He'll slip up someday, and we'll get him."

They trotted the boys into the Hashknife headquarters on Miller Creek about an hour after sunset. "This outfit's got spreads all over West Texas. Here in Baylor County, Nolan County, Taylor County, Throckmorton County, and a big spread out on the Pecos River that brands ten thousand calves a year. I bet the outfit has at least fifty thousand head a cattle. Probably more. And I hear they are negotiatin' on range in Tom Green County along the Concho River." Wes looked over to Jake to see if he was impressed. He was.

Jake let go a long and low-toned whistle. "That is impressive."

Wes led the way to the bunkhouse, where they were just in time for the last serving of supper. So, he arranged for them to eat right after they cared for the boys. After supper they sat with the cowboys around one of the two stoves in the large bunkhouse. Wes sat in tight with them. Jake stayed back and leaned against the wall. Wes smoked and joked with the cowboys and then got down to business.

"How many hands the Hashknife have now? Over a hunnert?" Wes blurted out to no one in particular.

"Oh, at least. Reckon we don't know fer sure. Boss knows. He keeps the payroll," one of the cowboys offered up, and the rest of them chuckled with him.

Wes was smiling and then went serious. "How many a the crew are rustlin' Hashknife cattle?" In a manner of speaking he threw it out like a challenge as if he knew the answer but wanted confirmation. The room immediately went silent. Not a cough. Not an *ahem.* Not a spur jingle. Nothing. Dead silence.

Then a particularly mean looking cowboy in the back piped up and said, "He a range detective, too?" He sent his hard stare over Jake's way.

Wes looked around as if he were surprised at the question and pretended he saw that the cowboy was referring to Jake. "Him? Nah. I picked him up on the trail a ways back. Said he'd like a place to bunk. I said c'mon. I got friends at the Hashknife." With the last statement he stared down the cowboy, who blinked first.

"Where yer headed?" The cowboy looked back up and said to Jake.

"Comanche Creek."

"What fer?"

"I'm signed on with the Flying XC. Just startin' out with 'em." Jake smiled pleasantly.

"Yer ain't from around here."

Wes looked disinterested but was watching everything real careful-like, especially concentrating on the gun hands.

"I'm from Kansas. Came to Texas to learn how to ranch."

"Well, yer come to the right place," another cowboy said. "We'll teach yer real good." He laughed, and the crew laughed with him.

"Flying XC's north a here. Kansas is north a here. Why ain't yer come south straight from Kansas to Comanche Creek?" the mean cowboy asked accusingly.

"Well, uh, I kinda got turned around. Guess I got to learn my directions, too."

"Wal, you ain't need to know directshuns in Kansas 'cause everythin's so flat. Out here on the range, it ain't no ocean. So good luck, pardner." Another cowboy chimed in and raised his coffee mug as a toast to Jake. "But we'll bunk yer fer the night, and maybe some good ol' Texas sense'll ooze into you whilst yer sleep, ha ha." That got the whole crew laughing. Jake raised his cup back at him, and the inquest was over. Wes decided to discontinue his line of inquiry. More important to keep Jake undercover. Cowhands often drifted from outfit to outfit. Top hands usually stayed in one place, but it wasn't worth the risk for Jake to maybe lose his cover.

In the morning, Jake and Wes sat at the chow table away from each other and acted like they hardly knew each other. After breakfast the hands went out to work, and Jake and Wes were in the bunkhouse alone rolling up their gear. "Best for us to separate. You go on ahead. Just head northeast outta here and keep goin' till yer hit the river. Then follow it north to Seymour. I'll see you in town if I don't catch up with yer first." He grinned. Jake gave him a droll smile.

Jake rode out of the barnyard alone on another sunny day. He left his coat unbuttoned because there was no wind, and the days were warming up. A few of the cowboys saw him go and raised their hats to him as he rode by. One yelled out, "Good luck, tenderfoot!" Jake dipped his hat and spurred Jasper into a lope. In short order, the headquarters was behind him, and he was out on the range headed for Seymour. Along the way he saw steers here and there and checked all their brands against Jim's book for the Millett brand and the Hashknife he already knew. About five miles into his ride, Jake saw a bunch of steers browsing on mesquite and juniper scrub in a shallow draw. He walked Jasper up closer to them so he could see the brand. It was one he hadn't seen before. It was on the sides of the beeves and looked like a *T* with an *L* over the top of the *T.*

Jake pulled out Loving's book and located the brand. It belonged to A. B. Edwards of Archer and Clay Counties. He thought they must be strays even though that was a long way for them to wander. At a minimum, they had to make it all the way through Baylor County down here to Miller Creek. And cross the river on their own. Could be rustled and holding here until late spring. Anyway, he thought he better wait for Wes to come along and figure what to do. So he rode up to the top of a knoll where he could see his back trail and keep an eye on the steers at the same time. It was quiet and still. Only when one of the steers snorted or bawled was the silence broken. He knew there were deer and birds and coyotes and other varmints around. He just couldn't see or hear them. Bet your boots they were watching him, though. He stepped out of the saddle and sat on a boulder. He lit a cigar and waited.

After two hours sitting in the warm morning sun, he was dozing. At one point he jerked awake and looked around. Jasper had wandered off down the side of the hill nosing around for some green grass. He looked to the sky. The sun was at its zenith. He looked toward where the steers were. They were gone. He pulled his watch from his vest pocket. It was indeed noon. *Gosh damn it,* he said to himself. Then he hurried down the hill and gathered up Jasper. He threw himself up into the saddle and spurred away to where the steers were last loafing. He found the disturbed ground indicating sign and determined the direction they had gone. Down a draw and up the other side, over the top of the hill and on the side of another draw, he found them lying in the sun on the grass chewing their cud. He counted them, and all twenty-five were there. Now what to do?

He decided he couldn't wait for Wes. He'd have to git these critters movin' if they were gonna git to the stockyard in Seymour before midnight. He figured when he got them up at least a few of them would try to make a run for the brush, so he rode around to get in between the herd and the brush, and then he started popping the whip and yelling and whooping. The steers bawled and clumsily got to their feet and looked around as if they were confused. And sure enough two of them ran together for the brush. Jasper was after them in a flash and almost dumped Jake from the saddle as he spun and lunged after the quitters. Jake was amazed. He basically let Jasper have his head, and, all by himself, he got the steers turned around and headed back into the herd. A few more pops of the whip and Jasper running back and forth got the bunch moving at a trot up the hillside. They chose a shallow angle for the ascent, and Jake let them follow their noses. When they reached the top they slowed to a walk and stayed pretty bunched up, especially since when any one of them tried to quit Jasper was right on top of them staying behind the dangerous long horns and pushing his body into theirs to get them back in the bunch. One rangy and wild steer tried to kick Jasper, and he bit a big chunk out of the steer's neck. The critter let out a big bawl, but he behaved after that.

At the top, Jake turned in his saddle and searched down his back trail. He didn't see anyone coming, so he kept the herd moving northeast. He sincerely hoped Wes would come along soon. He didn't know what to do when he got the herd to the river. The terrain was flattening out, and he guided the herd to stay on the flats. After about an hour and the hundredth time of looking back over his trail he saw a rider coming up on his left rear quarter. Too far off to be sure who it was. So he reined in Jasper, who was reluctant to stop, and he pulled his glass from his saddlebag and focused in on the horse and rider. It was Wes. Jake thought about firing a shot from his pistol to get his attention but thought better as it might have spooked the steers. So he just watched him instead, as Wes was heading straight for him, and, after a couple of minutes, he saw him stop. Jake put his glass on him and saw that Wes was looking at him through his own spyglass. So he waved his hand over his head, and Wes did the same and rode right at Jake. Jasper, however, was not happy. The critters were slowing down, and he wanted to git back on 'em. So he tossed his head and pulled on the reins and did little crow-hops. Jake gave up looking through the spyglass and let Jasper go. In no time he had the herd moving again.

Wes came riding up next to Jake and called out, "What the heck yer got here?"

"What's it look like?" Jake returned with

raw sarcasm. Wes was a little taken aback and looked at Jake, trying to figure what burr he had under his saddle. "What're you been doin'? Took you long enough to git here." Then Wes glanced at the herd and back at Jake, and he got it.

"Wal, I been busy workin' with Bill Vandevert. He's holdin' a bunch a strays 'bout five miles south of the headquarters with a brand he didn't recognize and wanted me to identify it for him. So I had to ride five miles south and then ten miles north to catch up with yer, dear. But, I'm here now, sweetie. Ever-thing'll be just fine now. Come here. Let me hug yer, ha ha."

Jake spurred Jasper and took off down the left side of the little herd. Wes followed, laughing all the way.

"So, yer got 'em bunched up and movin' all by yerself. Congratulations. That ain't easy."

"I got a good horse. What was the brand on the Vandevert strays?"

"Rocking TX out a Stephens County. He hadn't seen it before. Looks like yer got yerself some critters that's a long ways from home. That's the TL brand. E. B. Edwards," Wes said as he looked at the steers.

"Yeah, I looked it up in the book. Could be rustled, huh?"

"That'd be a good guess. Oh well, we gotta git 'em back to where they belong. Be long past sundown by the time we git 'em to Seymour, and then it'll be all the next day git'n 'em to Edwards's southern range. Cattle don't move fast. At least yer'll be 'speriencin' drivin' cattle even if it is a leetle herd."

It was three hours past sundown when, to their good fortune under a full moon, they arrived at the Brazos River. They were south of the crossing, and it was all they could do to keep the critters from falling into the river to drink. They rode the boys back and forth between the cattle and the river, yelling and whooping and Jake popping the whip. They pushed them upriver. The steers bawled like babies, thirsty as they were. But they kept them moving upriver and finally came to the crossing, where they let them wade in and fill their bellies. Then they wanted to get out of the cold water, but when they started doing that Wes and Jake spurred the boys and charged the steers, fired their pistols a couple of shots, and stampeded the critters across the river. It took about a half mile to get them slowed down and bunched up again, and then it was a slow walk to Seymour.

"Got a keep 'em tight goin' through

town," Wes hollered across the bunch to Jake on the other side. Jake waved his hand over his head to acknowledge the instruction.

They came up from the south into town on the east side to skirt all the buildings and drove the critters west at a walk on California Street toward the stockyards on the north. As they came to the Washington Street crossing, Wes galloped Noble ahead to open the gate to the stockyard corral. Jake and Jasper worked back and forth across the rear of the little herd and to the sides to keep them bunched up. He popped his whip at the steers that tried to turn up other streets instead of staying on California. He whooped and hollered and lashed out with his whip. The steers bellowed and snorted as they pushed against each other in response to Jake's whip. As soon as the gate swung open Wes spurred Noble around and galloped back to the herd, dug in his spurs, spun Noble in a hundred-eighty degree turn, and yelled at Jake, "Git on over ta the other side. We'll keep pushin' 'em from the sides. The stragglers'll follow the main herd!"

Jake gave a couple of last pops at the stragglers, and they tightened up with the rest of the herd. Then he gave Jasper a kick in the ribs and pulled the reins to the right. Jasper dug in with his muscled thighs and pushed off so hard to the right and ahead that Jake nearly got left in midair. Even if Jake didn't know exactly what he was doing, Jasper did. He went to the front steers and shoved his body into theirs in response to Jake's reining him that way so the lead steers were guided by Jake on Jasper and Wes on Noble to go through the open gates, and the rest of the cattle followed. Quickly all twenty-five of them were in the corral, and Jake threw a leg over and hopped off Jasper to jump down and shut the gate. Wes trotted Noble over to Jake. "Well, that was easy enough," Jake said with a grin up at Wes.

"Yup. That's 'bout the way it's done with any herd a cattle. Keep the lead cows movin', and the rest will follow. Course on a big drive yer got a few more hands ridin' point, swing, flank, and drag. We did it all ourselves. Let's head for the barn."

Jake reached in his coat pocket and slipped Jasper a piece of candy. "Good boy," he said as he stroked Jasper's neck. "You did a real good job today."

In the moonlight they trotted the boys down Oregon Street, and when they turned the corner onto Main Street they saw a small crowd on the street in front of the

Brazos Saloon. They were formed in an arch around a man facing the saloon. All the soiled doves and Alex the bartender were on the porch off to the side. Jake located Gracie and saw that she seemed to be out of harm's way. The man was yelling, and when Jake and Wes rode up they could see that it was Charlie Dalton. They held their horses just outside the arch of bystanders and remained in their saddles.

"Yer yella-belly horse's ass! Git on out here! I'm gonna shoot yer dead! Yer got the guts to face me, yer tinhorn card cheat bastard? Git on out here!" Dalton yelled at the top of his lungs. Tobacco spittle slipped down his chin, and he wiped it off with his left shirtsleeve. "Yer mother's a whore, and yer a bastard son of a bitch. C'mon on out, Waldrup."

At that moment from the saloon doors stepped a tall, heavyset man dressed in a dark-gray suit and a black and red silk vest, with a gold watch bob and chain hanging across it, over a white shirt with turn-down collar and a black brocade four-in-hand cravat. His shoes were shiny black leather, which Jake thought a little odd. He surmised the man had a room upstairs at the saloon and had changed his shoes from what he wore in the street. He had one thumb hooked in a vest pocket. Jake guessed that was where the derringer was hidden. Dalton, for his part, by contrast, was still in the clothes he had worn the other night.

"Now, Charlie. You know it ain't at all polite to insult a man's mother," the man said as he leaned against a post of the boardwalk porch in front of the saloon. The light from the lanterns in the saloon spilled out onto the boardwalk, and the man was silhouetted by them. Dalton was in the street awash in moonlight and light from the lanterns hanging on the posts of the covered boardwalk.

"That's 'xactly what *I'm* doin'! What're *yer* gonna do?" Dalton said menacingly and slowly let his right hand hover over his pistol in its holster. Everybody on the boardwalk stepped back further out of the line of fire.

"I ain't gonna do nothin'. You have me at a disadvantage, Charlie. I am not armed. I have no gun."

"Wal, yer better git one and give yerself a chance cuz I'm gonna kill yer either way. Armed or unarmed, yer bastard. Somebody give him a gun." Jake tensed. This did not look good.

In just a matter of seconds, a pistol flew out from someone in the crowd and thudded on the boardwalk at Waldrup's feet.

345

"Pick it up!" Dalton snarled between clenched teeth.

"Give your word you won't shoot while I'm pickin' up that pistol?"

"Yer got my word. I'll let yer get set to draw."

Waldrup thought for a long agonizing minute and then said, "I don't trust you, Charlie. I ain't gonna fight you, and, like I said, I ain't armed." He opened his coat flaps and spread them wide so everyone could see he was not carrying a gun. Then he turned his back on Dalton and started back into the saloon.

Dalton shook with rage and screamed, "Yer cheated me outta five hunnert in Dodge and got away with it cuz a yer pal Luke Short. Yer ain't gettin' away with it this time!"

Dalton drew his pistol. Jake threw his left leg over Jasper's neck and slid off the saddle. Dalton's Colt forty-five thundered and shot a red-orange flame a foot long out the muzzle. The bullet hit Waldrup in the back high on the right side. Jake still had his bullwhip in his hand, and he uncoiled it behind him as he pushed people out of his way. Waldrup was thrown to the boardwalk by the impact. The doves screamed.

Dalton lowered the pistol down from

where the recoil had thrown it up. He took steady aim at Waldrup and had started to cock the hammer when Jake's whip wrapped around the pistol. Jake jerked the lash hard and ripped the gun from Dalton's hand. Dalton stared at his hand in disbelief, then looked over at Jake and started to charge him. Jake's lash came again and slashed Dalton's face. Dalton screamed and clutched his face with both hands. Blood immediately showed between his fingers. He bellowed an ungodly roar and charged Jake. Jake quickly circled to his left and sent the lash around Dalton's ankles, and that tripped him hard. He landed in the street on his belly, and the air went out of him in a loud whoosh. And then Jake went to work. He lashed his head, his back, his arms, and his neck over and over again and again. He was breathing hard, and the doves were cheering, calling out, encouraging Jake. Dalton's green shirt was torn to shreds. Bloody slashes started to show through his shredded union suit. His head and neck were a bloody mess.

"Rip him open, Jake," Gracie and her girlfriends screamed amid their yells of delight. "Spill the son of a bitch's guts out on the street. Whip hell outta him."

Jake's eyes were glazed over as he put the

whip to Dalton, who was writhing in the street and trying to crawl to where his gun was in the dirt. "The fear of the Lord is to hate evil. You have no fear of the Lord because you are evil. You are a bad man. And this is what you get," Jake grunted out as he kept lashing Dalton, who was moving less. When he stopped moving, Jake let up and stopped whipping him. Breathing heavily, Jake said, "Yer lucky yer ain't dead. Only cuz I got a conscience, yer still alive."

Then one of the town's deputy marshals, Riley Crane, came running up. "What's going on here?" the deputy demanded in a loud voice.

"Charlie Dalton shot Wade Waldrup in the back, and Waldrup didn't even have a gun," Gracie called out, and everyone in the crowd voiced their agreement.

"And who are you?" he said to Jake.

Before Jake or anyone could answer, Wes, sitting astride Noble and holding Jasper's rein, said, "Why this here is Rawhide Jake Brighton. You ain't never heard a him? He single handedly stopped Dalton from puttin' another bullet in Waldrup. And if the first bullet ain't kilt him, the second sure would have." Again, the crowd voiced their agreement. Jake ducked his head to hide the smile on his face he couldn't suppress. Raw-hide?

"Why's he so tore up?" the deputy asked, looking toward Dalton sprawled on his belly, moaning.

"Because he was tryin' to git to his gun and start shootin' agin at Waldrup and Rawhide," Gracie announced from the boardwalk. "Rawhide was stoppin' him from doing that. Who knows? That crazy bastard Charlie Dalton might a started shootin' at us. Rawhide might a saved our lives."

"That's right, Riley. I seen it all. It happened just like Gracie said," Wes said matter-of-factly while still sitting Noble.

"You seen it, Wes? Look like he stopped a attempted murder to you?"

"Sure did."

"All right. Take your word for it since yer a stock detective and all. Charlie Dalton, yer under arrest for attempted murder. Now git on yer feet."

Dalton moaned and tried to protest, but his face was so swollen he couldn't speak. He shakily got up on his feet, and Deputy Riley pulled him along by the arm down to the jail. Jake stepped over to Gracie, came real close to her, and said, "Thanks, Gracie."

She gave him a long coy stare and then said, "Just the truth is all. Nothin' special."

349

And then she showed him just the right amount of white between her red lips as she smiled seductively and sashayed back into the saloon. The rest of the crowd headed that way, too. Someone had already helped Wade up to get him to the doctor. Wes had gone into the saloon with the crowd, and, when he got tired of waiting for Jake, he came out to find him gone. Noble was gone, too. He figured they were all in the stable. He figured right. Jake had both boys unsaddled and was getting their feed up when Wes came in.

"Wal, that's mighty kind a yer, Rawhide."

"You keep usin' that handle for me, it's gonna stick."

"Already has. Wait and see."

"Did Waldrup have a derringer in his vest?"

"Nope. Alex told me that Waldrup gave him the derringer before he went out through the doors."

"So, he really was unarmed."

"Wal, yeah. That's why you whipped hell outta Dalton, ain't it? Cuz he shot an unarmed man."

"Yeah. I just wanted to make sure, because he would have a derringer bein' a gambler and all. When Dalton shot him, in the back no less, I just saw red and went after him. I still had the whip in my hand from pushin' those cows, and so it was the handiest weapon. I can't abide innocent or unarmed people gettin' hurt by bad men. Can't abide bullying neither. And now, I'm gonna be Rawhide Jake thanks to that."

"Yer could do worse. Wal, speakin' a those critters it's gonna take a whole day tomorrow to push them back up to the TL. So I'm turnin' in."

"Me, too."

The detectives got back to Seymour Friday, just in time for supper. They were dead tired from the work of the day, so they both turned in early. Next day, they did their laundry and went to the barber shop. They got all trimmed up and soaked a bit in the bath and then washed up.

As they walked back to the Madison, Jake said with a grin, "You look like quite the gentleman once you are relieved of all that hair."

"Why thank ye, Mister Brighton. And I must say yer are becomin' quite the savvy cowboy." Wes returned the grin.

"Why thank ye, Mister Wilson." They backslapped each other and chuckled at their silliness.

That night after supper they went to the

351

Brazos. It was Saturday night. The line at the bar was tight but not shoulder to shoulder. Men and a few women were sitting at the dining tables, and three poker games were going on over at the other side of the room. Lanterns were lit on all the posts, tobacco smoke was thick, the sound of clinking glasses and bottles combined with loud talk and laughs to fill the place. The piano music played almost as if in the background. The doves were working the bar and the tables but stayed away from the dining area, where there were what Jake assumed to be more "respectable" ladies. Jake and Wes came in and moved up to the bar between two men who smiled graciously and made room for them.

"Hey, Alex," Wes said loudly to Alex, who was eight feet down the bar. Alex looked up. "Yer got any vodka?" Alex frowned and came toward them.

"What's that? Never heard of it," he said.

"It's Swedish," Wes said.

"This look like Sweden to you? Whatever it is, I ain't got it."

"It looks like white lightn' but is a lot smoother."

"White lightn' I got."

"Nah. Give us two whiskies."

In the mirror, Jake saw Dalton come into

the saloon and, like the people closest to the entrance, heard the loud slam of the doors against the jambs as he kicked them open. Glass shattered and fell to the floor. At the sound of the crash, the place quieted down a lot. Jake slipped his right hand over to the left between his body and the bar. He drew his pistol and held it concealed in front of him. Dalton had his pistol drawn and pointed at the floor. He was naked from the waist up except for a black hat pushed back on his head. He had his gun belt cinched tight around his waist to hold up his britches. His face was swollen bright red, and his back was a crisscross of angry blue and red welts mixed in with deep gashes that seeped a pink fluid. Slowly, he jingled step by step toward the bar, and as more people became aware of what was happening it got even quieter.

Jake hid his face under his hat but not so much as to be unable to keenly watch the mirror. He listened to Dalton's spurs and counted each jingle, adding them up mentally so he could gauge the distance between the two of them. The mirror could be distorted, but he used both sight and sound to his advantage.

Then Dalton loudly called out, "Where's that yella-belly son of a whore, the so-called

Rawhide Jake Brighton? I aim to kill him here and now. Step up, yer filthy Bible-preaching son of a bitch." The piano music stopped. A hush came over the room. He boomed a fiery shot at the floor from his forty-five that flashed red-orange and reverberated everywhere. Women screamed. Men yelled as they all dove under tables or crawled to the walls. They grunted and groaned as they scuffled across the floor sounding like walruses shuffling off the beach to the water. Men and the doves at the bar pushed to the ends of the bar and separated themselves from Wes and Jake like they were fleeing a train coming straight at them.

Dalton spied Jake, cocked and raised his smoking pistol, but Jake had already spun around to face him. He crouched low, focused entirely on his target, pointed his double-action revolver, and blasted two shots in one second's time even as a forty-five round screamed past his left ear and spent itself on the front edge of the bar. Blood sprayed in a five-foot, short-lived geyser from Dalton's chest before he hit the floor, dead from two forty-four caliber slugs entering his body within an inch of each other. The first severed his aortic artery, and the second exploded his heart. Dalton landed on his back, and his dead head bounced off the floor twice. Women screamed a crescendo of fear.

Smoke curled lazily from the muzzle of Jake's pistol, which he still had pointed at Dalton, when another cowboy ran in with his pistol drawn. He started to aim at Jake, and Wes's forty-five roared. The big slug hit the man in the right shoulder. He was slammed on his back and then rolled to his left when he hit the floor. He clutched his shoulder with his left hand as blood seeped through his fingers and pooled with Dalton's blood on the floor.

Wes walked over to him real casual-like, picked up the cowboy's gun off the floor, and stuffed it in his waistband. He leaned over him with his eyes blazing and said through clenched teeth in a low, calm voice, "Look at me."

The cowboy rolled over on his back and moaned, "Yer shot me."

Wes pressed the muzzle of his forty-five against the cowboy's forehead and said, "That's right, cowboy, and yer should thank yer lucky stars I didn't kill yer. I took careful aim at yer shoulder. What's yer name?"

"Whitey."

"Whitey what?"

"Whitey kiss my ass." He glared at Wes.

"Whitey Morgan," Alex announced from behind the bar.

"Wal, Whitey Morgan. I know yer name and yer face. Yer ever bother me or my friend agin and I'll blow a hole as big as Texas through yer. Yer see how the cat jumps?"

"Yeah. I need a doctor."

Wes holstered his pistol and pulled the man up by his shirtfront and threw him out the door, where he flopped on the porch, got up, and ran down the street.

"He needs help," another cowboy said. "What if he passes out and bleeds to death?"

Wes turned on him, fastened his still hot eyes on the feller, and said, "Yer run and help him then." The cowboy retreated back into the crowd. Then Wes drew his pistol and turned a slow circle to his left, holding his revolver and moving it as if it were a magic wand. He waved it through the gun smoke that, combined with the tobacco smoke, hung like a dense fog in the room. "Reckon there ain't gonna be no more gunplay here tonight," he snarled at the crowd. "Now git on back to what y'all were doin' before that yack came in here."

Three of the more "respectable" ladies held hankies over their noses and mouths as they bustled out the front doors along with their male escorts. Alex hollered, "Pinky! Start tickling that ivory. All right folks, all right. Let's all relax and try to enjoy ourselves. Ain't like we ain't seen it before."

Wes stepped over to where Jake was leaning with his back against the bar. Jake pulled a cartridge from his belt and loaded it into the cylinder of his pistol and then another. He shoved the forty-four back in its holster and turned to face the bar and the mirror. He grasped his whiskey and downed it.

Wes pulled in beside Jake, threw one boot up on the brass rail, and leaned on his elbow with his side to the bar. "Yer want another?" he said as he kept an eye on the crowd in the saloon. There could be other Dalton sidekicks in there.

Jake held his hands in front of him over the bar. They were steady as a brick, but inside he felt shaky. "Sure. You buyin'?"

Wes glanced sideways at Jake and chuckled. "Didn't I just save yer life?"

"What'd you say? My ears are all plugged from the gunshots."

"Yeah. Me, too. I said, didn't I just save your life?" Wes said louder but still smiled big.

"I had a bead on him. Lucky for you I didn't accidently shoot you in the back when you stepped in front of me." He finally cracked a smile at Wes and said, "Oh, all right. I'll buy *you* a drink." He motioned to Alex, who came with a bottle half full.

Alex said, "Keep the bottle on the house. Looks like you single-handily caused a spike in business." He glanced around the saloon, hinting that they should, too. "Plus, you got rid of some vermin I don't mind seein' gone. Course, now I got a big mess to clean up. Might even have to replace the floorboards. Guess it's worth it."

He laughed and gave Jake a light punch in the shoulder. "Here comes the marshal. Better late than never." Just as he said it, the marshal and both his deputies rushed in through the wrecked front doors, holding their pistols at the ready in their hands. Their eyes immediately went to the man lying on the floor in a big pool of blood.

"What the hell?" one of the deputies exclaimed loudly. The marshal gave him an irritable look. "It's Charlie Dalton, boss."

"I can see that, James. I ain't blind yet," the marshal said.

"He must a broke out a jail and come here."

"I can see that, too, James. I still got my wits."

"Alex," the marshal called to the bartender. "What happened this time?"

"Pretty simple. Dalton busted in here, broke the winders in my doors. City gonna pay for that?"

The marshal rolled his eyes and said, "Check with the mayor on that. What happened next?"

"He announced he was gonna kill Rawhide and pointed his pistol at him. Rawhide shot him dead just as he fired. Whitey Morgan tried to get in on it, but Wes shot him and chased him outta here. That's about the big and small of it."

"So, Whitey's probably the one who broke out Dalton. You say Morgan had a hole in him?"

"Yeah, said he was headed for the doctor."

"All right. James, you stay here and start taking names. Nobody leaves. Nobody."

"I ain't got no paper or pencil."

The marshal sighed and said, "Alex, would you per chance have paper and pencil you can give to James?"

Alex bent over behind the bar and came up with the goods. "Here you go, James."

"All right. Come on Riley. I gotta check on Barry. See if he's alive. You start looking for Whitey. We gotta find him and see what we gotta do with him," the marshal exclaimed. "James, you stay here. Don't let nobody leave. Nobody! We'll be back directly."

James tipped his hat. They ran out the door. He turned to the crowd and puffed out his chest. His big tin badge, highly polished, caught the light and shined brightly. "All right, y'all. I'm a gonna sit down at this table here by the door. Y'all line up single file and give me yer names, and then go back to what you was doin'. But don't nobody try and fly the coop," he said, almost growling and looking dead serious. He pulled his pistol and put it on the table with a thud. Wes and several other people snickered so that James could hear it, but he pretended he didn't.

"Might as well stay here. Marshal'll be comin' back once he finds that Whitey feller. Probably takin' names for the JP's inquest and stuff," Wes said as they stood in the line of people who were all in a hubbub, drinking, smoking, yacking. Several men came up to Jake and congratulated him on his shooting.

"Yeah. That was some damn fine shootin'. Yer a pistolero fer sure." Wes slapped Jake on the back. "Hell, I was aimin' fer that feller's heart and hit him in the shoulder, ha ha!" Jake didn't believe him.

Then Wes turned more serious. "A

course," he said quietly, followed by a pause, "now yer gonna have a reputation that'll follow yer all over northwest Texas. After the inquest tomorrow, it'll be on the wire and every newspaper from Abilene to Henrietta to Fort Worth'll pick it up."

"Yeah. That bothers me. I want to stay in the background. Undercover."

"Shoulda thought a that afore yer tore old Dalton to shreds with that whip."

"I know. But I just can't abide bad men. Something comes over me."

"Uh-huh. I can ride that horse. But, maybe this might make it easier to get with the outlaw gangs?"

"Maybe. I'll have to see how I play it."

Their turn came to sign in with James. "Wes, I know yer. What's yer name?" James asked Jake.

"His name is Rawhide Jake Brighton, and yer can write it down just like that," Wes said flatly.

Jake kind of liked the sound of that, but he was torn. How to play it? How to play it? "You said a justice of the peace runs the inquest?" Jake queried.

"Yeah."

"Thought they only did small crimes and marriages and like that."

"Not here in Texas. They's almost as

powerful as the circuit judge. The JP's ride drag, and the circuit judges ride point. So, ain't no circuit judge gonna investigate deaths. That's the JP's job. Our feller here in Baylor County is Joseph P. Anderson, and he is one mean sum-buck. He ain't gonna be at all happy to see me in front of his bench."

Just as James was finished taking names, the marshal came in. At the same time, the undertaker pulled up out front in a buckboard. He set the brake and sat rigid in the seat looking like a stovepipe in his black suit and black top hat. Jake saw him through the busted doors in the light of the porch lanterns and thought it was strange to have a bona fide undertaker in a small town like Seymour. But then the town was growing, what with the railroad comin' and all. And it was a pretty rough town being right in the middle of cowboy country with the Western Trail right next door. Probably going to get rougher, too, as it grew.

"Yer find him?" James asked loudly. "How's Barry? What'd yer do with Whitey?"

"Would you mind, James? One question at a time. Yes. We found him and took him to the doc. Riley's guardin' him. Barry's fine. They didn't hurt the old feller. Just scared hell out of him. Whitey held him at gunpoint and took the keys to open the cell. Let me see what you have there." James handed him his sheet of paper. "What do these two check marks mean?"

"They's the two shooters."

The marshal looked up at Wes and said, "All right. Wes, you stand over here, and your partner — Rawhide? — you stand with him. Alex, you come over here, too. All right. Who's the next two persons that were closest to the gun battle and saw everything that happened, beginning to end."

A man raised his hand. "All right, Clifford Brown." He put an *X* by Brown's name and said, "One more." Nobody answered. Apparently, they knew what was coming and didn't want to get roped into an inquest. "You might as well step forward because if you don't, old Judge Anderson will issue a subpoena, and I'll have to come and get you anyway. All right. There we go. Gracie Banan." He put an *X* by her name.

Jake smiled at Gracie. She batted her eyes and smiled back.

"All right now. Alex, which one of these cowboys is the killer? Or first, just a minute." He took Wes and Jake each by the arm and ushered them away from the crowd. Then he whispered, "Is Rawhide here a detective, too?"

"He sure is," Wes said proudly.

"Okay. Just wanted to be sure of that. It'll be in my report to the judge."

"Thanks, Benjamin," Wes said, and Jake nodded his head in agreement.

They stepped back to where they were, and the marshal said, "Alex. You were sayin'."

"Well, uh, I reckon that'd be Rawhide." Alex plainly did not want to answer but did when the marshal glowered at him with a look that meant he better cooperate. "All right. Wes, you shot Whitey, is that right?"

"That is currect, Benjamin." The marshal gave Wes a threatening side look like a mother about to scold her child. "Oh, and here is his pistol. I believe he dropped it. Don't know how that coulda happened, but I got suspicions." He handed the revolver to the marshal butt first. The marshal made a low growl and gave Wes another hard look as he took the pistol from him.

"Alex," he said. "Now tell me again exactly what happened in detail. Don't leave anything out." Alex went through the whole scene in extreme and melodramatic detail. Marshal Coregan was busy taking notes and didn't notice. All the others were dancing from one foot to the other, clearing their throats, coughing, licking their lips, looking anxiously at the bar. Alex, the thespian, saw them and frowned a *no* at them without missing a note in his story. There would be no drinks served unless he served them. It took him ten minutes to narrate the event.

"Marshal," someone called out, "I gotta use the privy." There were snickers and giggles all around that were immediately hushed under the fierce glare of Marshal Coregan.

"James," he said and motioned with his head for James to take the feller to the outhouse. "All right now. You all heard Alex relate the event as it happened. You two agree with it?" he said to Jake and Wes.

"Yes, I do," Wes said.

"Rawhide?"

"Yes."

"Gracie? Clifford? You both agree?" They nodded their heads *yes.* "I need to hear you say so." They answered. "All right. Anybody disagree? See it differently?"

Wes stared down the cowboy who wanted to help Whitey when Wes threw him out of the saloon. Nobody spoke up.

"All right then. You five be at the court-house nine o'clock sharp Monday mornin', and the rest of you don't leave town until after the judge's decision is announced. That is all. You can go about your business."

"Yer want another?" Wes said to Jake.

"Nah. I'm gonna brush out Jasper and hit the hay. That ain't the first man I ever shot. I was infantry in the war, yer know. And I killed a feller in Manhattan that was gonna kill me. So's that's the second one I ever shot and watched die. There was a feller in prison, but he broke his neck." He looked at Wes, searching for he didn't know what.

"It won't be the last if yer stay in this detective business. I guarantee it."

"How many men yer kilt up close?"

"Three. And another three far off with a rifle. It ain't never easy. But I ain't losin' any sleep over it. Yer'll get over it. I kin tell yer got true grit."

"Yeah. Don't suppose there is a priest anywhere around here." Jake hung his head and stared at the bar.

Wes slapped his back, grinned big, and said, "I think there is one in Henrietta, but that's fifty miles north."

"In that case, I'll have another." They laughed deep and long as Wes poured the drinks from the bottle.

The undertaker wrapped the body in a white sheet and then started to drag it by the arms when a couple of men hurried over to help him carry it out.

■ ■ ■ ■

Monday morning as Wes and Rawhide walked up the courthouse steps Wes said, "I don't take much to these inquests, 'specially with Anderson. He don't like me much."

"How come?"

"Don't know. Can't figure it out. I ain't a gonna say anything unless someone asks me somethin'. Yer gonna kinda be on yer own."

"That's fine. I been in court a lot. Ain't no never mind."

They took their seats, stood when the judge entered, and watched as he listened to the testimony. It took about thirty minutes, and Judge Anderson said, "I've read the marshal's report, listened to the testimony, and inspected the corpse at the undertaker's. It all appears to be in agreement. My decision is death by gunshot in the commission of the crime of attempted murder. In other words, self-defense by Mister Brighton. But I am curious. The deceased was clearly motivated by revenge. I understand there was an altercation between Misters Brighton and Dalton just a few days prior to the subject incident wherein Mister Dalton suffered a severe scourging at the hands of Mister Brighton, which surely must have been the cause for Mister Dalton's desire to seek revenge."

"Here we go," Wes whispered to himself. "He's gonna turn it all around on Jake just like he did on me."

"Don't you think so, too, Mister Brighton? I mean, such a severe beating. Was it really appropriate under the circumstances?"

Rawhide rose from his chair and said, "Your honor," and he smiled politely. He could easily see the trap the judge was attempting to set to get him to admit to the use of excessive force as an association detective and then arrest him for it. "As to Mister Dalton's motivation to attempt to take my life, I have no knowledge as to why he would do that, and we plainly cannot ask him given his current state of mind or shall we say no mind." There were brief chuckles in the gallery, very brief as Judge Anderson browbeat the chucklers into silence. "As to my actions on the evening of February 28, last, I can only say that I took what action I felt was necessary under the circumstances to prevent Mister Dalton from retrievin' his pistol since he had already just shot Mister Wade Waldrup in the back in the midst of a crowd of people. Mister Dalton seemed rather determined to reacquire his pistol and start shootin' again. I simply prevented him from doin' just that until the deputy arrived on the scene. And, I might add, there are many witnesses who have and will testify to the accuracy of my statement."

"But such a scourging, Mister Rawhide is it? Brighton. Could you not have subdued him in fisticuffs or clubbed him with your own pistol?"

"There is a higher risk in clubbin' either with fists or pistol. The victim is more apt to die from such wounds whereas a whippin' merely lacerates the skin. I am sure your honor will recall the case in Independence, Missourah, just last year wherein a suspect was pistol whipped by a town marshal and died. The marshal was charged with murder, tried, and acquitted. But the point still stands. The victim died from the clubbin' even though the marshal was attemptin' to avoid killin' him."

"I see. Do you have any experience at the bar, Mister Brighton?"

"Only as a witness, your honor." Again Rawhide smiled his affable smile.

"Very well. My decision stands."

Tuesday morning after breakfast at the table, Wes said, "Wal, we better get provisioned and geared up. Gonna be out for a week on regular patrol startin' tomorrow."

"What's that mean?"

"That means we're gonna be ridin' the range and searchin' for trouble. When we find it, we'll squish it like a bug." He grinned.

"Huh?"

"Don't you know what 'on patrol' means?" Wes frowned and threw his hand up. "Like a marshal walkin' the town streets lookin' for law breakers and jailin' 'em to keep the peace. Wal, we're gonna be lookin' for law breakers, too. Only they's gonna be rustlers. So we're gonna be out there jest lookin' for 'em. Yer savvy?"

"Yeah. I comprende."

"Thas what most a the job is anyway. 'Cept for you undercover detectives," Wes snickered.

"Well, let's get to it. What do yer have in mind?"

"We git a pack horse from Quincy and load it with all the gear and provisions we need for a week. Keep the horses light in case we have to chase down some rustlers. Usually I roam from bunkhouse to bunkhouse, but I don't want anyone to know we're out on the range. That's why we need the supplies to what-a-they-call-it?"

"Provide for ourselves."

"Yeah that. I'm bringin' a tent. We'll head southwest over to Long X range. I want yer to see the Herefords the Reynolds brothers are running out there. Their drives pass up Dodge and go as fer north as Canada. They go west to Utah and Nevada, too. They's smart that a way. Get better prices." He picked a piece of bacon out of his teeth with a toothpick and stuck the pick back in the side of his mouth. "Then we'll swing east to the river and follow it back to Seymour. That'll cover a lot a range. How's that sound?"

"Dandy. When do we get started?"

"Ride out tomorrow."

Wednesday morning at sunup they rode out toward the crossing south of town. The temperature was well above freezing, and the day was warming fast as the risen sun began its climb out of its rosy dawn color to its noontime apex. The air was still. It smelled like fresh spring was coming. But, thankfully, the insects were not yet on their ravenous foraging missions. A coyote ran across their path about fifty yards to the front, and a roadrunner ran off their right front quarter with a snake dangling from its beak. The boys snorted, and the detectives nudged them into a trot.

They had crossed to the other side of the Brazos as the day brightened, and Jake looked out over the rugged red cuts and the golden-brown swells of the land with the crawling green mesquite and scrub. The hue of the grass seemed to be a little more green than it was just a week ago. He looked closely at the ground as they trotted along, and sure enough the blades of the gamma grass were starting ever so slightly to turn green. That made him smile in appreciation of the coming spring.

By the early afternoon of the second day, they were on Long X range and came across the first of the Herefords they would see. They were coming up over a rise through some mesquite. Below them was a small valley, long and wide, slashed here and there by red ravines. The Herefords were on the downside of the rise, browsing in and out of the mesquite and scrub brush.

They rode over to the bunch of critters and looked them over. "All yearling heifers and steers," Wes said as they sat the boys. "Look to be in pretty good shape. They ain't as big as the longhorn, but they got more muscle fat. Supposed to be better. Brings a higher price, I guess. Me? Had me a Hereford steak in Abilene last summer. I like the taste of longhorn steaks more better. Anyway, yer gotta ride around a little and git used to 'em. Probably gonna be more a 'em every year."

"Yup. That the Long X brand?"

"Yep. Pretty simple, eh? Don't know why they use that one. It can be changed real easy, and if a feller is good enough with a running iron he could probably fool a lot a buyers and cattlemen, too."

"But not 'ol Wes Wilson, right?" Jake grinned at Wes.

"Wal, it does take a lot to get past me." He grinned back at Jake and then looked back to the bunch of Herefords.

Movement caught the corner of Jake's eye, and he looked out over the valley. "Ho. What's that a comin'?" he said.

Wes followed his line of sight and saw way down the valley a bunch of cows with two cowboys pushing them. They were heading north. "Let's get outta sight in the brush here," Wes said hurriedly. They jumped out of their saddles and walked the boys back under a mesquite tree. Wes dug his glass out of his saddlebag, and Jake followed his lead. They held their spyglasses on a tree limb to steady them and sighted through. "I'll be lassoed, thrown down, and branded!" Wes exclaimed. "I think one a 'em is that Jonesboro feller from the Circle

Bar B. What color a shirt was he wearing when we ran into him at the fence?"

Jake sighted in on him and said, "A maroon paisley just like this feller. That's him."

"They's longhorn and Herefords in the bunch. Can't see the brand this far away. Looks like 'bout a hunnert head. Let's think this out a minute."

"What's he doin' on Long X range?" Jake said.

"Wal, that's the first question. The Circle Bar B and the Long X border each other, but if he is here legit, what's he doin' this far northwest? That's the second question. The Long X headquarters is far to the southeast a here. I cain't think of why a Circle Bar B hand would be runnin' a bunch a cows this far north unless they are tradin' or sellin' to the L Bar or sumthin' like that."

"Or rustlin'."

"Or rustlin'. So let's git the answers. We can follow this line a mesquite to the bottom and wait by that clump down there until they come by and then jump 'em. Liable to be some gunplay."

They got into position, and Wes put the glass on the bunch of cows. "All yearlings," he said quietly and contemplatively. "I see Circle Bar B and Long X brands. That pretty much cinches it. Ain't no logical reason to be movin' both brands at the same time."

"Unless yer rustlin' 'em," Jake whispered.

" 'Xactly. Here they come. Figure they's 'bout fifty yards out. Horses won't see us or smell us. Let our boys nibble some grass if they can find it. Let's get ready. I want to come in behind 'em. Surprise 'em. So let's let 'em pass by first."

The two cowboys and the bunch of cows moved through in front of them. The dirt was just dry enough to raise a little dust. Neither Jonesboro nor his partner detected anything of Wes and Jake. They were too busy flopping their loops and whistling and calling out to the little herd as they kept them bunched up and moving forward. Wes let them go well past him and Jake so that when they came out of the brush, they could gallop the boys to the rear of the bunch without being caught in the rustlers' peripheral vision. And then Wes said, "Let's go." In a short few minutes they were trailing the herd about fifty yards behind and closing fast.

Wes rode right up behind Jonesboro and said in a loud voice, "Hey, Jonesboro! What're yer doin'?"

Jonesboro jumped in his saddle and spun

around to see who or what was behind him. Then he spurred and jerked his horse around in a hundred-eighty-degree spin and stopped to face Wes, who immediately reined in Noble to a stop. About five feet separated the two horses. Jonesboro pulled his hat down to shade his eyes from the sun while Jake eased Jasper up next to Noble. The other cowboy started over toward them and stopped about ten yards away from them.

"What's it look like I'm doin'. I'm pushin' some cows. That's my job. I'm a cowboy, jackass. Not a law dog like you," Jonesboro growled through clenched teeth, and a tic started up in his right cheek.

"Wal, cowboy, where yer pushin' the cows to and what fer?" Wes said, just as pleasing as a body could.

"Boss sold 'em to the L Bar. I'm takin' 'em up there to deliver and collect the money."

The other cowboy was easing in closer. Jake kept an eye on him with his peripheral vision, slipped his right hand under his coat, eased his pistol out of the holster, cocked the hammer, and held the gun out of sight under his unbuttoned coat.

"Olsson must trust yer an awful lot to carry cash fer him."

"Yep. He does," Jonesboro said with a wicked grin.

"He trust yer to pick up Long X cattle along the way?"

"What'er yer talkin' 'bout?"

"I'm talkin' yer a stinkin' liar, and yer a rustlin' right here, right now." Wes drew his pistol, pointed it at Jonesboro, and said, "Now throw up yer hands. Yer under arrest."

Jonesboro dug in his spurs and gave his horse two savage kicks. The horse lunged forward, and Noble reared, spun to the right to get away from the lunging horse, and let out a loud, wailing neigh. Wes got a shot off but missed, and Noble's spin took Wes's gun hand out of play.

Jasper flattened his ears, bared his teeth, and with the hair of his back standing straight up, charged. Jonesboro, who was left-handed, fired a shot at Wes and missed. The impact of Jasper's charge into his horse made Jonesboro's second shot fly off into the wild blue yonder. Jake stood in his stirrups, laid out over Jasper's neck, and gritted his teeth. With his eyes bulging in anger, he focused his complete attention, ignoring all gunshots, and pointed his pistol around Jonesboro's horse's head. A split second later Jonesboro's chest was full of forty-four caliber lead from Jake's blazing pistol. He blasted three shots at him, and they all hit in the middle of his chest, jerking his body in rapid succession. He flew backwards off the saddle, did a somersault off his horse's rump, and landed in the dirt on his head. His neck broke, but it didn't matter. He was dead before he fell off the horse.

The other feller fired a shot. It plowed into the dirt about twenty yards past everybody. He spun his horse around and fled at a panicked gallop up the other side of the draw, firing his pistol behind him as he went. Jake pulled his Winchester from the scabbard and jumped off Jasper, who was pushing Jonesboro's horse past the bunch of cows. It was a battle that Jasper was winning. Jake ran five yards to get away from the swirling dust rising from the whirling mass of horseflesh, kicking hooves, and froth flying from their mouths. He sat on the ground, bent his knees up, braced his elbows against the inside of his knees, and pointed the Winchester he held in his hands. He steadied the rifle, took a leading aim at the other cowboy about one hundred-fifty yards out, squeezed off a round, and immediately levered another round into the breech while still holding a bead on the cowboy, who fell off his horse to the right. His boot got stuck in the stirrup, and his horse drug him another forty yards before he stopped. The cowboy didn't move. Meanwhile, the cattle scattered in a panic from the noise of the gunshots, and Jasper was chasing Jonesboro's horse up the valley. Wes had backed Noble away from the fracas and was sitting his saddle, watching the show. When it was all over, he started clapping his hands.

Jake got up and started walking toward Wes. "What are you doin'?" he yelled with a hint of anger.

"Why I am applaudin' a hero. Yer saved my life and kilt two bad hombres all by yerself. I didn't have to even lift a finger, ha ha. Usually, I'd a chased that other feller down an' roped him. Tie him up and take him in alive. But he was shootin' at us, and I wanted to see how good yer shootin' is. Not too bad." Wes grinned.

Jake couldn't help it. He grinned and waved his hand dismissively at Wes. "You think yer could lift a finger and catch my horse for me."

"Oh, yer mean the other hero, Jasper?"

"Yeah. He was, wasn't he?"

It took them a full hour to catch the horses, throw the bodies over them, cinch them down, round up the cattle, and get them bunched up and headed south. While they were tying the bodies to the saddles of the outlaw's horses, Jake said over the back of the horse he was working on, "So let's see. That's about a hundred and ten dollars, right? Dollar a head and five dollars per rustler. Split two ways. Or maybe I should get the whole ten bucks for the rustlers since I am the one who kilt them." He said the last with exaggerated bravado.

"Fine by me if yer think it's fair."

"Ha ha. Just joshin' yer, detective. We are pards fifty-fifty. But we are even now. Yer saved my life at the Brazos, and I saved yer's here. Agreed?"

"Yer startin' to talk more like a cowboy now and less the civilizee. A song to my ear, ha ha. Yeah. We're even up. As long as we keep up this detectivein,' we're gonna be scorin' back and forth." He smiled at Jake and squinted the sun out of his eyes. "I been at this six years now, and it don't seem to be gettin' any better. Maybe worse. It's a sad thing to take a man's life no matter how bad he is or how much he deserves it. Oh, I ain't goin' soft. I'm just sayin' it's too damn bad it has to happen. I always feel a little guilty after. Not fer long though," he said as he went under the belly of the Jonesboro horse, came out the other side, and tied the dead rustler's hands and boots together.

"How 'bout yer?"

Jake stopped what he was doing and looked out over the range. "Well, so far I kin say no, except for Brinkman. He was the first shootin' close up like I told yer. The feller from Manhattan — I felt a little pang for that one. But I ain't sorry. Not for the one in prison neither. He was gonna bugger me, and I wasn't havin' any a that. And Dalton, well he was just a killer that needed killin'. So I don't feel sorry for them, and I don't feel sorry for these two fellers. They were tryin' to kill us. I hear what yer saying. I just can't quite git there. Damnation. Yer know I been at this stock detectivein' for only 'bout three weeks, and I already killed three men!" Jake said with a genuine astonished look at Wes.

"Wal, yer in northwest Texas, pard. Cowboys, rustlers, and outlaws everywhere. But, yer know, it mighta been different here if old gentle Noble hadn't shied from that wild-ass horse a Jonesboro's. I had the draw on him. He coulda surrendered and gone quietly, or I coulda shot him. That way yer woulda had only one killin' instead a two. But, thanks to ol' Jasper and yer, I'm standin' here flappin' my jaw. We better git goin'."

They had about three hours before sundown, so they headed right out. They left a lot of slack in the lead ropes they had tied to the horses loaded with the bodies so they could maneuver better around the herd and keep them bunched up and moving while still leading the horses with the bodies draped over them and their own pack horse. They were too busy driving the cattle, one of them each on opposite sides of the little herd, so there was no opportunity for more conversation, just shouts here and there to work the cattle.

Two hours had gone by when they saw four mounted riders and a pack horse coming up over a ridge about a half mile out through a gap in a line of mesquite. They kept coming right at them, and, at about a quarter mile, Wes pulled his glass from his saddlebag and focused in on them. "Looks like Bill Smith and Shorty and two other cowboys from the Circle Bar B. Probably comin' for these cows. When they git in rifle range, we got to raise our hands and hold 'em high cuz they might think we're the rustlers."

"Howdy, Bill. Shorty," Wes said as he held his hands high up. They were pointing their rifles at Wes and Jake. When Wes greeted them, they lowered their weapons.

"What the hell's goin' on?" Bill, the cow

boss, demanded.

"Wal, Bill. We're bringin' back to yer the cows yer hand Jonesboro stole from yer, and his body, too."

Bill looked past them and surveyed the scene. "Caught 'em, huh?" he said. "Guess yer beat us to it. Shorty here figured we got rustled a hundred head. One thing ol' Shorty can do is count cattle without countin' em. He know'd we was short, and sure enough we was. We took out after 'em two days ago. Been trailin' 'em ever since. When'd yer meet up with 'em?"

"Little after noon today."

"Damn. We was close then. Yer say Jonesboro was one of 'em. Had him workin' on the fence. He must a sneaked off. Well, guess he met his maker now. Yer gonna turn those critters over to us?"

"Yup, 'cept they's got Long X mixed in with 'em. We'll have to cut 'em out and take 'em to the Long X. Figger like Shorty says yer got a hunnert head a Circle Bar B and twenty Long X 'cordin' to my count."

"We got 'bout a hour before sundown. There's a small box canyon with a creek runnin' out a it jest a leetle ways back. We can bed 'em down there and make camp. Y'all can set out in the mornin' with the Long X critters if yer want."

"That'll be fine," Wes said. "And we'll let yer have yer hands, too, sech as they be, ha ha."

"All right. We'll take the bodies and plant 'em back at the ranch fer yer. Who's yer pard, Wes?"

"Why this here is Rawhide Jake Brighton. Jake, meet Bill Smith."

They tipped hats, and Smith said, "He a detective?"

"Sure is. One a the best. He singlehandedly kilt yer two hands there. I just sat my horse and watched as they tried to kill us and he kilt them."

One of the cowboys whistled, and the other said a subdued, "Wooee."

"Pleasure havin' yer out here on the range," Smith said, and Shorty nodded his agreement.

"Pleasure's mine," Jake said and tapped his hat. "Think we oughta git these critters a movin'?"

"Shore enuff. Let's go, boys." Smith and Wes took point, each with a pack horse, Jake and Shorty pulled along the sides to ride swing, and the two cowboys pulled in behind to ride drag. They got the herd moving.

In the morning, dark clouds were moving

in from the west, and it was a little breezy. Wes handed Bill a receipt book and pencil and said, "Here. Don't let it blow away. Make yer mark there fer the cattle and the two rustlers. It's fer the record fer the boss."

Bill took the pad, held it tight in both hands looked it over, and said, "Cain't read, but I kin sign my name. What's it say?"

"It says, a hunnert head a Hereford and two dead rustlers turned over to the under-signed, that's yer, by detectives Wilson and Brighton on March 10, 1883."

"Reckon that's akurat," Smith said, and he signed a wiggly *Bill Smith* at the bottom of the receipt.

"All right, we'll be headin' out. See y'all down the trail," Wes said as he and Jake mounted the boys. They waved their hats, and Jake popped his whip and got the bunch of Long X critters moving. By noon of the next day, they pushed the cattle through the corral gate held open by a hand at the Long X Throckmorton ranch. The headquarters was further south at Ft. Grif-fin, but Wes didn't want to drive the critters down there and then double back the same way to get to Seymour. So he got the receipt signed, and they got on their way back to Seymour.

In the early afternoon of the second day it was cloudy when they trotted into Seymour. "Think it's gonna rain?" Jake said.

"Nah. I told yer winter's over."

"Well, it doesn't have to be just winter to rain," Jake answered as if he were stating the obvious. And at that moment he felt some wet drops on his bare hands. He looked over at Wes and stared. Wes wouldn't look at him. Jake smiled and said nothing more.

After caring for the boys, they drug themselves into the Brazos. Nobody "significant" was in the saloon. Wes had two drinks, Jake had one, and they went home to the Madison. The rain had stopped.

"That weren't much of a rain, were it?" Wes said as they walked along in the damp dirt of the street. "I don't even see any mud." He stared at Jake, who wouldn't look at him, and said nothing.

In the parlor on the little table where Missus Madison left mail for the boarders was a telegram for Wes. It was from Jim Loving. Wes opened it, read it while Jake watched, and said, "Mmm. Jim wants yer up at the Flying XC now and me to the panhandle.

Cowboys from more than a few of the big ranches up there are threatenin' to strike. He's afraid rustlin's gonna git worse. Strike? That means they won't work, right?"

"Yup. Sound like it's urgent."

"Yer mean pronto? Yeah, it does. We better pull out first light tomorrow."

"All right. I'm gonna do my laundry. Clean my gear and shootin' irons," he said smiling, "and get a bath and a steak at the Brazos. How about yer?"

"Yeah. Sounds good to me."

CHAPTER SEVEN
ON THE WAY TO
THE FLYING XC

The stock detectives rode out of Seymour at dawn under a gray sky with just a slight breeze.

"Smells like rain," Wes said.

"Thought yer said winter was over."

"I did. But that's fer snow and freezin' cold. Like I said, it don't just have to be winter to rain."

"I think I said that." Wes turned his head and wouldn't look at Jake, who chuckled a low cluck.

"Just the same, think I'll pull on my slicker," Wes said as he reined in Noble.

"All righty. Yer the range boss. I'll put mine on, too," Jake said, still smiling.

"I ain't no range boss. Yer do as yer like," Wes grumbled as he shrugged into his yellow slicker.

"My, my. Kinda testy this mornin' ain't we, sweetie?" Jake's smile turned to a grin as he buttoned his black slicker. Wes stared at him for a minute and then busted out into a rolling laugh.

"All right. Sorry, dear," Wes said and smiled back at Jake. "How come yer got a black slicker?"

"Soaks up more sun."

"Ain't no sun."

"When there is sun and it's freezing cold. That's when."

"Uh-huh. That ain't gonna be today. Looks like we'll be in rain all day."

They remounted and urged the boys back out on the trail headed north and hadn't gone a mile when the clouds opened up. It was a steady rain going back and forth between light showers and heavy showers all day. The boys hung their heads as they trudged along the muddy trail, and rain water poured off their forelocks and down their blazes to their muzzles, falling off their lips in a steady trickle. Every once in a while, one or the other of them would stick his tongue out and take in a taste. They tried to suck, but it wasn't working. Jake and Wes didn't fare much better as the rain water dripped off the rims of their hats. And, if they got their heads out of position, it slid down their necks under their slicker collars and soaked their bandanas. Fortunately, it was a warm storm, uncomfortable but not miserable. They were already wet from the waist down, so it didn't matter when they had to swim the Wichita River at a place where it was narrow and too deep for the boys to balk when they plunged them in off the bank.

They planned to stop for the night at a line shack of the XC in the southern range. But if it was occupied, they would have to move on and find other shelter, because they did not want Wes, a known detective, to be seen with Jake. The shack had a corral with it that had a covered lean-to at one end so the boys could get under cover, too. A small creek bubbled along behind the corral. Although they weren't needed now, a couple of big mesquite trees were set to each side of the shack to shade it.

When they arrived it was still raining lightly. Jake rode on ahead, and Wes stayed back out of sight under a mesquite tree behind a thicket of scrub brush. From there, he had a clear view of the shack and corral. The light was real low, as the day was almost gone, and that helped conceal Wes as well. There wasn't a light showing anywhere in or around the shack. The plan was for Jake to reconnoiter the shack and corrals and, if all was clear, signal back to Wes. If not, then Wes would move on, and Jake would need to use his natural charm to play the cowhand heading up to the XC for a job.

Jake felt confident he could pass for a regular cowhand. His clothes were not brand new any longer, as they had been washed several times and had a bit of sun bleaching from drying on the clothesline and many days out on the range. The big Stetson he wore showed a little dirty sweat stain around the bottom of the crown. His leather vest showed weather wear, and his boots were scuffed and somewhat faded, as were his spur straps. He was falling naturally into the lingo and had picked up a lot of terms sufficient to get him by. And . . . he could even rope as well as the average cowboy. So, by most accounts he was ready to go to work and approached the shack confidently.

Jake walked Jasper up to the shack and took great care to observe everything there, which was not much. The shack, the corral with the lean-to, and that was it. He could hear the gurgle of a small stream, which he located to the rear of the corral. He circled the place once and then stepped out of the saddle and dropped Jasper's reins in front of and a ways off from the shack door that was closed. There was a hitching rail in front, but he thought it would be more cautious to keep Jasper back. There were no horses anywhere to be seen, but he had a funny feeling someone or something was inside the shack.

There were no windows in the shack, but he watched real careful in case someone stuck a rifle or pistol through a crack between the wall boards. He opened a button on his slicker, stuck his gun hand under the slicker and his coat, and pulled his pistol. He held it under the slicker and stood still watching. Jasper's ears were perked up forward as he stood very still, staring at the shack. Jake had taken one step toward the door when it burst open, and a little critter in human clothing flew out and ran for the corral. Instinctively, Jake pointed his pistol, then held back, grabbed the saddle horn, vaulted in one leap into the saddle, and spurred Jasper for the chase. He twirled his loop over his head and let it fly, catching the critter just before it got to the rails of the corral fence. Wes came rushing up on Noble and let fly his loop to catch the critter at the ankles. The boys held tight, and the critter screamed the most God-awful howl ever heard as he was cinched down good and not able to run. But he did thrash around like a snared weasel to try and loose the ropes.

Jake and Wes ran down the taut ropes, and Wes said, "What the heck we got here?" They were looking at what appeared to be a boy of about ten or twelve years of age with a mop of long brown hair down past his shoulders, dressed in a pair of dirty and torn bib overalls with a brown coat over the top, whose face and hands were nearly black with ground-in dirt. He bared his teeth at them and made low growling sounds like a wolf. Jake reached out to try and calm the boy, but he snapped at him and would have inflicted a severe bite wound had Jake not quickly jerked his hand away from the snapping teeth.

"All right. That's 'bout nuff a that," Wes said angrily. "We're gonna have to hogtie this critter." He grabbed a fistful of the boy's hair and pulled his head back. "Jake, yer got a piggin' string?"

"Yep. I'll git it." He hurried to his saddle and loosed a piggin' string, and ran back to Wes and the still thrashing boy. When Jake looped the piggin' string around the boy's wrist the boy let out that awful scream again. Jake pulled the loop tight and forced the boy's hands behind his back, looped the string around the boy's other wrist, pulled it tight, ran the string down the boy's back, bent his legs backwards, looped the string around his ankles, pulled it tight, and tied it. He stood and stepped back to survey the scene. Wes let go of the boy's hair and stood looking down at the dismal looking hogtied child, who was screaming and crying at the same time. Jake and Wes whistled the boys to slack off, and, while they were coiling their ropes, Wes said, "This here boy is gone plumb feral. Now that I'm lookin' at him, I member hearing Flying XC cowboys talk about a boy runnin' wild out here on the range. Question is, now we catched him, what're we gonna do with him?"

"Wal, first thing is to git him outta the rain and warmed up," Jake said. "Then take care a the boys." They picked the child up by the armpits and the feet. "Why he's as light as a feather," Wes said. They carried him to the shack, where they sat him inside.

When the detectives came into the shack carrying their saddles and gear, the boy was huddled in one corner. He stared at them like a trapped bobcat. Jake went to him and bent down to check the piggin' string. "Watch those teeth. He'll git yer," Wes said. Jake found that the boy had managed to loosen the tie around his ankles, so he rolled him over, untied the string, looped it twice around his ankles, and ran it up to the boy's wrists, where he tied it. "There. Like to see yer untie that one," Jake said.

The shack had a packed dirt floor with a ring of stones for a fire in the center and a flue in the roof for the smoke to escape. There was some dry firewood in one corner, so Wes used it and got a fire going. When the coffee was ready he poured three cups and let one cool while he and Jake studied their prisoner and sipped their coffee.

"Ain't much, but at least this ol' shack don't leak," Wes said.

"What're we gonna do with him?" Jake asked.

"Wal, we could git him dried out, feed him, and if he'll let us, cut his hair and turn him back out on the range in the mornin'. Sounds like the rain's easin' up. Maybe it'll be stopped by mornin'."

"Can yer talk, boy? What's yer name?" Jake asked. The boy shot dagger looks at them both and spit in Jake's direction. Jake made a big grin and said, "So yer name is Spitter." The boy spit again, and Jake thought he saw just an ever so slight smile crack the boy's crusty lips. He picked up the cooled coffee and held it to the boy's lips. "Here, try some a this coffee. It'll warm yer up." The boy sipped a little and then started gulping it down. He emptied the cup, and Jake said, "Yer want more?" Wes lit a cigar and silently watched the action while sitting on his saddle with his back to the wall and his legs crossed and stretched out to his front.

"Yer kin call me Spitter if yer want. But that ain't my name. I'll take some vittles if yer got any. Ain't et in three days."

"We got vittles, and we're gonna feed yer good. Ain't we, Wes?" Jake turned to look at Wes, who said, "Course we are. We ain't bad men."

"What's yer name then, boy?"

He blubbered with a heaving chest, "It's Lester P. Morgan, and my pa, God rest his soul, is Samuel R. Morgan, and my Ma, God rest her soul, is Eliza C. Morgan, and my brother, God rest his soul, is Eugene P. Morgan, and my sister, God knows where she be, is Julie Ann Morgan. My pa taught us to always be proud a our name." He looked up and went from face to face with a proud and defiant glare.

"Well, let's git that wet coat off yer, and, as soon as the chuck is ready, yer kin have all yer want," Jake said. "Then yer kin tell us all about yer troubles if yer want to. I got a couple a boys 'bout yer age. Yer won't run if we untie yer will yer?"

"No. Guess not. I can tell yer not bad

men, and I am awful hungry. But I cain't guarantee I'll be here in the mornin'."

Jake untied the piggin' string, and Wes stood and stepped over by the door. It was already getting warm in the shack, so he took off his coat and laid it on his saddle. Jake took off Lester's coat and his own. He spread Lester's coat on some firewood next to the fire and said, "Here, let's get those wet boots off to dry, too." He pulled off one boot to bare a foot with no sock, twisted up his face, and said "Whew. Yer got stinky feet. Put that boot back on and just hold yer feet close to the fire to dry them boots. Looks like yer 'bout to lose the sole on that boot." Jake nodded to the boot on Lester's left foot that had a rawhide strap around the ball and over the instep, while his big toe could be seen protruding from the detached toe box.

"Wes, yer got the chuck? Yer want another cup a coffee, Lester? No? All right. How 'bout some hardtack while we're waitin' for the rest to cook. What a we got, Wes?"

"Bacon and hardtack. And I'm makin' up a mash of dried apples and crumbled hardtack in hot water. Be like a steamed puddin'."

"Mmm boy, that sounds real good, don't it Lester? Here." He held out a big piece of hardtack, and in a blur the boy snatched it right out of his hand. "Goodness. Faster'n greased lightn,' huh, Wes?"

Lester ripped off big hunks of the hardtack, chomped them a few times, and swallowed it in big gulps. Saliva dripped down his chin, and he started the low growl again. Jake looked up at Wes, who shrugged his shoulders. "Yer gonna git that chuck goin', Wes?"

He could figure what Jake was doing so he said, "Comin' right up in a jiffy."

As the bacon was sizzling and the apples reconstituting in the hot water, they watched Lester drool uncontrollably at the aroma of the food cooking. "Sorry," Lester said self-consciously. "It's jest that I ain't et any sow-belly in over two years now, and it's a dern sight better'n raw rabbit."

"How long yer been out here on the range?" Wes asked.

Lester shrugged his shoulders and stared at the fire. "This last was my third winter out here."

"What —" Wes started to say, but Jake caught his eye and gave him a *No* signal.

"Wal, looks like the bacon's cooked and the puddin's 'bout ready. Yer don't want me to fix yer a plate do yer, Lester?" Jake flashed a big grin on him. Lester grinned back like he could tell Jake was joshing him. Jake scooped up chunks of smoking bacon and dumped them on a tin plate and ladled out some pudding next to them, put another hunk of hardtack on the plate, and handed it to Lester, who took it more civilized like. He fixed a plate for Wes and then himself. They all sat back and filled their stomachs. Lester started the low growl again as he concentrated on his food and then looked up and stopped it. In between mouthfuls he said, "Sorry, it's a habit. I fight coyotes for food. They always tryin' to snatch my kill away from me."

"What about the wolves?" Wes said.

"Wal, onliest time I ever come acrost wolves they wanted to et me, not my kill." He chuckled, and Wes and Jake joined him. "Three a them. Chased me down and ran me up a mesquite tree. They kept a circlin' that tree until I guess they got tired a me pissin' on 'em. So they ran off."

Jake and Wes laughed openly, and Jake said, "Finish yer supper, Lester. Ain't no wolves around here. Least wise none that want to et yer."

They finished their supper, and Wes took the utensils, plates, and pot and pan outside and down to the creek to wash them. The last of the dusk was fading, and the rain had stopped with the clouds breaking up so that a star appeared here or there in the sky. He came back in and put the chuck gear to set by the fire to dry. "Storm's bustin' up," he said. "Y'all git any talkin' done while I was out?"

"Wal, Lester's got him a full stomach and is ready to tell us his story, but we were waitin' fer yer so he don't have to tell it twice."

"It ain't much," Lester began. "We was farmin' corn and cotton on the east bank a the Wichita right at Beaver Creek. One day three men, bad men, mean and nasty, rode up and killed my pa, my ma, and my older brother and had their way with my sister. She were only fourteen. They went through and took whatever they wanted. Stole the horses and mules, burned the house and barn, and took my sister with 'em when they rode out. I ran to the woods while they was killin' and rapin', and I been in 'em ever since. I stay away from all folks. I don't trust nobody. Onliest reason I'm sittin' here now cuz yer seem like yer ain't bad men." He dropped his eyes and stared at the floor.

"Yer mean yer been runnin' out there on the range by yerself with no knife or gun for what, three years?" Wes said, sounding amazed. The boy nodded his head *yes*.

"How come yer didn't run to a neighbor's farm or git into town or sumthin'?"

"Too skeert I guess. I kin catch rabbits and prairie chicken an' sech. I got used to it — staying away from folks."

"Wal, yer ready to come back into town now, ain't yer?" Jake said. The boy looked up at Jake with big, excited eyes and nodded *yes* again. "All right then. Let's get yer bedded down."

Jake spread out one of his tarps, put his saddlebags down for Lester's head to rest on, and threw his saddle blanket over the top of the boy. Then he sat on his saddle and motioned for Wes to let him use his cigar to light his own. Once it was lit, he puffed it good and leaned back against the wall. He watched Lester and thought about Harry and Edgar. Lester even looked a little like Edgar. His boys were sort of abandoned, too. Oh, they had the surrogate parents but not their real ma and pa. If he hadn't got into trouble in Missourah he probably could have been working closer to the boys. Doing detective work. He smoked and thought, and, in five minutes, Lester was snoring, sound asleep.

Wes motioned for Jake to step outside with him. The night sky was turning brighter from the moon and starlight. It was just a cool evening now. No rain. Clouds were breaking up and scattering. They walked through the grass over to the corral. The boys nickered and came over to where the detectives leaned up against the fence. Jake slipped Jasper a piece of hard candy while Wes hung his lanky frame on the fence and reached out to stroke Noble's neck. "Yer want some?" he asked Wes. "Nah. Noble's gentle enough. He don't need to be spoilt." Jake didn't respond.

Wes tapped the mud with his boot and made a little puddle. "Sumthin' jest don't set right with this boy. Hard to believe he coulda been out there on his own with no weapons and live all this time. Better keep a sharp eye tonight. Sleep with our boots and pistol belts on. He could be lyin'. Settin' us up for his kin. They could be alive and sneak up on us." He puffed his cigar and spat a speck of tobacco.

"Oh. You don't believe his story?"

Wes shrugged his shoulders, held the cigar in his teeth, and shoved his hands into his coat pockets. "Big one to swaller."

"I know. Seems odd. But, supposin' he's tellin' the truth. Do you, er, yer know any families around that might be willin' to take him in?"

"Wal, there's the Adams family in Vernon.

They took on a couple a orphans awhile back. I guess this one here is a orphan. But, what if they cain't take him in? We cain't be saddled with no boy to look after. We got work to do. Speakin' 'bout, yer never told me yer had two boys."

Jake dropped his gaze to the ground, tapped his boot in the mud, and made a little puddle. "Wal, yeah. Their mother and sister were killed in a cyclone while I was in prison. My brother and his wife looked after them in Independence, Kansas, until I finished my time. I went to gather them up, but they wanted to stay there in Independence. Been there three years by then. That was in seventy-nine. Guess they were used to it. My sister-in-law thought it best they stay there, so I went on my way. Went back for Christmas last year, and they're doin' fine." He looked up at Wes and smiled. "The youngest one looks a lot like that one in there."

"Uh-huh. Wal, that's a sad story. Sorry fer yer," Wes said as he gripped Jake's shoulder like a father to a son. "That's normal. This," he nodded his head toward the door, "ain't. Best, like I said, to be on guard tonight." They smoked a while longer, and then Wes tossed his cigar. "Wal, reckon I'll git some shuteye. Yer kin have the first watch. I'll take the second. Sound all right to yer?" Jake nodded and tossed his cigar.

Jake sat on his saddle and rested his back against the wall while the other two snored away. A little after midnight Jake's chin bounced off his chest for the twentieth time, as he would doze and awake when his chin hit his chest. This time he heard Jasper whinny a warning. By the time he was on his feet and called to Wes, Jasper was neighing loudly and thrashing about the corral. They grabbed their rifles and were out the door in a flash, keeping low, Jake in the lead. A wicked orange and white flash came from the corral and at the same time the big boom of a shotgun. The buckshot whistled over their heads and sprayed them with splinters from the boards of the door.

The two detectives instinctively split apart, knelt, and fired their rifles, shooting foot long flames from their muzzles, sending bullets at the shadowy silhouettes crouching at the lower rail of the fence. The detectives poured in lead in a fusillade of fire, moving and maneuvering ever closer after each shot, levering and firing as they went. A scream pierced the night as one of the raiders jumped up and flopped on his back. That left only two sets of flaming muzzle blasts coming from the corral, and then they stopped. The boys were being backed out of the lean-to, and the culprits were hiding behind them.

"Hold yer fire," Wes yelled. Jake already had. "We're detectives," Wes yelled even louder. "Yer varmints better hightail it or we're gonna kill yer." There was some scurrying sound, and then two shadows ran off behind the corral toward the creek. Both Jake and Wes fired off a couple of rounds in their direction, but no response came. They were gone. Jake ran to the lean-to while reloading his Winchester at the same time. He ran as fast as he could. Wes hollered, "What'er yer doin'?"

"I'm gonna git 'em," Jake shouted back and disappeared behind the corral.

"Loco shave tail," Wes mumbled to himself. Then he hurried back in the shed. The boy was gone. "Figures," he mumbled. As he went back outside he heard two rifle shots. Then four shots, then silence. He waited and tried to figure what to do. The boys were most important, so he decided to stay with them. He talked to them softly and ran his hands over them. He didn't find any wounds.

In just a few minutes, he heard someone coming through the brush and then the creek behind the corral and then, "Yo, Wes.

It's me, Jake. I'm alone." That sounded strange. Wes pulled his pistol and crouched by a fence post. He waited and watched. "Yo, Wes. Yer hear me?"

Presently, Jake came into view. He tactfully walked real slow. One step in front of the other with a pause in between each step. Wes waited. No one was following Jake, so Wes said, "What happened? Yer git 'em?"

"Why'd yer wait so long to answer me just now?"

"Had to make sure yer was alone."

"Wal, I done the same. Yer coulda been a hostage yerself, yer know."

"Wal, I weren't. So what happened?"

"I caught up with them, and they fired a couple a rounds at me. I fired back, and then I saw 'em gallop over the rise in the moonlight and then the next one, too. They were runnin' fast. Pretty sure they's gone."

"Yeah, wal, so's yer little innocent boy."

"If that don't beat all. He was in with horse thieves."

"They weren't no horse thieves. They's jest thieves. Better check our gear and make sure nothin's missing. Probably been watching us the whole time we been here. Didn't see 'em when we rode in. We were too caught up in catchin' that boy. In fact, he probably run to take our attention away from his kin. Caught 'em right in the middle of a thievin' search. They's jest good for nothin' trash. Probably livin' in a shoddy sod house somewhere on the range, stealin' whatever they can find and sellin' or tradin' it off."

"Wal, they picked the wrong horse when they tried to wrangle Jasper." Jake chuckled, and Wes joined him. "Shore did. Ol' Noble woulda said howdy and walked right on out with 'em."

He waved off to the east and said, "They's probably from east of the Wichita like he said. Ain't from around here. This here is Flying XC range. No squatters allowed here. They's a lot a them dirt poor wretches out thataway. Oh well. One less now. We gotta rope him and hang him in that tree until we can plant him in the mornin'. Keep the coyotes and varmints away from him."

In the morning firelight inside the shack as they were waiting for the coffee to boil, Jake said, "He took my tarp and his own coat. Cain't see anything else missin'. Guess he ain't all that bad. Lucky that was my spare tarp. Got another one in my bedroll. The little rascal sure had me fooled."

"Yeah. Let's git that varmint outside in the ground. We could leave him hanged as a sign, but I don't guess that'd be Christian, eh?"

"No, we better bury him and say a word over the grave."

They finished their internment duties, saddled the boys, loaded their gear, mounted, and rode off north. About an hour past noon, they topped a high rise where they could see for several miles. The sun was warm, the sky deep blue with a few fluffy clouds floating around and a stiff breeze blowing out of the west. They stepped out of their saddles and let the boys rest and pull up grass. The terrain was mostly flat grassland with rolling hills here and there, sprinkled with bunches of mesquite. Four miles out there was a settlement in view.

"Mesquite looks thinner around here," Jake said and then took a swig from his canteen.

"Yep. Shore is, and this is where we part company, pard. I'll be headin' northwest to Vernon and then on to the panhandle spreads. Yer ride down to that settlement and then north to northeast to Comanche Creek and follow it east for a ways and then northeast to Flying XC headquarters. It's about seven miles from that settlement to the Flying XC. Can't miss it. Joins the Red.

That's where the headquarters is." Wes stretched his frame and squatted up and down a couple of times. "The cow boss is Walt Guthrie. He's a smart feller and tough as nails. Been on the range a long time. The owner is Xavier Calhoun. He's smarter but not as range tough. Course, he's the owner, so he don't have to be so range tough. He's business tough. Real good in horse breedin', too. Both a them are fair and honest fellers. They should be waitin' to meet yer."

"Yeah. Jim told me about Calhoun."

Wes stared off into the distance and continued, "I don't know when we'll meet up agin'. Don't know what's gonna happen in the panhandle. When the time comes, I'll find a way to git word to you. We can make this hill our meetin' place. Fer now, yer on yer own." He squatted and gazed out over the range. Jake squatted down beside him. Wes pulled a grass stalk and stuck it in his mouth. Jake copied him.

"Only been a few weeks, pard. Seems like years." Wes turned to look at Jake, smiled, and then was suddenly alarmed. "I mean good years," he said more serious.

"I was wonderin' there for a minute," Jake said very serious and then grinned. "Just joshing yer. Yeah, I know it's been good. I am very much obliged for all yer taught me."

"Aw shucks," Wes said, grinning. "Twern't nothin'. Yer a good learner."

"Yeah, wal, I still thank ye, pard." They shook hands vigorously and nearly knocked each other over, laughing as they regained their balance.

"Wal, good luck, pard. I'll be seein' yer when I see yer down the trail." Wes gathered Noble's reins, stepped into the saddle, tipped his hat, and rode off.

Jake waved and said, "Be seein' yer when I see yer down the trail, pard." A feeling came over him. Like there was something just went missing. Something he highly valued. Something lost. He hadn't ever felt like that before, not even when he was locked up at Andersonville or in the Kansas State Pen. Well, didn't do no good to mope 'bout it. Wasn't like it was the end of his life. There was work to do, and he would have to git after it best way he could even if he never saw Wes again. Of course he would probably see him soon enough. They'd be working together again. Out on the range there was plenty of the kind of work they do.

TO BE CONTINUED

Here ends Book I of the life and times of Jonas V. Brighton. But it is not the end of the story. Book II continues the adventure as Jake becomes more famous throughout northwest Texas. He is hired on at the Flying XC, working undercover as a line rider. He eliminates the rustlers plaguing the XC range, saves an important feller's life, and reunites with Wes Wilson to catch more rustlers. He is embroiled in the fencing wars, battles a range fire, fights racial bigotry, and he and Wes break up a major rustling operation targeting the Hashknife outfit. In the course of business, he is almost killed by a renegade Comanche, shot by a rustler, and nearly assassinated by a wanted murderer.

Along the way he meets a woman, Mary Jane, and falls head over heels in love with her. However, there is a problem. But it is overcome, and they finally marry.

Jake's troubles with Judge Anderson continue, and the judge eventually jails Jake. And that is the last straw for Jake and Mary Jane. They decide to quit Texas and head west, whereupon Book III continues the story.

ABOUT THE AUTHOR

Back in the day, as they say, there were plenty of Old West stories on T.V. to flood a boy's imagination as he played cowboys and Indians in the backyard with his siblings and friends. Those fanciful memories stayed with **J. D. Arnold** and, finally, now that he has quit his day job, came to fruition with this series on Jonas V. Brighton. More is in the works with a novel on Wes Wilson as the first Special Ranger of the Cattle Raisers Association of Texas; Walt Guthrie, cow boss; and a family saga set north of the Mogollon Rim in Arizona during the Progressive Era clear through to the 1960s.

J.D. lives by the polo fields in Indio, California, with Diane, his wife of half a century, and Sofie, their canine love.

Printed in the USA
CPSIA information can be obtained
at www.ICGtesting.com
JSHW020052200124
55311JS00005B/11

9 781432 889203